# REDEFINING
# NORMAL

## PAUL NANKIVELL

# TABLE OF CONTENTS

SPECIAL THANKS ..................................................... VII

DEDICATION .......................................................... IX

CHAPTER 1 - INTUITION ............................................ 1

CHAPTER 2 - LOVE BITES ........................................... 9

CHAPTER 3 - THE LINEUP .......................................... 17

CHAPTER 4 - GUEST SPEAKER .................................... 25

CHAPTER 5 - BULLIES & COWARDS ............................ 35

CHAPTER 6 - SLEEPING GIANT .................................... 47

CHAPTER 7 - DARE TO SMILE .................................... 57

CHAPTER 8 - DARE TO DREAM .................................. 65

CHAPTER 9 - THE MOLE ........................................... 79

CHAPTER 10 - THE INQUISITION ............................... 89

CHAPTER 11 - ENLIGHTENMENT DAY ......................... 95

CHAPTER 12 - THE GAUNTLET ................................... 101

CHAPTER 13 - TEAM 27 ........................................... 113

CHAPTER 14 - SPITBALLS ......................................... 119

CHAPTER 15 - DYING CATERPILLARS ........................ 125

CHAPTER 16 - NARC ............................................... 137

CHAPTER 17 - THE OTHER SHOE ............................... 143

CHAPTER 18 - DÉJÀ VU ........................................... 149

CHAPTER 19 - LONE WOLF ...................................... 159

CHAPTER 20 - EXILE ............................................... 169

CHAPTER 21 - CROCODILE TEARS ........................... 173

CHAPTER 22 - COLD WATER .................................... 183

CHAPTER 23 - COMPETITIVE DRIVE ......................... 191

CHAPTER 24 - COWBOYS ........................................ 199

CHAPTER 25 - SANS SHERPA .................................. 205

CHAPTER 26 - JAWS OF DEFEAT ............................. 213

CHAPTER 27 - END OF NIGHT .................................. 221

CHAPTER 28 - REFOCUS ......................................... 227

CHAPTER 29 - A NEW DAY ...................................... 235

CHAPTER 30 - SLINGSHOTS ..................................... 241

CHAPTER 31 - MOCKING MIMES ............................. 253

CHAPTER 32 - MOUNTAIN TOP ............................... 259

# SPECIAL THANKS

| | |
|---|---|
| Creative Consultants | Stephani Anderson |
| | Edmond Osepans |
| | Megan Henry |
| Advisors | Amy Downing |
| | Camille Block |
| Artistic Consultant | Veronica Dejesus |
| Cover Artist | Michael Crew |

A very heartfelt extension of gratitude to my dearest friend Mary Ann. After my mom passed away, I became lost in a dark emotional tunnel. Your compassion and support illuminated my path back to my normal life. I will always be grateful for your spiritual gifts and life lessons.

# DEDICATION

I wish to honor my late mother Martha Nankivell by dedicating my book to her memory. Besides being the best mom that a disabled child can possibly have, she was also my: best friend, advocate, and motivator.

# CHAPTER 1 - INTUITION

**M**s. Jones asked her eldest son, Thomas, to clear the dinner table. Bedtime was quickly approaching for little Alan. As she scooped her two-year-old son off the floor and tickled his belly, he squealed in delight. She turned him over and saw her maternal love reflected in his eyes. To her, he was an unexpected joy who captured her imagination with each passing day. To him, she was mommy, his universe, as the only person he felt tethered to, and safe with, in his young, challenged existence.

After their pre-bedtime bathroom ritual, she changed him into his teddy bear printed "jammies". Upon placing her boy in a special bed with protective side rails, his eyes lit up when she grabbed a book from a nearby table and sat by him. It mattered little that she read to him five times a day, he always was enthused when mommy read bedtime stories. Likewise, her heart soared whenever he displayed obvious signs of comprehension. Although she couldn't scientifically prove that Alan possessed at least average intelligence, her mother's intuition told her differently.

Due to a massive stroke suffered at birth, Alan's initial prognosis was so dire that he wasn't expected to survive his first weeks of life. Moreover, doctors grimly asserted that even if he lived, he'd be in a permanent vegetative state with brain damage classified as so severe that doctors predicted he'd never recognize people, or be able to interact socially. Therefore, it was recommended that Ms. Jones do the right thing by placing her son in an institution, as she would not be able to care for him properly.

Doctors are given expert status in society. Consequently, lay people trust them for not only medical assistance but also advice. However, Ms. Jones pesky gut told her to take her son home from the hospital—if he survived.

A fairly bright individual, with multi-tasking skills, Ms. Jones could complete three crossword puzzles and balance a checkbook before her morning coffee turned lukewarm. Yet, she knew that sometimes one's mind wasn't best at discovering all of life's answers. More often than not, her intuitive skills served her well. As she watched little Alan nod off to dreamland, something gnawed at her to find out, once and for all, if those doctors were wrong.

A little more than two years after his birth, her belief in him and what he could be finally motivated Ms. Jones to seek out other experts. She spent the next morning on the phone with pediatricians and other mothers. Just before office closing hours of five o'clock, her phone rang. Hoping to have some kind of response today, she pounced on the receiver like a hungry cat nabbing a wayward rodent.

"Hello?" she hurriedly blurted.

"Hello. Is this Ms. Jones?" a man's voice queried.

"Yes. And who am I speaking to?"

"Oh, sorry, I'm Dr. Howard Shasta. I've heard you've been looking for someone to evaluate your son's cognitive aptitude."

"Do you mean intelligence?"

"Yes, Ms. Jones."

"Well, yes, I suppose I have."

She went on in detail of what she'd been told of his condition by doctors who oversaw his birth and the subsequent complications. After telling Dr. Shasta of her desire to discover what her son's mental potential or limitations truly were, he agreed to see them both.

The following Monday, Alan's uncle Lou drove Alan and his mom to Dr. Shasta's office. Lou was a night supervisor at a manufacturing plant so he had a few free hours before his shift started. He and his wife, Ann, were always glad to lend a hand to his late brother's widow. Ms. Jones was a proud woman, however, and rarely asked for assistance.

Upon arriving, they found a waiting room packed with mothers and kids of all ages. Ms. Jones's interpreted this as a good sign. Apparently, Dr. Shasta had an excellent reputation in his field. After chatting with some moms, she found that her assumption was accurate. In a funny way, she became simultaneously settled and apprehensive by this revelation. On the one hand, she knew that by day's end she'd have a definitive prognosis on Alan's abilities. On the other hand, she feared that her hopes and his prognosis wouldn't correlate.

Back when she was a child, doctors were looked upon with great reverence. Oftentimes, people would only see a doctor as a last resort when home remedies and elixirs failed. Fearing a bad prognosis would mark a person for certain death, doctors were sometimes negatively stereotyped as doomsday predictors. As a result, even though on an intellectual level she now knew better, her initial god-like perception of the men in white coats still bedeviled her core being.

After a 45-minute wait, a feminine voice called out from the reception window, "Ms. Jones, Dr. Shasta will see you now." Springing out of her seat like a jack-in-the-box toy, Ms. Jones quickly wheeled Alan toward the doctor's open door. Uncle Lou trotted to keep pace. Just before they arrived, a short, pudgy fellow in a well-tailored three-piece suit greeted them. His pleasant mannerisms temporarily lessened her anxiousness about encountering another "expert". From young Alan's narrow perspective the balding middle-aged stranger looked like Santa Claus, shaved and out of costume.

"Come in, come in. Please, both of you. Have a seat." Dr. Shasta grinned.

After Ms. Jones and Lou settled in, Dr. Shasta positioned Alan directly across from his desk. The likeable fatherly figure casually chatted with the adults while showing a series of pictures to the youngster. Sporadically, he'd pause, conversing to ask Alan to identify objects in the pictures. Without much hesitation, Alan confidently pointed to and identified each object in Dr. Shasta's first test.

Alan saw this as a fun game with a new friend; similar to the games he played with mommy every day under their tree at home.

Ms. Jones wasn't completely comfortable with Dr. Shasta's apparent disinterest in evaluating Alan. Her perception of a typical doctor's persona was a straight-laced, no-nonsense, emotionally devoid person who was just interested in facts. His easygoing mannerisms, in her opinion, were very atypical behavior for a medical professional. She began resigning herself to the fact that he was just going to do his requisite time with them and regurgitate what Alan's first doctors had told her.

A few minutes later, however, Dr. Shasta made a statement that pleasantly surprised her.

"I'll need to have more extensive testing done on Alan." Dr. Shasta said.

"What kind?" Ms. Jones apprehensively exclaimed.

"We'll run him through a battery of standardized tests which will determine his cognitive function level."

"When can you do this, doctor?"

"Can you bring him in tomorrow morning at nine?"

"Why so early?"

"Because Ms. Jones, these tests will take a good part of a day to administer."

"Oh, okay. Well, I guess we'll just make it a priority. We'll be here tomorrow. Thank you, doctor." She slightly stammered, stood up, shook his hand, and wheeled Alan out the door with Lou trailing behind.

The following morning, at quarter to nine, Ms. Jones, Alan, and Lou were back in Dr. Shasta's waiting room. As soon as the office clock's minute hand reached twelve, Alan was called in. One of Dr. Shasta's interns quickly whisked him away.

Ms. Jones was stunned by her son's sudden departure. Until now, he'd rarely been out of her sight. Even though she was extremely unsettled by leaving him in the hands of strangers, she knew that testing protocols required Alan to be alone.

In an attempt to keep her mind occupied, during the next few hours she completed two crossword puzzles and read a good portion of a crime novel. Lou brought back lunch from a fast food place at 12:30 p.m. and chatted with his sister-in-law, over cheeseburgers. While their conversation didn't produce any tangible outcomes it did serve as a much needed distraction for her. However, ten minutes after chewing her last bite of ground beef, her anxious musings grew more acute. With no more puzzles to solve or books to read, her thoughts now obsessed on her baby boy.

All kinds of "What if?" scenarios floated in her head. Her mind became a popcorn machine of thoughts. What happens next if he's smart? What happens next if the original diagnosis is proven correct? Can I send him to school if that's the next step?

Finally, she picked up a magazine and immersed herself in a topic she had no interest in.

Soon after reading Popular Mechanics from cover-to-cover, her name was called. Looking up, her eyes caught a clock face that read 2:35 p.m. She instantly turned and apologized to Lou knowing that now he'd miss a part of his shift. He assured her that a mea culpa wasn't necessary. Slowly, they walked down a hallway and into Dr. Shasta's office.

As they entered, Dr. Shasta greeted them with a smile from behind his desk while Alan sat directly opposite.

After all parties settled in Dr. Shasta placed a wooden box in front of Alan. The hollow box was a perfect cube, nine inches high, wide, and deep. Five sides were solid but its remaining side was a hinged door with five shaped holes cut into it. There were also five multi-colored solid shaped blocks: cube, star, cylinder, pyramid, and rectangle.

As Dr. Shasta gestured for Alan to play with it, he took a relaxed pose in his office chair, chin resting in hand.

"Watch what Alan does here," he said.

Without being prompted, Alan picked up a cube and tried to fit it into a cube-shaped hole. Even though he successfully identified what shape belonged to which hole, lack of coordination prevented him from completing his goal. After dropping the cube several times, a pained expression went across Ms. Jones face. In her mind, he'd already failed. All that remained was taking her son home. Finally, Dr. Shasta picked up the cube and smiled at young Alan and then at his anxious mother.

"Do you know what this means?" Dr. Shasta mused.

"What, doctor?" Ms. Jones nervously inquired.

"Well, Ms. Jones, in all of our tests, your son demonstrated a unique ability to quickly identify problems and formulate solutions. Furthermore, despite his coordination problems, his intestinal fortitude won't allow him to quit trying," he said.

"But he can't get the cube in the hole," Ms. Jones lamented.

"Ms. Jones, Ms. Jones, I'm afraid that you can't see the forest for the trees," he lightly chuckled, "The point of this exercise was to see if he could correctly identify which shapes belonged to what holes. Whether or not he could make the blocks go through was of little importance. Furthermore, the speed in which he figures out answers speaks volumes about his analytical skills."

"So, intellectually speaking, you'd say he's at least as smart as an average kid?"

"Oh, no, I wouldn't say that. I would say that he's smarter than an average kid. Moreover, with all due respect to you and your brother-in-law, I'd say that he's smarter than the two of you put together."

"What do you think we should do next?"

"He should be enrolled in school now," he emphatically asserted.

"But he's not even three yet," a slight tone of panic was evident in her voice.

"A child's prime learning years are before they turn five. The longer you wait to send him to school, the harder it will be for him both academically and socially. Now is not the time for half-measures and compromises, Ms. Jones," he chided, "You have to give consideration to what's best for Alan's long-term interests."

"But he'll be the youngest one in school, other kids…" she rationalized.

"I'm not saying that there won't be an adjustment period. Will he struggle at first? Yes. Will he miss home and cry some? Sure. Will you have days where you just can't stand parting with him? You bet! However, over time, both you and your son will adjust and he'll be further ahead in the long run."

A silence fell upon the room as Alan's mother gave consideration to his words. Even though she just heard the best possible news regarding her son's intelligence, a new reality hit home. Before Dr. Shasta's tests had confirmed her hopes, she never had to concern herself with the next step. She loved having him home; teaching him what she could while being able to protect him like a mother lioness. However, now that there was documented proof of her intuition, her only recourse as a responsible, loving mother, was to do what was best for her son.

"Okay, what kind of school can he go to?" she relented.

"The nearest handicapped elementary school in your area is Ramsey Elementary School. They have everything Alan needs in regards to teachers, personal attendants, door-to-door school bus pick up, facilities, etc…" he said.

"Okay, I guess I'll call their principal tomorrow and tell him or her about Alan and how to proceed from there. Thank you, doctor," she sighed.

---

Dr. Shasta stood up and walked toward the door, "Well, it was a pleasure to meet you all and if I can be of any further assistance, please don't hesitate to use me as a reference," he smiled.

Two weeks later, Ms. Jones and Alan waited in front of their apartment for the school bus. A series of phone calls and a meeting with Ramsey's principal led them to this fateful day. Her heart never wanted to let him go. Yet, that same heart also knew that she had to do right by him. Whatever temporary pain about to occur was going to be more than offset by long-term academic achievement. To that end, she steeled herself in this moment for his sake. Regardless of what happened today, he wouldn't see her falter.

The bus arrived on time and she gently handed her baby boy to a kindly driver who seated Alan directly behind him. At this point, everything was okay because he thought mommy was coming too. However, as soon as the bus began pulling away, he thought that he was being taken from his mommy forever! His sudden crying didn't dissuade the driver from doing his job.

Ms. Jones saw her son's pain through the window. She kept smiling and waving, smiling and waving, until his bus vanished from sight. Then, she leaned on the mailbox, put her head in her hands, and wiped her eyes. Alan's future had begun.

# CHAPTER 2 - LOVE BITES

Mr. Washington had been driving school buses for over 25 years. The last eight of those years, however, he drove kids to and from Ramsey Elementary School for handicapped children. Now, in his mid-sixties, he was looked upon by: parents, children, and faculty alike, as a kindly, respected elder. He was as important to Ramsey's foundation and success as the first brick ever laid, or when the first child entered its doors in September of 1959.

He greeted everybody with a charming pleasantness and old-world respect. Being an old pro, Mr. Washington also knew his job very well. You see, a school bus driver's job isn't simply a matter of transporting kids to and from school. Anytime a group of twenty youngsters with varied personalities rides a bus, a driver must wear many hats. At any given time, he may have to be a: baby—sitter, consoler, disciplinarian, friend, joker, or referee. When those kids are disabled, however, another dimension is added.

At Ramsey, on one end of the spectrum there were children who had severe physical disabilities, yet were fine mentally. On the other end of the spectrum were children whose bodies were fine, but they had an array of mental and, or, emotional disabilities. Like the proverbial lion and lamb conundrum, Mr. Washington inherently knew which kinds of kids absolutely couldn't sit together.

As he pulled up to young Alan Jones's apartment building, Mr. Washington gave a wave and a wide smile to Alan's mom who was standing curbside for her three-year-old son. Coming to a halt, Mr. Washington opened the hinged bus doors and greeted her in his usual gentlemanly way.

"Good afternoon, Ms. Jones. How are you this fine day, ma'am?" he said.

"Oh, not good, not bad, just getting along the best I can today. If you know what I mean," she sighed.

"Oh, yes, ma'am, I hear ya, I hear ya. Some days it's all I can do to coax these old bones of mine out of bed in the mornin'."

"So, how's my boy today? Is he behaving himself?" she chuckled lightly.

"You're funny, Ms. Jones. Alan never causes any problems. I wish more kids were as well behaved as him," he broadly smiled.

He then walked towards where Alan was seated, which was always in the first row, and unbuckled Ms. Jones' weary-eyed tyke. Next, he carried Alan's limp body to his mother's waiting arms. Even after a long, exhausting school day, Alan always perked up when he felt mom's nurturing touch. He wrapped his little arms around her neck and squealed excitedly, "Mommy, mommy!" She instinctively gave him a big squeeze that she knew made him feel loved, safe, and happy. Mr. Washington was always moved whenever he saw evidence of a close bond between mother and child.

As he went back behind the wheel, Ms. Jones shouted, "See you tomorrow!"

Mr. Washington thought for a moment and replied, "I'm not working tomorrow."

"Oh, is everything okay?" she frowned.

"Got some personal business that needs tending to, no big thing, ma'am."

"How long will you be gone?"

"Just a day, ma'am, a substitute will drive tomorrow."

"Who? Do you know?"

"No, but I'm sure it'll work out fine." He nodded reassuringly at her.

As was customary, when he drove off, Ms. Jones and her son waited for their beloved driver to turn around at the cul-de-sac's end. As the bus passed their building again, all parties happily waved at one another.

A new driver took Alan to school the next day. Fortunately, there were no unexpected incidents that morning. Everybody, more or less, behaved themselves and didn't exploit a golden opportunity to rattle a substitute driver. Maybe they found their collective compassion and decided to cut the new driver some slack. Or, perhaps they were scared because their bus ran two red lights and seemed to be moving at an erratic pace.

Alan had a typical day at school. Arts and crafts with naptime thrown into the mix highlight an average kindergartner's day. He made a kid cry, another kid made him cry, nothing out of the ordinary. With his teacher's helping hands he made a bear out of clay. He was told that he could take his masterpiece home tomorrow after it was glazed in a special oven.

When Alan's day was over, all of Ramsey's students raced to their respective buses. A droopy-eyed, middle-aged lady, whose metal nametag read, "Ms. Clark", quickly lifted him out of his chair and carried him onto the bus. After depositing him in the back row, she motioned for all able-bodied kids to sit wherever they wanted.

A tall, hefty girl named Maggie found her way next to Alan. Even though Maggie was 13 years old and big for her age, she was relegated to going to Ramsey because of her severe mental retardation.

Five minutes after they departed Ramsey, Maggie became fascinated with little Alan. She grabbed his left thigh and began kneading it like dough. When her rubbing started to hurt, he yelled and feebly flicked at her hand, given his underdeveloped mobility at that time. Since he was too small to hurt her, Maggie grinned and probably interpreted his light tap on her hand as a playful gesture.

Right after drop off number one, Maggie became even more adventurous with Alan. She put her head on his left thigh and rubbed it like a cat. Next, emulating a hungry lioness she bared her teeth and slowly gnawed at his thigh. Alan's body writhed, and his pain began to mount. With her head in his lap, he repeatedly hit her on the back in an attempt to make her stop. Unfortunately, his actions seemed to backfire as she went into a chomping frenzy.

Now very desperate, and not knowing what else to do, Alan repeatedly shrieked in pain as tears streamed uncontrollably down his face and onto Maggie's back. However, Ms. Clark ignored his cries. She only seemed interested in doing this route as fast as possible. After she dropped off kid number four, she finally became visibly annoyed by Alan's persistent screams. She marched halfway down towards him and warned loudly, "Pipe down or I'll tell your mommy that you were bad today!"

As Ms. Clark's bus resumed its course, Maggie resumed making Alan's thigh her main course. Like a ravenous savage, her nibbles slowly became deep bites. Normally a placid child, his ear-piercing screams had everybody, except Ms. Clark of course, holding their ears. He only had to endure one more drop off before he would be home. Unfortunately, by this point, his pain had become excruciating. As he saw his street approaching he felt a damp area where she was chewing.

Finally, as the bus stopped in front of his home, Alan knew that his anguish would soon end. Ms. Clark robotically lifted him from his seat while his sobs and screams continued. Ms. Jones expression was a mixture of fear and confusion as her young son was delivered to her arms crying and yelling. Knowing her son's personality, she feared that something was terribly wrong. He wouldn't carry on like this unless he was in utter agony. She stood in the vehicle's doorway as she grilled Ms. Clark for answers.

"Why is he crying? What happened?" Ms. Jones vehemently demanded.

"Oh, I don't know, maybe he thought I passed his house." Ms. Clark dismissed.

"My boy doesn't cry like this without a good reason!"

"What can I tell ya lady? I have to go."

Ms. Jones had barely lifted her foot from the bus step, when Ms. Clark carelessly slammed the door. As soon as the bus headed toward the cul-de-sac's end, Ms. Jones grabbed Alan's head firmly between her hands. She looked him in the eyes and got him to focus. He quickly settled down enough so that she could ask him a question. As the bus started turning around she got her answer.

"Tell mommy what's wrong right now." She said firmly but calmly.

"It hurts! It hurts!" He sobbed while pointing at his left thigh.

She hurriedly unbuttoned his pants yanking them down to his ankles. She gasped at the sight of his left leg. Pools of blood and layers of flesh had been exposed and there were teeth marks all over his left thigh. Instinctively, she scooped him up in her arms and dashed out to the street. Ms. Clark's bus slowed to a stop as it approached them.

"Hey! What are you doing, lady?" Ms. Clark bellowed out her window.

"Look at this, damn it! Look at this!" Ms. Jones held Alan up to the window.

"Oh my god, I had no idea. I, I ..." Her face turned pale.

"What the hell happened? Who was sitting by him?"

"Uh, I don't know, one of the retarded kids, I guess." She stuttered nervously.

"Are you stupid? You never sit kids like that next to helpless kids. Is this your first day on the fuckin' job?" She fumed.

"What, what can I do? I'm so sorry. Just tell me what I can do to fix this?" She pleaded.

Ms. Jones took a couple of deep breaths but when she spoke again her rage still seeped through her attempted veil of civility.

"Just point out and give me the name of the kid who did this to my son."

Ms. Clark motioned for Ms. Jones to enter. As soon as Alan's enraged mother came on, the guilt-ridden driver pointed at Maggie while saying her name in a sorrowful tone. When Ms. Jones saw that her son's attacker was adult sized, her anger was renewed. Seeing Maggie's infant-like demeanor and mannerisms, she couldn't very well focus all blame on a girl who seemed barely aware of her surroundings. Conversely, as the adult in charge, she figured that Ms. Clark was supposed to know better. As mother and son stepped back off, Ms. Clark tried to appease an obviously seething mom.

"I promise to tell Maggie's mom what happened." Ms. Clark stated firmly.

"Then what?" Ms. Jones snapped back.

"I guess her mom will punish her in some way."

"And all will be right in the world and your conscience will be clear."

"Look, I'm sorry. What more can I do?"

"What more can you do? What more can you do? Try owning up to your mistake. Try offering to pay for his impending doctor visit. I'll deal with you later. Right now, I've got to get him to the hospital." She stormed away to call a taxi.

Alan's pediatrician saw him immediately. He carefully examined Alan's leg, treated his wounds, and administered a tetanus shot. After bandaging Alan's thigh, he smiled while giving Alan a lollipop. He turned toward Alan's mom and informed her of his findings.

"The surface damage is bad, but all things considered, he's very lucky."

"Lucky? What do you mean lucky?" She yelled.

"Well, she was just about an inch from shredding a quadriceps muscle."

"What would've happened then?"

"Worst case? He could've lost at least some use of the leg."

"But now?"

"It'll heal in a couple of weeks. Just change the dressing every day and I'll prescribe a course of antibiotics. He should be fine. If there are any signs of infection, come right in."

Next morning, Ms. Jones took five buses to Ramsey elementary. She knew what she had to say to principal Rifkin. Usually, she feared authority figures such as teachers and principals. However, today, her protective instincts dwarfed any of those fears. When it came to protecting her young, this mother had no equal in either the human race or animal kingdom.

When principal Rifkin saw Ms. Jones enter Ramsey's reception area, she walked up to her and invited her into the office. After pulling out a seat for Ms. Jones, she shut the door and sat behind her desk.

"May I offer you a cup of coffee?"

"No, thank you."

"Okay then, I understand that there was a major problem on the bus yesterday."

"I guess you can say that. My son almost lost the use of his leg."

"Did a doctor say that?"

"Yes. Are you calling me a liar?" She fired back.

"Well, no…"

"Good, because the doctor's report is right here!" She held a copy in her hand.

"I know that you're upset, Ms. Jones, and you have every right to be. Now, let me assure you that this will never happen again."

"How can you do that? What are you going to do to make sure my boy won't be cannibalized again?"

"I'll make sure that all our substitute drivers are aware of the situation."

"You mean that girl isn't going to be expelled?"

---

"Well, she has nowhere else to go, no other school…"

"I wonder why?" Ms. Jones said, sarcastically. "Look, I have to watch out for my son. I don't care if she can't go to a regular school. All you need to know is my son won't be coming back to school until that girl is gone!"

"Okay, I'll talk to the girl's mother, apprise her of the seriousness of the situation and try to persuade her that her daughter needs a facility which can better serve her daughter's needs."

"Alright, I guess that sounds fair. Alan has to rest his leg for a few days anyway. I'll keep him home until the situation is resolved to my liking."

They shook hands and parted amicably. Three days later, Ms. Jones was making lunch while Alan was entranced with an educational puzzle. Her phone rang and she casually trotted to the living room to answer it. Alan, having excellent hearing, overheard mom's end of the conversation.

"Hello. Yes, she's been taken out of school permanently? Good, good, he'll be back in school on Monday."

# CHAPTER 3 - THE LINEUP

Ms. Hampton's nose twitched as she put down her chalk holder. There was a foul odor emanating from one of the 12 boys and girls in her kindergarten class at Ramsey elementary school for the handicapped. She knew that somebody had an accident; now her task was to identify the culprit. As a psychology intern who had no formal training as a teacher, let alone special education, she often displayed ignorance in dealing with the realities of young disabled students. Scowling with hands on hips, she glared back and forth among the five-year-olds in order to ascertain who dared to soil themselves and interrupt her class. A hushed silence fell upon the students, as they anxiously anticipated her next move.

"Okay, who dirtied themselves?" she forcefully demanded while banging a clenched fist on her desk.

Predictably, since nobody wanted to become a target of a tirade, there was no answer. She then ordered her aides – Ms. King and Ms. Jackson – to line up the wooden wheelchairs in a row side by side. "Alright ladies and gentleman, we'll do this the hard way!" she shouted.

The terrified dozen started to cry almost in unison, as the two aides began to unceremoniously slam the chairs together until a queue was formed. Earlier, Alan had tried to go potty at the designated restroom time of 10.30, but no matter how he desperately pushed and strained he couldn't go. He knew that Ms. King hated to clean up his "White boy shit" as she put it.

She had told him recently that: "Listen here boy; I got no patience with your soilin' yourself. One of these days I'll whoop you behind so bad you won't shits for five days. Ya hear me boy!" So with Ms. King's admonishment still fresh in his mind he frantically tried to clench his buttocks hard against the chair. But alas his body betrayed him once more as he felt fecal matter escape into his shorts.

While holding hands behind her back, Ms. Hampton bent down to smell the bottom of the first student. She always sniffed three times to ascertain guilt or innocence. Alan was sixth in line and he was hoping against hope that someone else, in the first five also had control issues today. However, when she was done sniffing number five, he knew that his fate was sealed. As he felt her hands painfully clench his shoulders a sick feeling wound through him. At this point he hoped she would assign Ms. Jackson, instead of Ms. King, to change him.

"Mr. Jones, how many times do we have to go through this with you? You were given a potty break at 10:30, yet here we go again!" Then lifting her gaze to Ms. King she continued, "Ms. King, would you be so kind as to clean up Mr. Jones?" Ms. King glared menacingly at Alan and hissed, "Yes ma'am."

As soon as she wheeled him into the hallway, Ms. King let Alan know – in no uncertain terms – that she was prepared to make good on her threat. "Boy I told you last time I've had it with you! Time for me to teach you a lesson!" Fearful of her wrath, Alan's legs began to shake involuntarily. Seeing his fear, Ms. King bellowed, "Boy you know what's coming don't you! I warned you."

Upon entering the attendant's room she noticed that there were two aides on duty. "Hey Marcia and Nancy. Why don't you guys go grab a snack and I'll hold down the fort here for a while. Take your time," she smiled.

Since none of the aides at Ramsey could be mistaken for an anorexic, Ms. King's offer was like offering vodka to a Russian.

When the women left, Ms. King shut the door. Then she wheeled Alan into the smaller changing room and slammed the door! "Now Mister times up for you!" she roared. Alan knew that she meant business, however he didn't yet appreciate her anger's acute nature. "Let's get you up on this table and sees what kinds of mess you made this time!" she said with disgust. As she lifted him onto the table, the odor grew more pungent, "phew boy, you out did yourself this time!" she recoiled.

She violently tore off his parts and underpants in one motion. Upon seeing the extent of his accident, Ms. King's rage surpassed safe levels for a woman of her huge size and genetic disposition. "I can't believe you shit this much you stupid little asshole! What does your momma do when you do this? Huh? I bet she don't do nothin', right boy? I'm askin' you a question boy!" Alan quivered and began to cry, as he never before, in his young life, been victimized by such a vile tirade.

Ms. King shook her head at Alan's tears as she admonished him: "Best save your tears boy! When I get through with you, I'll make you bawl your little eyes out!" That revelation only caused him to cry harder as he knew he would be beaten. His only recourse now was to beg for mercy. "I won' poo no more, poo no more!!" he plaintively sobbed. Ms. King would have none of it, "Too late for promises boy." she grumbled.

After cleaning him up with cold wet rags, she grabbed both of his ankles with her big left hand until his legs were perpendicular to his torso. Then without any fanfare, she proceeded to spank his exposed bottom repeatedly with her right hand. Alan's little body writhed in pain as he was helpless to stop the violation. Tears gushed down his face as Ms. King continued a sadistic rampage against her miserable existence by abusing poor Alan until all semblances of spirit and dignity, instilled in him by his mommy, vacated his eyes.

Finally, it was over but Alan's tears wouldn't ebb. Ms. King ignored his sobbing while putting on clean briefs and pants. When she got him back in his wheelchair, she bent down – to his eye level – and put her right index finger an inch from his nose. "Listen here boy! Don't you dare tells nobody I whopped ya!" she warned. "Your momma will think yous lyin' and whop ya for lyin," she stared into his eyes, "Now when we go back to class, you keep your mouth shut, or I's haul you back in here! You here!" she demanded while making sure his misty eyes met with hers. "Yes, ma'am." he frightfully stuttered.

For the rest of the day, Alan appeared downcast, quiet and withdrawn. When Ms. Hampton tried to include him in class projects, he just turned away and lightly wept. Although, certainly alarmed by his atypical behavior there were still 11 other students who needed her attention as well. At day's end, she wanted to ask him what was wrong; however, time got away from her and Alan departed for home before she could talk to him.

On the bus ride home, Alan weighed Ms. King's threat against what his mommy had always told him every day before he left for school: "Honey, always remember that – except to help you go potty - no adult is allowed to touch your hiney or pee pee other than me or daddy. And if they do something that you don't like, you tell mommy right away!" When he arrived home, he realized that his decision wasn't that hard at all. He knew that he could only trust his mother. She was his first and best teacher.

After the bus dropped him off, Ms. Jones smiled at Alan, then hugged him and inquired about his day. Upon embracing him, she felt his unusually tight body and cold skin. "I have a problem mommy." was his muffled response. Alarmed at her normally happy boy's subdued offering, she immediately knelt down on the lawn and met his eyes with hers. "What's wrong baby?" she gently broached with her hands lightly stroking his arms. Young Alan recalled his assailant's warning and became hesitant about telling his mom what happened. "I can't tell you momma," he sobbed.

At this point, her mind started racing with all sorts of nasty possibilities. However, she had to keep a cool exterior for her son. After taking three slow deep breaths, she lowered her voice and reminded him of their first rule: "Remember sweetie, you can tell mommy anything. If someone hurt you, you tell mommy right now." She purred softly. Alan however, needed a tad more convincing. Struggling with his words he unknowingly gave her all the information that she needed. "If ..If I tell you…the lady said that you beat me too!" he wept.

There are no words that could come close to describing how Ms. Jones felt at the moment Alan – her baby – revealed his assault to her. She hugged him while trying to suppress tears beget from an unholy union of fear and rage. She had to calm down internally, before asking him the next question. Once composed, she softly asked: "Who hit you baby, it'll okay, mommy will fix it."

He looked into her soft, warm eyes and rediscovered what he'd always known, he could tell mommy anything. He then went on to detail what Ms. King had done to him and her justification for it. After he finished, Ms. Jones inspected his bottom and discovered a noticeable bruise. She then put on her happy face and told him: "Guess what! You get to play hooky tomorrow!" She smiled. "Tommy will play with you tomorrow, while mommy goes out for a little while. Alan loved his cool older brother – a high school junior – who'd helped take care of his younger brother since Alan was born.

The next day Ms. Jones – who didn't drive – took five buses before arriving at Ramsey School. While en route, she rehearsed what she was going to say to the principal. Once on school grounds, she strode with unmistakable conviction towards the principal's office. Greeting her, at the front door, was Mrs. Rifkin a short, rosy-cheeked lady in her late fifties nattily attired with a gray and black plaid jacket and matching mid-calf length skirt, and a white ruffled blouse underneath. The two women knew each other through PTA meetings. "Hello Ms. Jones, how are you today?" Mrs. Rifkin, had already parsed Ms. Jones body language from across the hall, was just attempting to keep things light. "Not good, not good at all." was Ms. Jones somber retort.

Upon seeing the seriousness of Ms. Jones demeanor, Mrs. Rifkin escorted Alan's mother into her office and quietly shut the door. When educator and parent settled into their respective seats, Ms. Jones took a deep breath and proceeded to relate what Alan had told her yesterday. After she told Alan's portion of what had transpired, she added her own commentary. "You know part of the problem is that the attendants dictate bathroom time, instead of the kids. They give them a strict 10:30 potty break and if a kid has to go after that, too bad!" During her monologue, she only had to pause once to compose herself. When she finally finished, Mrs. Rifkin's hid her face in her hands as she came to grips with the gravity of the situation.

Summoning up her courage, Ms. Jones asserted her wishes on Alan's behalf. "I'm sorry Mrs. Rifkin, but I'm not sending Alan to school until that woman is gone!" she stated with a practiced coolness masquerading her inner rage. Clasping her hands tightly together, she continued: "Let me be clear, I don't want her transferred to another class. I don't want her assigned to another part of the school! I want her gone! I don't want her anywhere near my baby boy ever again!" she punctuated the last word by slapping her right hand on Mrs. Rifkin's desk. Then Ms. Jones slowly leaned back in her chair, awaiting Mrs. Rifkin's rebuttal.

To Ms. Jones surprise, Mrs. Rifkin totally concurred with her recommendation. "I completely agree with you Ms. Jones, we cannot tolerate that kind of unprofessional conduct from our attendants." She stated with steely-eyed conviction. "Be rest assured, I'll handle this matter personally," she paused, "Thank you for bringing this matter to my attention." She stood and extended her right hand and Ms. Jones shook her hand. "Always remember Ms. Jones, feel free to talk to me anytime regarding Alan." They smiled at each other and said their goodbyes.

When Alan arrived in class the next day, he noticed that Ms. King was gone. In her place, was a new attendant who quickly walked up to him sporting a wide grin, "Hi Alan, my name is Barbara," she gushed. Then, kneeling down to meet his eye level, she stroked his thighs with her hands. Using a soft, comforting tone, she told him how things would be on her watch. "Listen Alan, from now on, whenever you've got to go potty, you tell Barbara right away and I'll take you right then okay!" Alan didn't believe her. "But Ms. King said . . . "Barbara hugged him and gently cooed, "You don't have to worry about her anymore baby. What mean old Ms. King did to you was wrong! And don't worry if you have an accident. I understand you hate them. I'll just change you as needed." She then hugged him again before standing back up.

Upon arriving home, Ms. Jones asked her son about his day. Alan laughed and exclaimed, "Susie got paint all over her face!"

# CHAPTER 4 - GUEST SPEAKER

"**I** don't believe this crap," Principal Rifkin—a normally genteel lady of extraordinary grace—shouted. Yelling at no one in particular, she frantically scoured Ramsey Elementary's halls looking for a solution. She had 200 college kids in the auditorium waiting to hear why they should dedicate a career path to special education but there was a fly in the ointment.

The speaker just called, three minutes ago no less, to tell her that he overslept. "What a flake!" she giggled hysterically. The aforementioned flake possessed two special education Doctorates and a Masters in a related field. "What will those kids think? What a bad first impression of this field," tugging a handful of her previously well-coifed silver locks.

Meanwhile, Alan's mom, Ms. Jones, was walking towards the front doors having just left a parent—teacher meeting. By happenstance, she nearly collided with the wandering leader who, by now, needed to breathe into a paper bag. The two women exchanged pardons before resuming on their separate paths. Just before Ms. Jones left the building however, a hand strongly grabbed her left arm spinning her around.

Principal Rifkin and Ms. Jones had high regard for one another. Alan's mom was very active at Ramsey, advocating for her son on many occasions. Some parents, of disabled children, thought of the hours that their kid is in school as a respite from their onerous burden. But, Ms. Jones couldn't wait for her boy's school day to end.

She genuinely loved Alan and wanted to make available every chance to maximize his life's potential. Nobody could definitively forecast what he could or couldn't do. So, she decided to let him continue to surprise her without any preconceptions on supposed limitations.

"You have to help me," Principal Rifkin's speech alternated between words and very audible gasps for more oxygen.

"What, what's the matter? Are you okay?" Ms. Jones still stunned by the Principal's minor physical assault.

"I… I have an auditorium full of college kids…" Principal Rifkin blurted.

"Okay, so, what's the problem?"

"Well, um, you see, um…"

"Wow, calm down Principal Rifkin," Ms. Jones rubbed the distressed leader's shoulders, "Now, how can I help?"

Alan's mom's nurturing touch temporarily relaxed Principal Rifkin just enough so she could compose herself, take a couple deep breaths, and reveal the nature of her predicament in a calmer fashion.

"Okay, thank you Ms. Jones, let's try this again," she sheepishly grinned, "This morning, an expert in special education was supposed to give a speech on career opportunities in the field to the college kids," she sighed again before continuing, "But, the inconsiderate bastard called me about five minutes ago to tell me that he can't make it!" she huffed.

"Alright, I see your dilemma, but I still don't know how I can be of any help?" Ms. Jones shrugged sympathetically.

"Well, um, you see," Principal Rifkin's nervous hesitation returned, "I was sort of hoping that you would, uh, how can I put this…uh…"

"For goodness sakes spit it out!" Ms. Jones smiled lightheartedly.

"Well, I don't want to put you on the spot but I was hoping that you would save my bacon and talk to the kids…" her eyes fearfully darted like a leopard-chased gazelle as she began heading for the auditorium while Ms. Jones instinctively kept pace.

"You're kidding right?" Ms. Jones face fell in disbelief at the Principal's seemingly preposterous idea, "I've never given a speech before and I don't know anything about public speaking," she nervously exclaimed while shrugging and raising her palms skyward while beads of perspiration formed on her forehead, "Besides, I'm just a mom. Aren't those kids waiting for some expert with a P.H.D. to impart them with wisdom?"

"You have the wisdom Ms. Jones," pitched Principal Rifkin like a Sunday morning preacher, "All someone with a P.H.D. after their name has is a list of studies and some unproven theories. On the other hand, you've been there, done that. You taught Alan how to read before he entered pre-school," her voice grew in volume and conviction.

"But, I…" Ms. Jones tried rebutting to no avail.

"Don't underestimate yourself," Principal Rifkin stopped and looked Ms. Jones in the eyes, "I bet you can offer some unique insights and give those kids a hands-on perspective into your experiences raising and advocating for a disabled child. Come on, you'll do great!" she cheered.

"Uh, well…" Ms. Jones sighed in resignation, "I suppose you've got a point, besides, what's the worst that can happen?" At that moment, she realized Principal Rifkin's right hand was gently pushing her through the auditorium's doorway.

"That's the spirit," Principal Rifkin smiled optimistically, "Now, let's go!" With her Shanghai maneuver now complete, they exchanged knowing glances and wry grins.

Upon entering the auditorium however, their warming optimism was chilled by a distinct frosty aura emanating from the students. Arms crossed, feet tapped, and heads shook in disbelief. Disapproving stares shot laser beams through Ramsey's principal.

Making them wait nearly a half an hour without any explanation was unacceptable. As a group, they were livid and became more unreceptive with each passing minute. At this point, even an experienced orator would have their work cut out reaching this mob. As she absorbed the atmosphere, Ms. Jones felt like a lamb whose shepherd led her into a den of wolves for slaughter.

The women walked onto stage and Principal Rifkin stood at the podium. She knew, all too well, that her next step was going to be a whopper. Convincing Ms. Jones to give a speech was hard enough. Now, she had to find a way to persuade these kids to listen to a mom instead of an expert.

"Ladies and gentlemen, may I have your attention please," she began, "Unfortunately, our scheduled speaker won't be able to attend today," mumbles were heard amongst the crowd, "However, I have found a fine substitute speaker who can give you a view from the trenches. We have a mother of a disabled child to talk about…"

"Hey," a voice from the crowd interrupted, "We were promised an expert in the field. Not some dumb mom." Other voices seconded the opinion.

Dismissive rumblings and chatter brought about a sudden change in Ms. Jones attitude. In her mind, evidently, they weren't going to place any value on anything she had to say. As a result, nervous feelings were being replaced by a new found determination fueled by the audience's disrespectful vibe.

These kids were just a couple years older than her first-born child. She wouldn't tolerate such flippancy from her own kids; therefore, she now couldn't wait to sermonize to these wet-behind-the-ears punks. As Principal Rifkin continued to struggle in appeasing the crowd, Ms. Jones gently pushed her beleaguered friend aside and whispered in her ear, "I've got this."

The mother of three seized control of the podium, giving her unruly audience that classic "mother's glare." A glare usually reserved for children who are one careless word away from a severe attitude adjustment; a glare that sends icy chills down a child's spine. This look says much more than a thousand words and is better versus a lecture at communicating a point.

In no time at all, what was once a raucous, belligerent, mob full of righteous indignation transformed into a disciplined platoon of army privates awaiting orders. The silence was so acute that you could hear a scalp being scratched six rows away. Ms. Jones was well aware however that this truce would be fleeting unless her words were impactful and resonated truth.

She scanned her audience one last time before delivering an impromptu recitation of whatever popped into her head. At this point, half the battle was maintaining some semblance of that glare. If she showed any hesitancy, or any other signs of weakness, this crowd would sense it instantly then brand her incompetent and tune her out.

"Let me introduce myself," beginning with a measured delivery, "My name is Ms. Jones and I am the mother of a six-year-old boy who has a condition known as Cerebral Palsy," she paused, "Okay, um," she cleared her throat to gather her thoughts, "I have a word that I would like you to remember today," speaking more commandingly into the microphone, "That word is adversity."

"Today's incident, with a speaker cancellation and substitution is your first lesson in special education." Pausing again to monitor the audience's pulse, half still seemed disinterested; half liked her opening statement.

"Special education is a new concept. Ten scant years ago, there were no schools for disabled children. Back then the so-called 'experts' categorized most physically disabled children to be mentally disabled as well. So, these kids weren't educated at all because it was deemed a pointless drain on resources. They either stayed home or were institutionalized all of their lives..." A raised hand interrupted her speech.

"Excuse me ma'am," a squeaky male voice interrupted, "with all due respect, what qualifies you to criticize experts in special-ed. I mean, I know you're a mom of a disabled kid and all, so I guess you're an expert on how to take care of a disabled kid but you're not an educator. So, like I said, how can you speak to this topic with any intelligence whatsoever—ma'am?" he said sarcastically.

She momentarily ignored her verbal assailant and attempted to stay on topic, "Because it's new, special education has no tried and true methods or standard textbooks outlining what to do if certain situations arise …" she stopped, mid-sentence, realizing an undeniable truth. She couldn't continue without first responding to anyone who dismissed her experience just because she lacked a sheepskin or two. This group wanted examples of where she knew more than the experts. Her confidence swelled once more as a fantastic example came to mind.

"Okay, I'm going to change topics for a moment," she pointed towards the room's center, "May the student who questioned my qualifications please stand up?"

A short, thin, baby-faced lad stood and raised his hand to further compensate for his small stature. "Here I am Ms. Jones. How can I help you?" his smile bordered on a snicker.

"What is your name young man?" Ms. Jones calmly inquired.

"Norman ma'am, my name is Norman," was his snarky response.

"Well Norman, I think you're right. I think that I do need to give you guys an example of where I knew more than the experts," saying the last word with an obvious implication that she didn't think much of the experts.

"Well, here's my story," she continued, "When my son was born he had a massive stroke due to a lack of oxygen during a difficult and prolonged birth. This caused major damage to the left side of his brain. The doctor who delivered him told me that he would probably be a vegetable," she groaned recalling that moment, "and never recognize me or his surroundings. He said that my best course of action would be to put him in an institution as soon as possible so that I wouldn't get too attached and I could get on with my life," there were pockets of gasps in the room as a tall blonde girl raised her hand.

"Excuse me, Ms. Jones, it would seem that the doctor had a logical solution to your problem. Why didn't you heed his warning?"

Ms. Jones gave the girl a sideways glance as she contemplated how naïve and self-centered young people are sometimes. Finally, she responded with a query of her own, "Logical solution to my problem?' she chuckled, "Young lady, let me ask you a question first, if I may?"

"Sure, yes ma'am," the girl cautiously offered.

"Are you planning on having children someday?"

"Why, yes ma'am. One of the reasons that I want to get into teaching is because I love being around kids," she flushed with pride.

"Do you have any preconceptions about what kind of people they will become? Do you want them to be a doctor, lawyer, or teacher?"

"Uh, no, I guess as long as they're healthy and good people, that's all I could ask for. I'd let them choose their own career paths like my mom and dad did for me," she said cheerfully.

"Well, what if you had a son who was a healthy, happy boy until his legs are permanently mangled in a car accident at age nine. Would you then put him up for adoption because he wasn't 'healthy' anymore?" Her question sounded more like a cross-examination.

"What a terrible thing to say," the girl gasped, "As his mom, I'd never… Oh, oh…" she trailed off as she realized flaws in her argument.

Ms. Jones continued her speech, "Having a child isn't like going to a shoe store, buying new shoes, and taking them back the next day because they don't match your dress," she gestured at her outfit, "When you become a parent, that child isn't just another responsibility," she straightened her stance, "That child becomes a part of you, your core being," pounding her chest with an open palm three times while speaking the last three words, "You see both the best part of yourself and the worst part of yourself through them." She admonished.

"So, you see, when that doctor looked into his crystal ball and nonchalantly said that my son would never recognize his surroundings, I didn't take his word as gospel from on high," her disdain for people who see doctors as gods couldn't be missed, "I owed it to my boy to seek out the best cognitive testing I could find," scanning her audience as the last remnant of trepidation flew away.

Now, her delivery took on a professorial air, "When he was two, I took him to a doctor who specialized in cognitive analysis for children. He did a lengthy evaluation of my son and concluded that my son had well above average intelligence for any child, disabled or non-disabled," the crowd let out a chorus of surprised sounds, "Based on these results the recommendation was to put my son in school although he wasn't three years old yet. Any questions?" she asked with a swagger.

"Why did he want you to enroll your son at such a young age?" An unidentified girl's voice asked tentatively.

"Well after the evaluation, I was told that before age five a child's brain is like a sponge and absorbs every new concept it's exposed to," she stated authoritatively, "For that reason, he said that it was critical to get my boy in school as soon as possible." She straightened her stance again, proud as a peacock mother, and further prepared to deliver a crushing blow to anyone who mindlessly went along without questioning expert opinions, "So, now, as you can see, this was an example of where the first 'expert' didn't know what the hell he was talking about. Like I said before, special education is still a new field and sometimes you have to go with your gut and seek out a second opinion."

Ms. Jones continued relaying details of her ongoing mission to get her son educated by offering hands-on knowledge; Principal Rifkin rested her head in her hands trying in vain to suppress a smile. What began as a tiny seed of an idea, born out of pure desperation, was actually bearing plentiful fruit. Yes, at first, Ms. Jones was a reluctant speaker. But, now, Principal

Rifkin saw a strong woman confidently orating from a platform of real life experiences as a parent of a disabled child.

The guest speaker became aware of the audience's transformation. They were enraptured by her stories—hanging on every word. She made them laugh by sharing funny slices of life with a disabled child that will never be found in any textbook. Yes, this once standoffish group had been won over but, in reality, the battle's outcome was never really in doubt. She had slain much bigger and scarier dragons during her crusade for Alan—with more dragons looming on the horizon.

# CHAPTER 5 - BULLIES & COWARDS

Mrs. Knight looked desperately around her fourth grade class for any signs of life, any glimmer of hope that, for all intents and purposes, she wasn't just the private tutor for Alan and Nick Nicholson. Out of sixteen 4th graders, only two responded to her questions. Both boys were always eager to make their teacher happy by proving their knowledge to her, time and again. Whenever two boys find something to compete over, a rivalry develops.

There were similarities between Alan and Nick that went beyond mere coincidence. Both of them were born on the same day. Nick was older by three hours and constantly teased Alan about that fact. Each had the same type of cerebral palsy affecting them in almost identical ways. They also had similar body types: long and lanky, but with wiry strength. Alan was a hair more gifted intellectually, while Nick possessed slightly better coordination and strength. So, naturally, ever since their preschool days their relationship was fiercely competitive.

"Can anyone tell me who the first man on the moon was?" She asked.

Nick knew that if he didn't rush his answer, Alan would beat him to the punch. "Neil Young!" He hurriedly shouted.

"I'm sorry Nick, but that's incorrect. Neil Young is a musician. Anybody else?" Her gaze purposely avoided Alan.

With the poise of a seasoned gunfighter whose opponent had shot too soon, Alan slowly raised his hand and kept it in the air until Mrs. Knight had no other options; she was aware of the history between Alan and Nick. Whenever one boy would answer incorrectly, his foe not only provided a right answer but also would throw in some creative sarcasm towards his rival. Finally, she couldn't ignore Alan any longer. With a tone of exasperation, she surrendered to the inevitable, "Okay, Alan, what's the answer?"

A slight smile—or smirk, depending on your point of view—appeared on Alan's face, "Mrs. Knight, the answer you are looking for is, Neil Armstrong."

He winked Nick's way after she turned away again. Nick responded with a steely-eyed scowl that Alan instantly interpreted as a beating he would get at recess. At this point in their relationship, Alan knew that it didn't matter if he made Nick angry or not. Nick always relished any opportunity to pound his rival into submission.

As class let out for recess, Alan tried to find an open space of playground so that he could keep an eye on all of the angles. Before he could reach his intended destination, he felt a punch to his upper back. Then, Nick spun his chair to the left of Alan's until their big wheels touched. Nick held Alan's arms down with his right arm, while locking his victim's brakes while using his left hand. This was done, of course, to prevent Alan from escaping.

Nick possessed superior reach, coordination, and strength—as well as the element of surprise. He jabbed at Alan's jaw, nose, and eyes until the latter was forced to cross both arms over his face.

Alan knew he'd have to sacrifice his torso to protect his face. A marked up torso was easier to hide than facial abrasions. Nick proceeded to tenderize Alan's gut like a baker pounds at dough. Each punch was delivered with such impact that Alan rose slightly from his chair.

After about 20 punches in a row to the stomach, Alan's wailing could be heard across Ramsey's playground. Finally, Nick was satisfied that he'd gotten his revenge.

"Don't you ever make fun of me again! Got that?" He warned, while clutching Alan's shirt. "I can beat you up anytime I feel like it and don't you forget it!" He wheeled away leaving Alan sobbing and publicly humiliated on the blacktop.

Peer pressure prevented Alan from seeking adult intervention. Boys, in his age group, who tell an adult that they're getting beaten up at school, are seen as outcasts. They were labeled, "Tattle tales" or, "Momma's little diapered baby." There is an unspoken rule that once a boy reaches a certain age; they're expected to be able to stand up to bullies.

For the rest of that day, whenever a question was asked in class, Alan hesitated. He kept one eye on Mrs. Knight and another on Nick. If Nick vied for an answer, Alan would keep play dumb. Otherwise, he'd feel free to answer without fear of retribution.

Subjugating his will to his rival gave him a sick feeling. He wanted to get back at Nick—some way, somehow—but finally resigned himself to his existence as a coward.

Riding the bus going home, he was seated next to Joey, a second grader. Along with being significantly smaller than Alan, Joey's form of cerebral palsy left him unable to move his arms or legs without tremendous effort. In addition, he could barely talk above a whisper; which made him an easy target for almost any of his peers. On the other hand, his sweet demeanor and friendly smile made him everybody's protected little brother.

Alan's feelings of helplessness, anger, and self-esteem issues had only intensified during the day's progression. He was sick and tired of being constantly victimized by Nick. He was sick and tired of having to behave subserviently or pretend to be stupid just to appease a bully. For once, just once, he wanted to know what it felt like to give a beating rather than get one. He needed to find someone who he could dominate, his own patsy.

Alan and Joey were seated on the right side, seventh row. The former had an aisle seat while the latter had a window seat. When the bus started to move, Alan instantly seized an opportunity to vent his emotions. Without any consideration of potential consequences, he swung his right fist back as hard as he could and punched his helpless traveling companion in the gut. Joey's little body reacted convulsively and his doe-like eyes looked at Alan as if to ask, "Why!"

The unexpected endorphin rush Alan got from delivering that initial salvo sent him into a punching frenzy. He landed a series of punishing blows all along Joey's torso leaving the younger boy crying and whimpering, "No more please; no more please." The little boy's pleas shook Alan from his rage.

He recognized himself in Joey's sorrowful plaints and a new kind of nausea washed over him. At that moment, a revelation that Nick and him weren't so similar after all. While his rival was a sadist, he was unable to find that quality in his own soul.

Alan felt like a coward's yellow stripe had just been painted down his back. A nice, happy little boy got beat up because he couldn't beat up the one who needed a beating—Nick. Little Joey's sunny disposition became ruined because Alan needed to pass along pain to another poor soul. One moment of selfish rage cost him the friendship of someone who looked up to him as a role model. "A role model? What a joke! I'm a joke." Alan remorsefully thought.

Upon arriving home, he felt guilt-ridden and extremely conflicted over what to do next. There weren't any witnesses to his evil deed and there wasn't any way Joey could tell on him. But, mom had instilled a strong sense of right and wrong in his consciousness. Consequently, he knew that awful pang of guilt wouldn't abate until punishment had been given in some way.

On the other hand, a kid asking his mom for punishment would be akin to a Fortune 500 company asking the IRS for an audit, or a motorist driving up alongside a motorcycle cop and confessing that he sped. Absent any witnesses, most people will seek to avoid punishment for their acts and live with varying degrees of shame depending on their own moral compass.

Once home, he acted atypically bratty and very disrespectful to mom. He felt a need to test limits with her like never tried previously. They had a great mother-son relationship and rarely crossed words. The worst punishment she'd ever given him was sending him to his room a couple of times for 20 minutes.

Even as he was sassing her, his mind couldn't believe that he was actually saying such harsh words out loud. It was as if being possessed by another entity, an entity who wanted to get him in trouble.

"Come on, Alan, honey, time to sit down and do your homework." She said

"Not now, ma." He growled.

"What do you mean? Not now?" She wondered, "We always do homework after school."

"I don't want to do it now, okay! And you can't make me!" He snapped.

She leaned towards him, one hand on her hip while wagging her index finger on the other one hand at him, "Now, you listen here, young man, I don't know what's gotten into you today, but I don't like it! You get your behind in that chair right now and we'll do homework!" She gnashed her teeth as her face flushed red.

"What are you gonna do, send me to my room again? Big deal." He mocked.

At this point, Ms. Jones knew that, for whatever reason, Alan was testing her authority. This was parental poker and she had to either fold and leave him alone, or bluff back by raising the stakes. Normally, he'd comply and go to his room to serve out punishment. But now, she felt forced into an uncomfortable corner. She never gave him a spanking—and never would. However, she couldn't let him know that.

"You've got until the count of ten to get yourself into your room." She coolly said.

"Yeah, or what? Old lady!" He oozed sarcasm.

"You might have a hard time sitting down for a while." She opened a closet door revealing a leather belt.

He looked at the belt and gulped, "You never spanked me before."

"There's a first time for everything, one..."

"Okay, okay, I'll do my homework." He became frantic.

"Too late for that, go to your room, two, three..."

He quickly turned around and scooted down the hallway as fast as his knees would take him. Upon entering his room, mom just finished yelling, "Eight!"

Although almost positive that she was bluffing, he wasn't completely sure. While indeed scared of getting spanked by mom, for the first time, something else became scarier. How would a spanking would affect their relationship as mother and son? Would they both be traumatized by such an event so that they'd become hesitant strangers from that point forward?

"I'll be watching that door, young man. Don't even dream about coming out before I say so, understand?" She yelled down the hallway.

"Yes, ma'am!" He said in a respectful tone.

After thirty long minutes, Ms. Jones entered his room and sat next to her son on the bed. His whole body sagged, slumped shoulders, watery eyes cast downward towards the floor, an obviously somber little boy. Alan's previous behavior caught her off guard. He'd always been a very good kid with a pleasant nature.

During that half-hour cooling off period, she surmised that something happened at school. Her mother's instincts told her that he needed a hug. As soon as she put her arms around him, he found her shoulder and sobbed for five minutes. No words were spoken of their argument ever again.

Lying in bed, before falling asleep, Alan agonized over the day's events. Nick was ruining his life. Not only was Nick making him miserable but his tormentor also caused him to act badly towards people he liked and loved. He beat up Joey out of frustration and purposely baited mom to punish him because of guilt about hurting Joey. He couldn't sleep, until deciding that tomorrow—one way or another—Nick wouldn't want to bother him anymore.

Upon arriving at school, Alan knew what he had to do. This problem with Nick had evolved into something bigger than simply getting beat up. His frustrations had now caused him to lash out at other people. And, in his mind, that was just unacceptable. Consequently, he simply lacked fear, because the desire to exorcise this abuse cycle far outweighed any fear of Nick.

As he wheeled himself into Mrs. Knight's class, he stopped at Nick's empty desk and waited. A couple minutes later, Nick rolled in while talking to one of his friends. When Nick saw his patsy violating part of their unwritten agreement, he wheeled up to him nose to nose. During a brief stare-down Alan never flinched.

By now, all but two of Mrs. Knight's students had filed in. They became an impromptu audience to an unfolding drama. They held their collective breath as the two rivals traded glares. Finally, Nick broke the silence.

"You must be suicidal today, Alan." Nick growled.

"Why do you say that, Nicky?" He smiled patronizingly.

"You're sitting at my desk and you've got a dumb smile on your face." He sneered.

"I don't care what you want anymore; you don't matter to me anymore"

"Does that mean that you're not afraid of me anymore? Come on, I've known you since preschool. You can't fool me. I can see it in your scared little eyes. I'll pound you at recess again just to make sure you understand." He squeezed Alan's arm hard.

"Good, let's invite our whole class and anybody else that you want." He yelled.

"Why?"

"Because, Nick, I've finally figured you out and you don't scare me anymore."

"What do you think that you've figured out, little boy?"

"You're nothing but a coward who has to sneak attack people to win a fight. Maybe you're taking out your frustrations on me because you're getting the crap beaten out of you by your mom at home. I've seen her and she always looks pissed. I don't envy you at all."

"Don't talk about her! Don't you ever tttalk…" He stammered.

"Whatever. Just meet me in back of bungalow B at recess."

Turning toward the rest of his classmates, he shouted, "Everyone's invited, spread the word!"

Both combatants had to wait two hours before they could have their version of "High Noon" to settle the score. During the interim, Alan had his way with Nick by rattling his rival in class. Every time Nick would try to answer Mrs. Knight's inquiries, Alan would tell his teacher, "If Nicky messes up again, I know the answer, it's easy." He'd accompany every statement by looking at his watch and motioning Nick to hurry.

After awhile Nick stopped attempting to answer questions. He was so thoroughly flustered that words weren't coming from his mouth, just gasps of air. To add insult to injury, Alan backed up his boasts by correctly answering each one of Nick's misses, causing the latter to turn red and shoot daggers at the former.

At precisely 10:30 a.m., Mrs. Knight excused her class for recess. Alan and Nick locked stares as they peddled themselves backwards out to behind bungalow B. The rest of Mrs. Knight's class followed them quietly. They didn't want any attendants to become suspicious and intercede prematurely. So, no words were exchanged until they reached the show-down locale.

Once ensconced at their destination, Alan and Nick's remaining class-mates formed a loose circle around them.

Nick sidled up to Alan's left, craned his neck around and said loudly for all to hear, "Look at him. We all know what's gonna happen here. The same thing that always happens. I'm gonna beat him up 'til he cries like the little baby girl he is. He's so smart in class but so dumb with his mouth." He smirked, "Now watch what I do to this guy. I'm going to show you all what happens when someone forgets who they are and mouths off..."

As Nick's incessant belittlement slandered his character, Alan's logic and reason went on vacation and his rage took center stage. The more Nick bragged, any lingering doubts Alan had were rapidly dissipating. Suddenly, feeling overwhelmed by a strange sensation that—until now—he'd never quite experienced, a fist flew. A surge of fury totally focusing mind and body on destroying his adversary engulfed him.

Right in mid-sentence, Nick was rudely interrupted. Alan's left fist suc-cessfully connected under Nick's jaw in rapid-fire fashion causing his head to whiplash violently three times. As soon as the besieged boy protected his face, Alan spring-loaded his body in order to put all his force behind seven punishing gut blows that made Nick double over in his chair. Seeing that he was, at long last, getting the better of his long-time oppressor, Alan didn't let up relentlessly pounding on Nick's back until he heard loud sobbing and begging for mercy. Even then, with his adrenaline still pumping, he wanted to make sure that there had been a lesson learned. With his enemy in a defenseless position, Alan jammed an elbow between Nick's shoulder blades and grinded away.

"Please, please, no more! Oww! Oww!" Nick cried.

"Why should I stop? Tomorrow you'll just sneak attack me again, you coward!"

"No! No! I promise I won't. Just don't hurt me no more!"

"I want you to say that to everyone here, so that you can't back out," he grinded Nick harder.

After Nick let out a series of deep, wailing sobs, he spoke loudly enough for all witnesses to hear. Moreover, his promise had a ring of sincerity to Alan's ears.

"Alan, I'm sorry, I really am. I promise not to hurt you again, really." That one statement, combined with the sorrowful tone that it was delivered in, satisfied Alan momentarily. He released the vanquished foe from custody, shoving him away.

As Nick rose up revealing a red tear-stained face and runny nose, Alan suddenly wondered why he had ever let this guy bully him. He wheeled from the scene with his classmates leaving Nick alone to compose himself.

Later that day, Alan met little Joey and one of Joey's friends in the hallway. Still feeling awful about hurting the loveable tyke, Alan was determined to make amends. As soon as he got near the smaller boy, Joey yelled, and his friend pulled him away. While his friend peered down at his tray, Joey pointed furiously at his letter board. After a minute or so, the friend spoke harshly to Alan.

"Joey says you're a bad boy. You hurt Joey bad and make him cry. Go away now!"

"I'm very sorry, Joey. I wasn't feeling good yesterday and I hit you because I was mad at someone else."

"Joey doesn't like you no more. You're a meanie and your mommy ought to know what you did. Joey never like you ever again, now go away before we tell a teacher you bad."

As Joey's friend wheeled him away, Alan was left to grapple with the fact that he was seen as nothing more than a bully by a boy who he used to inspire. He had become another's tormenter just as Nick had been his. Just as he ultimately saw Nick as a coward, he surmised that Joey saw him the same way.

To make matters worse, Joey didn't want any part of his attempted apology. All of a sudden, a wave of hopelessness and self-loathing washed over him. He broke down and sobbed inconsolably against a wall. That day, he learned the difference between a bully and a coward… nothing.

# CHAPTER 6 - SLEEPING GIANT

Alan's family moved out to the suburbs just before his tenth birthday. This meant not just a new town, but also a new school and new kids. There was a comfort zone at his old school, Ramsey. All of the variables were known: from bullies to wimps, good attendants to borderline child molesters, teachers who exhibited passion for their chosen profession - to those who kept one eye on the minute hand; he knew the players and their tendencies like a chess master with a long time rival.

The moment that a mechanical lift descended out of a yellow bus onto the curb in front of Alan's house, he knew things would be different. No such technology existed on Ramsey's fleet. Once aboard, it was hard not to notice of an eerie lack of sound even though there must've been at least 25 kids on board. Moreover, upon first inspection, there wasn't a sense that the driver was an oppressive ogre who beat a kid for making a noise. To the contrary, Mrs. Alexander oozed gentleness and warmth.

Just before arriving at the new school, Steinback Elementary, a realization hit that a new kid's presence might cause uneasiness amongst Mrs. Alexander's passengers. He fretted this "cold shoulder" treatment would continue at school. Figuring new kids probably received some kind of initiation; he steeled his emotions for what could be a rough first day.

Upon departing the bus, he headed straight for an assigned classroom without meeting quizzical stares from other kids. The new goal was to just to get through "today" as emotionally detached as possible. Sooner or later, every kid who changes schools is forced to deal with some sort of initiation rituals. Before that came to pass, however, maybe he'd be given today to soak in the new environs.

He patiently waited outside room eight for a new teacher to come and start class. While waiting, a crowd slowly formed around him. One by one, they tentatively approached, asked usual questions like name and previous school. Politely, he introduced himself as Alan Jones, but not bothering to divulge any further facts. Sticking with his Uncle Ron's credo of name, rank, and serial number, he was wary about divulging information to strange kids who might use it as a future weapon.

Finally, a silver-haired lady in her early 60's came strolling towards the door with keys in hand. She had fine wrinkles on her pale face and hands. She was attired in very appropriate conservative clothing for a teacher of her years and stature. Sporting a white button-down, long-sleeve sweater, and a full-length ankle skirt, she was the dictionary definition of prim and proper. She was an epitomized exemplification of an old-fashioned schoolmarm.

Alan noted how the kids reacted to her sudden presence. Conversations ceased, backs straightened at attention, and, "Good morning, Mrs. Watson," was echoed by every student. Alan's initial impression was that his new teacher didn't put up with any sass. As soon as class commenced, and everyone settled behind their assigned desk, Mrs. Watson pointed his way in the back.

"Class, we have a new student today, if he would do us the honor of introducing himself." She slightly nodded Alan's way, waiting for him to take her cue.

Alan nervously hesitated, then clasped his hands together tightly, and with strained speech pronounced the words, "Alan Jones."

Mrs. Watson then turned toward the blackboard and wrote his full name in foot-high cursive letters; at which point, he felt an instantaneous urge to crawl into a corner and die. Sure, Mrs. Watson was expected to take a moment to introduce him to the class, but being a shy, socially stunted nine-year-old, he was embarrassed to see his name up there like a billboard advertisement. After gazing at their new classmate for what seemed like an interminably long period, for the object of their collective wonder, she redirected their focus toward normal class business.

"Please retrieve your mathematics text books and open them to page 129," she ordered, "today, we're working on our times-tables. I know that all of you have mastered the seven's. As usual, I'll randomly go around class and ask each of you to give an answer."

Alan's mind raced and his palms became damp as each student confidently supplied solutions to Mrs. Watson's queries. Panic hadn't set in as yet, but it had definitely staked a beachhead on his frontal lobe. "What the heck is a times table?" he wondered frantically.

Just a couple weeks before, at Ramsey, daily homework included subtraction, but apparently this class appeared to be well beyond that topic. What was known was that his turn would be coming soon. What wasn't known however was how to answer a question, which he fundamentally couldn't grasp.

"Tracy, what's seven times six?"

"42", a rail-thin, bespectacled girl smartly asserted.

"Correct! Kenny, what's four times nine?"

"36", squeezed from the lungs of a boy with obvious signs of muscular dystrophy

"Correct! Donald, can you give us nine times nine today?"

"Yes, Mrs. Watson. That would be 81."

"Fantastic, Donald, bravo!" Mrs. Watson enthused.

As students accurately answered their posed questions, Alan's anxiety worsened. The feeling was akin to being suddenly stranded in a foreign country sans interpreter. It was bad enough that he didn't have an inkling of what times tables were, but the numbering scheme baffled his brain. How five and six could be combined in any way, shape, or form to make 30, was beyond him. More troublesome, was that every student correctly, quickly, and confidently answered their respective questions.

Then, a sick feeling quickly radiated through his body. He was a dummy who'd been put in dummy classes at Ramsey. Now, he was in a real fourth grade class, taking actual grade level subjects. Perhaps, Steinback didn't have dummy level classes. When he got home, perhaps mom would fit him for a dunce cap so he could at least look stylish while taking up permanent residence in the classroom's far corner.

After every other student had their turn, Alan felt the fingers of doom squeezing his neck. Mrs. Watson looked him dead straight in the peepers, and without hesitation, asked for the solution to three times four. Maybe, if he didn't answer, she might move on to someone else. But doing so might give Mrs. Watson a false impression. Never being a troublemaker, but in his mind, looking stupid was worse than making her angry.

"Mr. Jones, I'll ask you once more," she spoke in succinct, monosyllabic speech, "What is three times four?" putting emphasis on "four"

Alan noticed how suddenly quiet it became. Panicked at the thought that his breathing had become very audible, he purposely held his oxygen intake for short spurts to limit embarrassment. Looking around, there were concerned expressions coming his way. It's the "you're gonna get it look" siblings flash each other when one of them pisses off mommy.

"Mr. Alan Jones, please make no mistake. I will not harbor disrespectful behavior in my classroom. If you persist in not answering me, I promise you that there will be severe consequences forthcoming. Am I perfectly clear, young man?" She clenched her teeth while glaring lasers his way.

"Yes, ma'am," bowing his head fearfully.

"Very well, then. I'll ask you one final time. What is three times four?"

Having no other face-saving options left, he just threw a number out and desperately hoped for a miracle. "16", he meekly offered.

The classroom exploded in a chorus of mocking laughter and jeers. The next chorus in his humiliation was a wave of derisive insults, "dummy", "retard", "lame brain", "idiot", and "moron".

The onslaught of hurtful comments overwhelmed him, and he wondered why these kids hated him so much. As tears streamed onto his textbook, a third chorus of "cry baby, cry baby, wear your diaper," rang out. Suddenly, a booming thud brought silence once again.

"Enough!" Mrs. Watson screamed, before picking her thrown book off her desk. "The next person who says another word is going home with a note to their parents. Now, Alan, I'll talk to you at recess. As for the rest of you, the only sounds coming from any of you will be when I ask a question."

The students responded with a sharp, unified, "Yes, ma'am."

Alan watched the clock as recess grew closer. At Ramsey Elementary, no one really cared if you answered a question right or wrong. Everybody still got a gold star at day's end, and teachers didn't seem to mind repeating themselves day-after-day. All that was asked of a student was that they try their best, even if they could never correctly add three plus two. However, he got a sinking feeling that Steinback was a more competitive school. Yes, Ramsey and Steinback were both elementary schools for the disabled, but their philosophies resided at polar opposites.

The bell finally rang and Alan's classmates headed out to the playground. As soon as he and Mrs. Watson were alone, she slowly strode to his desk and pulled up a chair. Before speaking, she studied his nervous expression for a few awkward seconds; he grew increasingly uneasy at what he interpreted as wordless disapproval. Sensing her new pupil was just short of terrified, she reached out and gently held his right hand between her hands.

"Alan", she began softly, "I want you to relax as much as you can. We're just going to have a nice little talk, okay?"

"Okay," he anxiously uttered.

"Now, at your last school, what math subject were you working on last?"

"Minuses."

"You mean subtraction?"

"Yes, ma'am."

"Oh, I see now why you had problems today."

"Uh huh," Alan, feeling tears well up again, bowed his head with shame.

She lifted his head back up with her hand, "Oh, no, you don't, mister, no self pity in my class. If one of my students has a problem, I'll work with them until it's fixed. Got that?" Her eyes moved back and forth within his gaze, making sure her new pupil understood her sincerity. He nodded affirmatively while drying his eyes.

"From now on, instead of going out to play during recess, you'll be in here with me getting caught up on math—agreed?

"Yes, ma'am," he almost gratefully exclaimed.

"Good, now I'm also assigning you extra math homework because I firmly believe that practice makes perfect."

They spent what remained of recess studying basics of multiplication. She broke down concepts into smaller more digestible segments until she saw flickers of comprehension in his eyes. Even though she had to repeat herself again and again, her patience never waned. Whenever he showed frustration or self-deprecating tendencies, she immediately refocused him with a sharp rebuke.

"Oh, what's the point? I'm stupid," he whined.

"Hey, hey!" she yelled, "Stop that right now, unless you'd like to sit in the corner for the rest of the day!"

The unexpected ferocity of her tone shocked him from defeatism. Never before had he encountered a teacher who possessed such passionate resolve. Recess was also staff coffee break time. Yet, here she was, eschewing that for him. He knew teachers who yelled just to vent personal frustrations on helpless kids. Mrs. Watson's admonishments, on the other hand, seemed to be given when a student, or class, lost focus on the objective at hand.

As recess wound down, she asked him about his favorite school subject. When informed about his knack for spelling, she gave him an impromptu spelling quiz of six progressively harder words. After he spelled all six correctly, her eyes widened as she let out a thoughtful and mischievous snicker. He spelled at a level not yet attained by their best spellers.

As soon as everybody settled back into their seats, they were hit with a nasty surprise. "Okay, I think it's time to find out how everyone is progressing on their spelling. Just like last hour, during math, I'll go around the class randomly and ask you to spell a word," she said.

Her announcement didn't seem to arouse a hint of suspicion in their young minds. They'd grown accustomed to her daily challenges and competing with one another for academic bragging rights. However, based on their collectively rude treatment of Alan the preceding hour, Mrs. Watson thought her charges were long overdue for a slice of humble pie, and increased the difficulty level to new heights. Not wanting to embarrass mediocre spellers, she rotated her inquiries only amongst the top four: Tracy, Donald, Susan, and Julie.

"Julie," she began, spell substantiate."

Julie frowned intently before her hesitant offering, "Um, s u b s t a n t e a t e."

"Sorry, Julie, that's incorrect. Anybody else?" she scanned for raised hands.

As the rest of them exchanged puzzled gazes, one hand slowly rose. When they saw who it was, chuckles couldn't be suppressed.

"Yes, Alan. Would you please tell us the correct spelling?" She softly intoned.

"Yeah! Right! Ask the moron!" The interruption came from a left side seat.

Knowing all her students voices by heart, she whipped out her notepad and scribbled furiously. Then, as she tore her freshly composed prescription for behavior modification from her pad, she verbally warned the offender, "Mr. Ferguson, you will take this note home and have it signed by your mother by tomorrow. Otherwise, I'll be forced to call her at work, and she has expressed to me that if I'm forced to do that, you'll be a very sorry young man. In the meantime, you can spend a half hour sitting in the corner!"

After some tension had passed, and Alan's heckler shamefully took up residence in the front right corner, Mrs. Watson serenely reiterated her question. "Alan, please tell us how to correctly spell substantiate."

With all eyes fixed on Alan, he instantly recalled how they'd mocked him just an hour before. All his young life, he felt betrayed by his imperfect body and speech. This, he felt, led many children to draw inaccurate assumptions about his intellect as well. After such a pitiful performance on the multiplication tables, initial impressions of him couldn't have gone worse. Now was his chance to prove that he belonged here. Spelling the word wouldn't be a problem; however, nervousness may cause a letter to be pronounced wrong and thus seal his fate as class dummy.

Fully aware of the momentous implications his answer would have, he took a deep breath and subsequently paused between each letter, "s u b s t a n t i a t e."

Mrs. Watson didn't feel a need to add a pregnant pause to a moment already rich with suspense and ramifications, "Correct, Alan. Good job."

He simply accepted her praise blankly, not wanting to show any satisfaction over a lone correct word. While his ability to spell the word raised some eyebrows, not all were convinced that it wasn't a fluke, but after Susan,

Donald, and Tracy all suffered the same fate as Julie by subsequently going down in flames and having their Alan correct their errors, he felt a new sensation come alive within him.

With each successive word, he saw a gradual change in their stares. Finally, his self-doubt had completely transformed into a confident swagger that evidently he couldn't conceal. While previously interpreting mocking glances, now he read fear in their eyes because they'd awoken his sleeping giant.

# CHAPTER 7 - DARE TO SMILE

Cerebral palsy aside, Alan Jones was a shy kid by nature. And, like most other introverts, being the center of attention in a crowded room didn't hold any appeal whatsoever. Events such as today's grammar school commencement ceremony are usually a time for celebration; but anxiety muted other emotions. He wished for chameleon powers so that blending into the stage could be a viable escape.

Further complicating matters, trying to be calm is nearly impossible when you're also dealing with a condition that causes twitchiness and involuntary flailing of limbs. Stressful times pour gasoline on the fire causing these symptoms to intensify proportionally. Consequently, he simultaneously looked forward to and dreaded sixth grade graduation day.

Typically, clammy palms, grinding teeth, and uncontrollable hand movements give an appearance of a kid about to be punished rather than praised. Steinback Elementary's auditorium was probably a little smaller than most other schools. But, on this day—to Alan—it felt more like a standing room only Broadway theater. The tummy butterflies were flapping furiously during this agoraphobic moment.

From Alan's perspective, even moving too much or breathing too loud would bring festivities to a screeching halt, thereby making him an object of ridicule and shame. As each speaker prattled on and on however, he gradually became aware that nobody else on stage had trouble maintaining poise. While envying their nonchalant demeanors he felt ashamed for being so wimpy. He thought that every parent could spot the only kid who was struggling with handling the moment. So, given his mindset, it was a great task to treat this as a celebration—not a trial.

Just when labored breathing caused light-headedness, a small hand gently began rubbing his back.

"Shh, shh… It's okay Alan. I'm here sweetie. It's okay. Relax," a soft lilting girl's voice whispered reassuringly in his ear.

Instantly recognizing who was soothing his troubled mind, a transformation took place. Alan's anxiety melted rapidly away, replaced by calming energy radiating from her hand. The kind soul in question was Emily Robertson—his Emily. In reality though, he was her Alan because she staked her claim when he transferred to Steinback two years ago.

Although standing just 4'10" tall and weighing maybe 70 pounds, Emily was a beautiful girl inside and out. She smiled at him and he could only focus on her shoulder blade-length black hair, blue eyes, and dimples. These traits unmasked a girl full of life and mischief. Ironically, poor circulation caused pale skin giving her an angelic-like quality—further enhancing her allure. Meanwhile, his body slowly began loosening up as her magic began to take effect.

Unfortunately, her heart and immune system were very fragile. A simple childhood cold required a hospital stay. Possessing chronic illnesses, coupled with a slight stature, forced her to miss so much school that she was nearly two years older than the rest of her class.

As a result, she often joked about being class babysitter whenever their teacher needed to leave the room. One time playfully telling a classmate that she would spank him if he misbehaved. Moreover, classmates knew her unassuming personality belied an inner strength and spiritual serenity of a wise elder.

Alan sighed, allowing muscles to relax as they went from a state of near spasm to normalcy. Emily kept rubbing his back and whispering calming phrases just to make sure her guy felt fully joyous during this day of honor and recognition. Whenever music played during transitional phases she would mumble quick, derogatory, jokes about the last speaker to further lighten his mood. Her spell worked wonders because for ceremony's remainder he beamed a natural smile of a boy who had just met Santa Claus.

Emily pushed Alan's wheelchair down the aisle as graduates received their diplomas. When they reached the podium, principal Smith attempted to hand Alan his diploma. Alan refused and indicated that Emily should receive her diploma first. Upon taking possession, she hugged her guy and cooed, "You're such a sweetie." Her public display of affection woke him up to the fact that others were watching—making him blush. But, those panicky feelings lasted only an instant due to her presence.

At ceremony's end, Alan and Emily sneaked outside for a moment of solitude before their respective sets of parents whisked them away for summer vacations. She eased herself onto his lap as he held her snugly. Then she raised his head with an index finger until their eyes met.

Looking upon her, every impulse told him to steal a kiss, consequences be damned! But, as luck would have it, just when he summoned up enough courage to make a move, Murphy's entire law library came crashing down on his plan. Their parents simultaneously arrived on the scene.

"Hey boy, what do you think you're doing with my daughter?" Emily's dad joshed with a fake snarl.

"Yes, it looks like a we got here just in the nick of time," Ms. Jones concurred solemnly without breaking stride.

Usually, emotions of anger and awkwardness arise when parents catch their kids being affectionate. And, truth be told, crimson colorization in Alan and Emily's faces revealed embarrassment. Yet, despite feeling understandably uneasy, the boy and girl stayed very comfortable in a natural embrace. Neither felt as if any grievous wrong had been committed. Both had terrific relationships with their parents.

Besides, the vibe couldn't be categorized as a typical situation where children are being defiant. Holding Emily without a single twitch, using hands that were dancing a jig a little while ago, Alan exuded serenity. She leaned back, letting her head come to rest on his right shoulder. They just wanted to have one last moment alone before a long summer of unknowns came upon them.

These were a couple of disabled kids dealing with severe and ongoing physical maladies. Alan, now, just age 12, already experienced the passing of several school chums. These classmates in particular were born with a variety of life-threatening conditions or diseases. In some cases, acute natures of certain conditions precluded any thoughts of becoming a teen-ager—let alone an adult. Other kids look forward to: first dates, proms, marriages, and children of their own; in contrast, disabled youngsters learn to savor every slice of happiness each day.

Mrs. Robertson knew this dreadful reality all too well. Her darling daughter's grasp upon life was tenuous at best. Emily had more sunsets in her past than sunrises in her future. Thus, with full understanding and motherly love, Mrs. Robertson wanted her girl to enjoy one of life's precious experiences.

"Why don't we give them a moment," she whispered while escorting her significant other and Ms. Jones surreptitiously away. Ms. Jones understood but Emily's mom had to resort to using an "evil eye" glare to get her hubby to capitulate.

Emily immediately recognized and appreciated her mom's gesture. As soon as the adults were a comfortable distance away—Emily beheld Alan with a soft, warm smiling gaze. Instinctively, he took that as a cue and put her head back on his right shoulder while hugging her torso firmly. Then, passion temporally overcame shyness as he impulsively gave her left cheek a quick peck. She countered with a mock stare of disapproval before eventually reciprocating with a cheek kiss and an amused giggle.

"Hey you," she cooed, "Did I ever tell you what a terrific boyfriend you are?" her eyes glistened.

"Uh, no, but I don't care. You're great too, " he grinned easily.

"I'm gonna miss you during summer vacation but we'll see each other at our new school in the fall," she spoke quietly while stroking his hair, "Say, what are you doing this summer?"

"Oh, I think our family is driving up the coast to San Francisco," he smiled, " How about you sweetie?"

"Oh Alan, you're so handsome!" She hoped that her caress would render him absent-minded.

"What are you going to do this summer? Are you going to camp?" Reaffirming the inquiry, like a dog with a bone.

Her expression turned serious, pondering her response.

The instant hesitation and discomfort in her mood set off all kinds of alarms in Alan's head. They only knew each other for just under three years. Yet, in that small amount of time, an intuitive sense of each other's feelings had been developed. So, now, she wasn't going to be allowed to just slide by with a weak excuse.

When she glanced down without saying anything, he lightly snapped at her out of fear, "Emily, you tell me what's going on right now!"

She felt like she owed him a truthful answer. At the same time, maybe this truth would be too much for him. Still, openness had always been a hallmark of their relationship. Moreover, he was well aware of her condition and all nasty monsters lying in wait.

His expression and tone softened upon sensing tension in her little body, "Come on Emily. We don't have secrets, right?" he smiled, "Whatever it is I can handle it," proclaiming with ignorant confidence.

One reason why Emily fell for Alan to begin with was personality. He came across as a caring soul with whom she felt strongly connected. Whenever she encountered a problem, he would be her first counsel. But, because of that initial quality she found so endearing, today she decided to reveal only a sliver of truth so that her guy wouldn't worry too much.

"Okay, here it is," she groaned convincingly, "Next month, I'm going in the hospital and they're going to run a few tests…"

"What, what kind of tests?" He interrupted with a panic filled inquiry.

"Well, if you let me finish I'll tell you!" She chastised with a glare.

"Sorry," he uttered uncomfortably.

"Alright, now as I was saying, when I'm in the hospital they'll run tests to see if they can improve my health," she plastered on a grin.

Everything about Emily's body language told Alan that she was fibbing. Her eyes fluttered and she seemed uncharacteristically tense. His first impulse was anger and fear—quickly rationalizing that her health must be rapidly deteriorating. However, instead of saying something hurtful, he played dumb. By not completely revealing everything, she had already communicated that her health problems were serious. So, for both their sakes, he opted for the path of least resistance.

"Oh, wow, that would be great!" He excitedly exclaimed with a wide smile.

After reading Alan's expression, Emily stroked his hair and shoulders and let out a sigh. She knew that he didn't believe a word of her fairy tale. But, sometimes, words are unnecessary when two people are close. The bottom line was that she knew his heart; he was tuned to her soul.

"Anyway, our folks are walking back here so…" she looked away, hoping he wouldn't press the issue further.

"Okay, um, good luck with the doctors Emily. I'll see you in the fall," he sneaked another peck before letting her off his lap.

"And you need to smile more Alan. You're always so serious," she giggled.

He blushed a grin while mumbling, "I know."

As Ms. Jones wheeled Alan to her car, he kept looking back at Emily as long as possible. Tears welled up in his eyes because he had a bad feeing that she wouldn't see the next iteration of autumn leaves or experience one day of middle school. On the other hand, her strong spirit had seen her through other health crises. So, perhaps her inevitable premature demise would be postponed yet again.

# CHAPTER 8 - DARE TO DREAM

The first day of junior high is both exciting and stressful. A junior high or high school kid falls into one of three social categories: a nerd, a part of the "in crowd", or just an average kid trying to get by without drawing too much attention to themselves. Alan intuitively knew that good grades would probably seal his fate as a nerd. Still, he couldn't wait to be a cool guy who went to junior high instead of a snot-nose elementary school kid. Running parallel to this desire is an aspiration of being able to excel in at least one area at your new school.

Dillon was a school for disabled kids grades seven through twelve. Although, calling Dillon any kind of "school" is a euphemism at best but that topic is more thoroughly explored in later chapters. Anyway, during orientation, Alan searched for a comforting, familiar face amid a sea of strangers. Knowing at least some former grade school pals would be matriculating here eased his angst. Finally, he espied three friends from Steinback Elementary. To his delight Emily Robertson glowed amongst them.

Up until this moment, he didn't really know if he'd see her again. They last spoke after sixth grade graduation when she spilled the beans about her upcoming hospital stay. At that time her tone indicated that serious, life-threatening implications might arise. Consequently, one of his anxieties for today was finding out whether or not she'd passed away during summer break. So, now, seeing her smiling face made it difficult to remain composed; he couldn't wait to be in her presence.

After orientation broke up, students scurried to reconnect with old friends or introduce themselves to new acquaintances. Alan aggressively pushed through to reach Emily and didn't hear people swearing at him for running into their ankles. His focus was on her and everybody else faded to gray. She was also trying to maneuver through traffic but had to be more nimble and avoid collisions due to her slight frame. At last, they were face-to-face and instinctively reached out for one another's hands.

"So, Alan, you're looking good. How was your summer vacation?" She smiled with her eyes as well as her mouth.

"Oh, alright, I guess," he shrugged, "but, I'm very happy to see you right now Emily!" He beamed enthusiastically.

As people were noisily bustling past the two lovebirds it quickly became apparent that their conversation would have to be suspended for a later, more private time.

"Well Alan, we both have first period classes to go to anyway," she yelled over the commotion, "I'll look for you at lunch, okay?"

"Okay, Emily, be careful getting out of here," he yelled back as she coquettishly winked, turned, and glided away solely for his benefit.

Only when she finally disappeared from sight did he start heading toward class. Yet, even backpedaling around other students became secondary in his mind. Fortunately, he was proficient at multitasking and routinely did two puzzles at once for fun. Meaning daydreaming about Emily, while not running over anybody in the process, turned out to be a fun challenge.

The daily format at Dillon was unlike any other junior or senior high school. Usually, you have six different classes over six periods as you rush from one room to another. However, at this institution, students stayed with the same teacher for three straight hours. Then, after lunch, standard high school norms applied with a different teacher each period. Alan looked around his new environs in order to acclimate and adapt. First day nerves came back and set in as the teacher spoke in admonishing tones reserved for first days.

"Okay, ladies and gentlemen, class, class, may I have your undivided attention please!" She smacked her hands together for effect, "My name is Mrs. LaFontaine," she turned and wrote her name forcefully on the chalkboard.

"Let me make myself perfectly clear," she scanned her new charges intensely, "I've been teaching for over three decades and I teach the same way now as I did to start my career," she paced through each row, "I set the rules in this class and you obey them! You will respect me as you would respect your parents. Do I make myself clear!" She posed rhetorically.

She continued, "I highly recommend that all of you take what I'm telling you now very seriously," she leaned over her desk, "There will be no second chances or warnings. This is your one and only caution. If you disrespect me, or your classmates, you will be sent to vice principal Stern for disciplinary actions and then she'll contact your parents or caregivers. Any questions?" She stared dead-eyed to the room's center.

Alan felt her conviction radiating within him. She wasn't a young, idealistic, teacher fresh out of college, full of naïve enthusiasm. Mrs. LaFontaine's eyes told a story of someone who had been broken by a broken system some time ago. Maintaining a semblance of control in a classroom full of mixed disabilities and intellects took priority over conveying any academic instruction to this group.

By quick observation, he didn't sense that there would be much competition for him. Almost everybody else appeared to be off in his or her own little world. The ensuing three hours confirmed his initial impressions that this was in fact a dummy class filled mostly with mentally disabled kids. She "taught" first grade arithmetic, spelling, and even drawing in coloring books. He wondered if this was some kind of hidden camera prank being pulled on him. But, alas, at least for now, this was reality.

After serving over three plus hours in Mrs. LaFontaine's version of purgatory, Alan found salvation in the bell for lunch. That wonderful clanging noise brought about two welcome, events. First, obviously, a cessation from suffering in a class where he felt insulted to be trapped in. Second, lunchtime means spending time with Emily. And, perhaps if they finish eating early they can find a secluded spot where he can hold her on his lap.

Once again, he skillfully backpedaled past a disorganized mob of students, pushing and shoving their way towards the cafeteria like a pack of mindless zombies. By observation, one might conclude someone weaving a wheelchair with such precision had some ballet or tap dance classes. Simultaneously, swiveling your head like an owl is required in order to navigate a good path. Deep down he liked the challenge of a moving slalom course.

He glided into the open cafeteria doors and threw a fist skyward to celebrate a well-run race. Alan and Emily quickly spotted each other then she signaled him to go to a table in the back. They rushed towards their eventual rendezvous spot and sat side-by-side, unable to wipe smiles off their faces. They temporarily forgot reality as their eyes kissed with a deep tenderness of two people whom although young by typical standards were old souls nonetheless.

"I bought both of our milks," she smiled.

"Oh, thanks Em…" he began

"No problem, you can pay for mine next time," she interrupted.

"Okay," he nodded.

"Your lunch is in your backpack," she asked rhetorically while slyly withdrawing his lunch bag from said backpack like a magician with a rabbit and a hat.

Alan's assigned feeding attendant came to their table. The man automatically sat on Alan's other side and reached for the lunch bag. Then, Emily pulled the bag away while politely letting the attendant know that she would be feeding Alan today. By the time she got done talking to him, he turned and walked away looking bewildered and a tad intimidated. Alan giggled, shook his head, and gazed at his girlfriend with admiration and awe.

"Boy, I think you almost made a grown man cry Emily," Alan giggled, "I think he's still wondering what happened."

"Oh Alan, how could you say that," Emily feigned anger with him, "I'm a sweet girl, and you know it," she pouted, "Now, say you're sorry!"

He mentally replayed what he said to her and couldn't understand why she got upset. After a few tense moments, he decided to employ rule number one in the boyfriend handbook: 'If your girlfriend's upset, say that you're sorry even when you've done nothing wrong.' Before starting to apologize though, he recognized a telltale sign betraying her otherwise flawless poker face.

"You know brat, you really had me going there," shaking his head, "But, you forget that I can read your eyes better than anyone else," he grinned, "And, when you're bluffing or fibbing your beautiful eyes smile," he firmly patted her nearest thigh twice. When his hand came down on her thigh, her smile burst forth and hysterical bellows emanated from her gut.

"Oh, you," she struggled to speak while laughing, "You've just busted me and complimented me at the same time," she hugged him, "Even when I want to kick your butt you always give me that look you have and I lose it."

Anyone seeing Emily for the first time would draw erroneous conclusions about her. Disability and related illnesses stunted her body's growth and development. As a result, she could easily have been mistaken for a precocious nine-year-old girl rather than a fourteen-year-old young lady. At 4'10" tall and hovering around 70 pounds, she looked like a fourth-grader on a field trip to a school she would attend in a few years.

On the other hand, if someone were to have their initial meeting with her through a phone call, that individual might think of Emily as a young mom in her mid 20's. She already possessed an intangible maternal quality of helping others either by action or spoken word. Due to many close calls with death she had gained adult maturity and an appreciation of just being in the here and now. So, Alan simply was grateful that this loving spirit saw value in him and cherished every second that they could spend together.

Emily took turns feeding both Alan and herself with her right hand. Meanwhile, under the table, she surreptitiously nestled her cold left hand in his big warm paws. Her healing touch always soothed whatever troubling thoughts were trying to scar his soul. She was one of those people whose simple presence made those around her more hopeful and compassionate. However, her cold hand also reminded Alan of her frail state and sparked him to ask about her hospital visit over the summer.

"So, Emily, um," he nervously hesitated.

"What Alan? Don't talk before you swallow," she teased.

"Oh, okay, I'll just say it," he sighed, "How did your hospital visit go?" he pushed the words out as fast as ripping off a bandage.

Without missing a beat she nonchalantly put the next bite of sandwich in his mouth. Then, Emily quickly took a gigantic chomp of her meal, slowly masticated, and looked away. She didn't want to acknowledge his query before thoroughly formulating a response in her own way, in her own time. Upon turning back to Alan and seeing those big, hopeful puppy dog eyes she knew that he wasn't truly ready for any possible answer about her health. Sometimes when a person asks a question about an emotionally difficult subject they are only prepared for an affirmation of good news.

After swallowing her last crumb of a big mouthful she smiled and hugged him, "If we eat fast, we can go out to the patio and I'll sit on your lap," she whispered seductively in his right ear.

All of a sudden, his focus shifted toward gulping down whatever remained of lunch. When your girlfriend promises to make out with you after lunch, you do everything in your power to expedite food intake. At this point, Alan adopted a simple mantra: chew, chew, chew, swallow, and repeat. He did have a foggy recollection of asking her some kind of serious question. But, her enticement pushed all other thoughts into the archives of his mind.

Emily could tell by Alan's body language that her ploy worked. She had a hard time feeding him fast enough before being signaled for the next bite. Her feelings about his response to her proposal were mixed. On the one hand, having your boyfriend love you so much touches any girl deeply. On the other hand, given her tenuous health circumstances, she felt somewhat guilty that he might be investing too much of his emotional health in someone who might not be around much longer.

"Slow down, slow down," she laughed, "We've got plenty of time and I can't have you choking on me," she smiled and shook her head.

"Okay, don't worry I won't make an embarrassing scene," he winked while polishing off the sandwich and slurping down milk.

After Emily bussed their table, she surreptitiously pushed Alan's wheelchair out of the cafeteria and down a hall. Since this was their first day at Dillon, Alan trusted that Emily knew where she was going. He still didn't know his locker combination—let alone the school's layout. But, before he knew it, they were in a secluded section of an outdoor patio.

As always, Emily was in charge, and as always, Alan loved every minute of it. She locked his wheels, slowly wiggled sideways onto his lap, and wrapped her slender, supple arms around his upper back. Instinctively, he reciprocated by cuddling her body snugly and easily. They shared a loving gaze while their faces drew tantalizingly closer until their noses kissed.

"You know what," Emily cooed softly, "I'm so lucky to have such a great boyfriend like you," she tilted her head and smiled.

Alan looked into those glimmering blue eyes and couldn't comprehend how this angel saw value in him, "I'm the lucky one," he sighed contentedly, "I hope that you never wake up and realize you could do much, much better than me," he chuckled.

She lightly stroked his hair and grinned, "You have no idea do you?"

"What are you talking about sweetie?" He kissed her chin.

"Alan, we've known each other for almost four years," she began, "I was in all of your classes in grade school and I used to watch you take over a class, answer question after question until the teacher had to ask you to let other people try. But, I got the feeling that you never wanted to embarrass anybody. You just become very intense when there's anything resembling competition," she spoke admiringly.

"But, I've always wondered why you…"

"Oh Alan," she smiled, "Like I said, you don't have a clue?" she paused, "You're going to do such great things…"

The bell sounded signaling the end of lunch and curtailing Emily's answer. Soon, everybody would be streaming out of the cafeteria to fourth period classes. Alan kissed Emily's neck and lips before she got off his lap. They didn't have any classes together so he suggested meeting tomorrow outside of her first class. She nodded in approval, rubbed his thigh, and winked before gliding away.

Falling asleep that night two distinctively different emotions were toying with his mind. On the one hand, when she told him that she sees value and potential in his life, he felt loved. Besides his mom, nobody had ever validated his worth and potential impact on this world. On the other hand, he just now noticed that she somehow managed to avoid a direct question about her health and began mixing those feelings of love with unpleasant thoughts. His heart already knew the answer to a question that he didn't want to ask because he still wanted to live in a fantasy for a little while longer.

The following day, Alan went to a bungalow in back of the school where Emily's first period class was located. He had just settled against an outer wall when she came out of nowhere and jumped on his lap. She wrapped her arms around him and gave him a long luxurious smooch. Then, she ever so slowly eased back until she saw his entire face. As she was pulling away, he couldn't help noticing that her expression had taken on a serious tone.

"What's wrong sweetie?" He rubbed her hip.

"We have to talk about something that's difficult to discuss," she groaned lightly.

He studied her eyes for a few moments and hoped against hope that his gut was wrong, "Emily, listen to me carefully," pausing to ensure that he had her full attention, "Whatever it is that you're having a hard time telling, me, you don't have to say anything right now," forcing a smile, "Let's just hold each other before your teacher gets here, okay?" His usually steady voice quivered a bit.

She stroked his arms pondering what to say. The weakness in his aura told her that he already knew something was gravely amiss with her health. Moreover, considering their ability to read each other so well, perhaps he was right and there is no need to verbalize her health situation. But, in her mind, that was a coward's road and she owed him more.

"Alan honey," she cast her eyes downward and sighed, "Yesterday, you asked me about my hospital visit during summer vacation and uh…" She clasped her hands together, "Anyway, the doctors say that my heart is very weak and there's nothing more that they can do for me."

"I… don't understand, 1 thought you said that they might be able to improve your health," his face flushed apprehensively.

Peering into Alan's eyes Emily knew that he was at the tipping point of crying. However, no matter how she cushioned the gut-wrenching reality of her fate, she would do something awful—cause her boy pain. Despite their youth, Alan and Emily had forged deep emotional and spiritual bonds from fourth grade. When you feel connected to that special someone, who you cherish and adore, their joys become your joys; their sorrows become your sorrows. So, as she finally mustered up the courage to speak, a tear escaped from her right eye slowly trickling down her cheek.

"Alan, sweetie, we've always been honest with each other even when it was uncomfortable," she held his hands firmly while making strong eye contact, "Well, today, I need you to be strong—okay?"

"I'll try," he swallowed hard and nodded.

Emily looked up to the sky and took a deep breath before uttering, "Boy, this is tough," she took yet another deep breath and continued, "Anyway, as you know, my health has never been that great from the time that I was a baby. And, as the years have gone by, I've had more sick days and less good days. My doctor said that as my body continues to grow, my heart won't be able to keep up and I'll get weaker and weaker until..." She trailed off.

Alan impulsively rubbed her fanny, "Are you dying Emily?" Using every emotional dampening resource to sound calm for her.

"There you go again Alan, you won't let me finish," she stung his face with a sharp slap, "Now, as I am trying to tell you," she glared, "over the summer my doctor had an idea for an experimental procedure that could make my heart stronger and improve my health," her eyes softened once more, "when I went to the hospital, they ran some tests to see if I would be a good candidate for the procedure. But, after running the tests, my doctor said that my heart is a lot worse off than he realized. He said that I wouldn't survive the procedure. Now, you can ask questions sweetie," she caressed his slap mark.

"Are, are you dying?" He stuttered, "And, if you're dying, how long..." he couldn't mouth the words to complete his thought.

"Well, there's an outside chance that I'll be around for my sweet sixteen party in a couple of years but don't hold your breath," she giggled attempting to lighten the mood.

Although she just confirmed what he instinctively knew, Emily's announcement of her grave outlook still stunned Alan. Before learning the cold hard facts, he could occasionally toy with a fantasy of being with Emily for a longer period of time. But, now, those delusional escapes had just been slaughtered by a cruel reality. Their future wouldn't be played out over a number of decades or years—but in months.

A wave of despair churned within his soul as he mightily fought back tears. There would be time to deal with emotions later. At this moment however, she needed him to be strong. He hugged his girl firmly, stared at wall, and tried to stifle a moan.

"Hey, mister, you stop that crap right this minute," she yelled while wagging her left index finger in his face, "Do I need to slap you again?'

'No, I'll get it together," he sighed with a pained expression.

"Okay then, let's just take a day at a time and not worry about what we can't control," she said, "Can we make that promise to each other?"

"You're right, we can be happy now," he conceded.

Autumn passed its torch to winter, which ran its leg in the perpetual relay of seasons. Winter gave birth to the season of new beginnings and hope—spring. Unfortunately, with each passing season, Emily became weaker and more ashen in her appearance. The young couple kept: talking, laughing, kissing, and hugging even when it was apparent that her time on this planet was drawing to a close. By now, her absent days far outnumbered her present days; however, she willed herself to see Alan on the last day of school.

As she approached her classroom Alan was positioned against a wall, "What are you doing in front of my classroom sweetie? I haven't been to school in a long time," she hugged him.

I always come here because it's our tradition," he said with a smile, "You don't know how happy I am to see you baby!" she became enveloped by his exuberant joy.

"I needed to give you a message today and I told my mom that nobody could stop me from going to school today," she stated firmly.

"What do want to tell me honey?" He stroked her legs.

"Do you remember when you asked me why I wanted you to be my boyfriend?" She smiled softly.

"Yes, and you just told me that I had no idea or something," he said.

"Well, I know that I kind of avoided answering you because I've always felt like I was the lucky one. You have something special inside of you," she began her pep-talk, "You're going to do good things with your life, I have a strong feeling that you'll help people. And, even if you don't see your potential, I see it inside of you right now," she said while firmly tapping her index finger on his chest.

He blushed and his eyes began pooling, "I love you Emily," he softly uttered.

She delicately dabbed his damp eyes dry and pulled his head onto her shoulder, "Oh my boy, my boy," she gently rocked him back and forth, "I love you with every bit of my soul. You have made my final years of life very happy," she released him, got off his lap, and stood facing her soul-mate, "I need you to make a promise to me," she stared through him.

"Anything honey," he averred.

"As I said before, I know that you're going to do very good things with your life," she bent over him with her hands clasped behind his neck, "Well, I need you to promise me that whatever obstacles come your way, you'll keep pushing and pushing and pushing until you've broken through," she slowed her speech and rested her finger upon his nose, "Don't let anything stop you! Dream big! Do I make myself clear?"

"Yes ma'am," he grabbed her hands.

Two months into summer vacation, on an atypically cool August afternoon, Alan's mom answered the house phone. Five minutes later, she approached her son with a solemn demeanor. She knelt beside him and stroked his legs, "Alan, mommy has some bad news about Emily," she hesitated, "Emily's mom just called and told me that Emily passed away in her sleep last night. Do you want to talk about it honey?"

After reassuring her that he was fine, Alan spent the rest of the day calmly watching television to distract his mind. As bedtime arrived however, stark reality couldn't be escaped. As soon as mom hugged him good night and closed his door, the floodgates opened and his pillow became drenched. He knew two things at that moment: no girl would ever love or understand his heart like Emily; and nothing would ever stop him from achieving his goals.

# CHAPTER 9 - THE MOLE

When a 12-year-old enters junior high it marks a rite of passage from childhood to adolescence. The opposite sex becomes more appealing than say, the latest "must have" toy. Self-awareness comes to the fore as one begins to take pride in or, worry about appearance, peer acceptance, and being respected. One week before Alan began his junior high experience at Dillon Junior and Senior High for the handicapped, he eagerly anticipated taking this next exciting step toward adulthood. A month later, however, he was dazed and confused.

In Alan's final year of elementary school, he'd been taking such courses as: social studies, U.S. History, and pre-algebra. Now, looking around Ms. LaFontaine's Level I seventh grade classroom, one had to wonder what crime he committed to be banished to a cramped bungalow in back of the school. His first three-and-a-half hours were spent here doing kindergarten type activities such as finger painting, arithmetic, and spelling. Most of Ms. LaFontaine's students weren't cognizant of their surroundings; let alone what was happening in class. He was mystified as to how he had been miscast so badly.

"Okay, class. Two plus seventeen is…?" Ms. LaFontaine asked.

Alan raised his hand and waited for the inevitable.

"Come on, class. What's two plus seventeen? Anybody besides Alan have a clue?" she pled despondently before finally acknowledging Alan,

"Alright, Alan, give us the answer." Her voice meekly trailed off with a tone of defeatism.

"Nineteen," joylessly answering and understanding his role in this twisted farce.

The next hour offered more of the same. Ms. LaFontaine would pose a question to her class and like a compulsive gambler who doesn't know when to cash out, hope against hope that anyone not named Alan Jones would answer.

"Please, somebody must remember what we talked about yesterday," she whined. "Okay, once again, if Margo has three eggs and Lucy has four eggs, how many eggs are there?" she sighed.

Alan kept his hand down because at this point he was more fascinated by his classmates' utter ineptitude than his own abilities. Then, after exhausting all other options, she called on him to end her angst.

"Alright, Alan, I know that you know the answer so…" she sighed.

"Seven eggs, Ms. LaFontaine," he deadpanned

Over time, he became her security blanket. His presence and competence allowed the beleaguered teacher to delude herself into believing that even in the twilight of her career she was actually a teacher instead of an elevated babysitter. So, naturally, she became very fond and protective of her star by keeping him by her at all times during class hours.

At first, his ego was fed by being Ms. LaFontaine's star pupil. She'd float a question to her students and he was always first to raise a hand. A competitive kid is always eager to demonstrate not only aptitude but superiority as well. As time wears on, however, cold reality tells you that being the best student in the dummy class in a school for mostly mentally challenged kids is a dubious distinction at best. After awhile, disillusionment set in as he saw Dillon for what it was—a glorified day-care center.

Frustration with an incompetent school system wasn't new to Alan, because whenever he went to a new school, he had to prove his worth all over again. Administrators, faculty and staff, always drew conclusions about him based on body spasms and impaired speech. Therefore, until they discovered his true talents, he'd be treated as just another useless retard taking up space. The realization that this was how teachers and attendants saw him left Alan feeling hopeless.

Other sensory perceptions told him not to take pride in hollow victories. A true competitor needs a challenge from those who are equally talented. Otherwise, accomplishments cannot be truly measured in a quantifiable way and are just meaningless mental masturbations.

Moreover, experiencing Chinese water torture in the form of an overwhelming permanent daily stench of urine, and on those very special days shit, emanating from three other students: Doris, Ned, and Ken, A.K.A. the three Stinkateers, kept him grounded in reality. Every day piss puddles formed ever expanding circles under their wheelchairs. Yet, he marveled at how Ms. LaFontaine and her aide had grown numb or oblivious to this perpetual occurrence. On this day, her olfactory senses were truly tested.

"Okay, class. Who can identify California on this map?" she pointed.

Almost on cue, the three Stinkateers made synchronized piss puddles beneath their wheelchairs. Although the opening act was impressive, ten minutes later, their encore redefined gross. All three made a moaning sound, scrunched up their faces and shit their pants at precisely the same time. Alan didn't know whether to barf or be amazed at such precision teamwork it took to pull off such a feat. If smells were visible, a big wall-to-wall brown shit cloud would've filled Ms. LaFontaine's classroom. From that day forward that act alone earned them the distinction as shit gods.

After his barfing reflex passed, two things totally stumped Alan, which is an unusual occurrence to say the least. First of all, he wondered how three tiny kids could produce such a nauseating stench. Secondly, he figured that Ms. LaFontaine must've lost her sense of smell or had accepted this as part of her punishment for past misdeeds. He worried that the odor would permeate his pores. Other smells come and go, but like visiting in-laws and three day old fish, shit smells linger until you see the merits of being a hermit. Then, just when his eyes began watering, Ms. LaFontaine finally, mercifully, walked over to the door and opened it wide. The smells abated somewhat and he survived.

From age three, Alan was very aware of others' judgments. Whenever mom would take him out on a simple stroll, invariably some well-meaning soul crossed their path for a chat. At first, they'd screw up their face and engage him in baby talk. Mom would then try to enlighten each stranger as to how bright her boy actually was by having her son perform a mathematical trick. After witnessing evidence of Alan's cognitive talents the stranger's persona towards Alan would take on a more respectful tone.

Upon reaching seven years of age, however, Alan tired of this trained monkey vaudeville act. One day, after mom recited her usual spiel, he let his tongue fall out of his mouth and mimicked the responses of a severely retarded child. Alan's mom looked at him with a mixture of horror, amusement, and respect. From that day forward, she never asked for another performance.

So, by the time that he entered Dillon, he didn't see any point in enlightening people who were just cogs in a broken machine. He naïvely figured that school administrators did their job professionally and actually examined each incoming student's transcript from their previous school. Instead of checking transcripts, however, administrators at Dillon made snap judgments about students based on intuition. He couldn't fathom that, in this day and age, new students would be assigned to certain classes based solely upon initial outward appearances. Instead of cursing the fates, however, he decided to have a little fun. During this wasted year, he purposefully decided to observe and experience how people act when they think nobody's watching.

Every day, around lunch hour, he used a restroom. Usually, all six urinals and four toilets had long queues of boys. Assuming that all of their charges were cognitively impaired certain restroom attendants felt free to goof around or take other liberties. Occasionally, an attendant would "playfully" rough up a kid and Alan wouldn't react because he wasn't sure what was happening. All that he knew was that it didn't look like a fun activity for the recipient.

Mostly, however, attendants were toileting their respective kids and talking openly about many subjects. Oftentimes, conversations would center around females on campus. One day, whilst relieving himself at a urinal, Alan overheard an exchange between attendants Rob and Steve. They both had similar backgrounds and attire for ex-hippies, denim jeans, t-shirts, sneakers, and four-day facial growth. Among other topics, a side bet was made on who could score first with a young female attendant.

"Hey, Rob, did you see the rack on that new girl attendant, what's her name?"

"Melissa?"

"Yeah, she's a prime piece of ass." Steve whistled.

"Hey, Steve, watch the language man, kids are here." Rob expressed panic

"Ah, don't worry, man. These kids don't understand nothin', they're morons."

"Oh, yeah, stupid me!" Rob laughed.

Alan thought that it really wasn't in his best interest to let these clowns know the truth. Still, anytime you're condemned or profiled based on a stereotypical construct it takes an emotional toll. It hurts when reckless assumptions are made that one is not worthy of respect, compassion, or dignity. At twelve years old, one is on the cusp of developing awareness and value of self. So, at this crucial stage, any input positive or negative has an impact on forming personality and self-esteem.

"Yeah, anyway, about Melissa, I betcha 50 bucks I can hit that before you can, dude." Steve boasted.

"You're on!"

Alan's attendant, Sam, zipped his pants and sat him down again. He lingered to hear other tantalizing tidbits. Twelve-year-old ears are rarely privy to such scandalous sexually oriented dialogue. So, naturally, he desired to soak up all of the "adult talk". Next, Rob and Steve speculated on which blossoming 13 and 14-year-old disabled girls were ripe for picking based on the perkiness of a certain body part.

"Hey, Steve, speaking of fine little plump behinds, some of those eighth grade crip girls have grown great booty curves since last year. Man, if it were legal…"

"Say no more, man, say no more. But, I certainly understand."

"Yeah, you're right. Anyway, if Vice Principal Stern caught us we'd be in big trouble."

Some attendants liked to weave fantastic tales of Vice Principal Lauren Stern in a leather suit.

"Yeah, she's one mean bitch. I wonder if she's mean to her lover. Sometimes, I imagine her in one of those black dominatrix outfits with a whip…"

"What the hell? You've got a boner for old lady Stern. You're sick, dude."

"No, I don't! I, I'm just saying…"

"Relax buddy, I'm just bustin' your nuts."

Meanwhile, Steve had grown impatient with Stanley, a slightly built seventh grader whom he was assisting at a urinal. The shy boy had difficulty peeing with an audience.

"You've got until the count of ten to start peeing, man, or else…" Steve screamed.

Stanley began crying.

"Hey, man, cool it, cool it." Rob tried calming his buddy.

"Yeah, man, if little dude can't go, threatening him ain't gonna do no good," Sam added.

Ironically, crying finally distracted Stanley, his bladder instinctively relaxed, and Steve got his wish. Alan felt a certain kind of rage reserved only for people who take advantage of their position to abuse and or belittle disabled kids. What happens when poor little Stanley is alone with nobody watching Steve? Alan thought Stanley's reaction to Steve's threat seemed predicated on a past encounter. Maybe, Steve had a history of hitting kids but given that most of these kids weren't capable of speaking up, who'd be the wiser?

After lunch, Alan was finally let out of his daily three-hour sentence in Ms. LaFontaine's nut house. He enjoyed finding and talking to other kids who had their wits about them. This subculture only represented about 17% of Dillon's 250-student body. Still, he took solace that he wasn't alone as experiences were related and shared among these kids who thought that they'd been summarily cast into scholastic purgatory and forgotten. He cherished a small ten-minute slice of time between the last bite of lunch and fourth period. Bobby, a friend from elementary school and a fellow seventh grader, was in a similar situation only he'd been bumped up to Mrs. Franklin's Level 3 class.

"So, what's going on with you," Bobby inquired.

"Oh, same old crap, teacher's having me answer all the questions," Alan sighed.

"Well, what do you expect, she can't call on anybody else," Bobby snickered.

"Yeah, I suppose so, but still it's weird, the whole freakin' thing is weird,"

Bobby saw frustration in his pal's eyes, "Come on, Al, what's up?"

"Look, I'll never say that I'm better than anybody else or anything like that…"

"What, Al, what?" Bobby implored Alan to vent.

"I just don't belong there, it's a god damn zombie class," Alan's face flushed.

"Zombies?"

"Yeah, everyone else in that class isn't there. They're off in their own world, eyes rolling around, people pissing and crapping stinking up the room, one guy just won't stop staring at me,"

"Man, that is freaky," Bobby shook his head, "at least in Mrs. Franklin's class everyone's somewhat on the ball."

Alan saw students rushing by which instinctively told him fourth period was rapidly approaching. Bobby punched him in the arm and said, "Hang in there," as they parted ways.

Alan laughed and replied, "Thanks, dick wad."

Three days later during, Ms. LaFontaine's first hour, class was interrupted. Mrs. Hathaway a school official stood in the doorway. The two women huddled briefly and separated slowly. Mrs. LaFontaine walked over to Alan, bent over and spoke softly.

"Alan, you need to go with Mrs. Hathaway now," she smiled knowingly.

"Why? What did I do wrong?" Panic entered his voice.

"No, no, my dear boy, you're not in trouble, you just belong in a better class,"

"Will you be okay?" he saw a sense of loss in her eyes.

"Oh, me, don't be silly, now you get out of here," she forced a smile.

As he slowly back peddled from Mrs. LaFontaine's classroom, he studied her one last time. As Mrs. Hathaway escorted him to the new class, he wondered how much more competitive his new environment would be. Their trek turned out to be a long one ending at the main building. As he entered room 15, there were a lot of familiar faces from elementary school. One of those faces belonged to Bobby who flashed him a wink and a grin.

Upon finding an open spot, a petite middle-aged red-headed woman walked up and greeted him, "Hello, Alan. My name is Mrs. Franklin, welcome to our class," she smiled.

Although Mrs. Franklin's class did indeed turn out to be vastly more competitive than Ms. LaFontaine's, Alan still came out on top. By this time, Dillon's administrators knew that they'd screwed up their evaluations of the freshman class. Moreover, academic calendar constraints forced administrators to wait until next year to explore Alan's mainstreaming possibilities into a regular junior high.

# CHAPTER 10 - THE INQUISITION

There were 15 students in Mrs. Franklin's level 3, seventh grade class at Dillon High School for the handicapped. Most of the students had disabilities including a developmental, as well as, a physical component. Consequently, as discussed previously, Dillon's primary purpose was not to prepare students for adulthood but rather to play a day-care function. There were a few students who only had physical disabilities. One of these students was Alan Jones.

Over the P.A. was heard Mrs. Wright's familiar voice with an unsettling message, "Alan Jones, please report to the principal's office immediately!" A hush fell upon the class as all eyes tuned towards Alan, realizing that he could be in trouble.

To a seventh grader, a summons to the principal's office is slightly more terrifying than an I.R.S. audit is to his parents. Then, predictably, someone began chanting, "You're gonna get it. You're gonna get it." Of course, the rest of the class felt obligated to copycat. When the chants died down, Mrs. Franklin gave Alan a hall pass and excused him.

As Alan started back-peddling his wheelchair through the long maze-like corridors of the school, his mind retraced events of the past two weeks. He couldn't recall an incident that would qualify him to show up on the principal's radar.

Now it must be understood that even though Alan was the smartest kid in his class, he could by no stretch of the imagination be labeled a "nerd". Although, he never got into "real trouble," Alan became quite adept at defending himself.

In a typical high school setting, bullies can be appeased through reason and, or, extortion. However, given the typical student at Dillon, defending oneself was a matter of necessity rather than an option. When he finally arrived at Principal Wilkerson's office, his stomach was, understandably, tied in knots.

Meanwhile, Alan's mother had asked the school to place him into the mainstreaming program Dillon had with Sylvester middle school. The program places the top 20 middle school-age students from Dillon into Sylvester for two periods each day. The administrators at Dillon were reluctant to grant Mrs. Jones' request for testing because they'd already done an evaluation of Alan based solely on his speech.

At the time, Dillon's basic method for determining learning potential was speech pattern. Consequently, Alan's speech disability led the school to make assumptions that he was mentally limited. Eventually, however, the school decided they would only be able to quiet Mrs. Jones by testing her son. Still, Alan was unaware of his mother's request as he approached the principal's office.

As Alan rolled in, five school administrators fixed their attention on him. Two secretaries simultaneously pointed at him, and giggled, "Yeah, he's the one." Then, Joan Hawthorne, a tall thin woman with horned-rimmed glasses, in her mid 30's, approached Alan. She bent down and talked to him as if she was an aunt talking to a four-year-old nephew.

She asked, "Hello, Alan, do you know who I am?" Alan had to crane his neck to meet the gaze of the inquisitor. As he answered, he responded by stuttering the words, "MMs. HHaaawwthorne, ssschool psychiatrist."

Obviously stunned by the young man's awareness of not only her name but also her position, Ms. Hawthorne exclaimed excitedly, "That's right!" Staying in her aunt persona, she clapped her hands while smiling patronizingly.

At that moment, all Alan could hear was the beating of his heart which he swore was keeping time with the throbbing in his head, as he wondered about the motives of this meeting. "Was Ms. Hawthorne to decide whether Alan needed to be institutionalized! In a padded cell! While bound in a straight jacket?" After all, he rationalized, "psychiatrists are the ones who send people to the nut house!"

Then, Ms. Hawthorne's secretary, Nancy, approached her with a piece of paper in her hand. As Nancy met Ms. Hawthorne's gaze, she handed her the note while stating, "Oh, yeah, almost forgot, your boyfriend called. He wanted to know if he could take you out to lunch, should I call him back and confirm?" Ms. Hawthorne said, "I have to give a test to this young man and I don't know how long it will take. So.." She shrugged.

Nancy interrupted, "Isn't this the kid whose mother thinks is the next Einstein?" she said, with a mocking eye roll. Ms. Hawthorne nodded. Nancy continued, "This kid can't even talk straight, you'll be done evaluating in no time flat. I'll call your boyfriend back and confirm your lunch date."

Then Ms. Hawthorne warned, "I'm not sure, Nancy." As Nancy walked back to her desk she replied with a laugh and a wave, "Oh, Joan, you're such a kidder!" All the while, Alan silently fumed at the secretary's insults.

Next, Ms. Hawthorne motioned Alan to her small office, "Please come with me," she said. Upon entering a windowless room, Ms. Hawthorne waited for Alan to settle behind a desk then she closed the door. Suddenly, all noise from the administration office and hallway became muted.

Ms. Hawthorne tossed three huge three-ring notebooks on the desk. As each notebook landed it made a resounding thud—causing Alan to jump.

Then, she sat down and informed Alan as to why he was here and what was expected of him. "Alan", she began, sensing his nervousness, "all I want you to do today is to answer the questions that I ask you. There are no 'right' or 'wrong' answers, so try to relax." Alan took some solace in her words but still was convinced that this test had potentially grave implications for his future.

Before opening the notebooks, Ms. Hawthorne asked Alan standard questions such as, his first and last names, the day, date, year, who the president was and so on. To Ms. Hawthorne's ever-growing surprise, Alan had answered all of her initial inquiries correctly. She complimented him, "Very good Alan! Some adults don't know the names of government officials."

She opened the first notebook, the title of which was simply, "Inkblots". Upon opening the notebook, she mistakenly surmised that the images would befuddle young Alan and quickly bring this charade to an end. However, Alan's astute interpretation of abstract figures left her mouth agape.

After disposing of the inkblot notebook, Alan's next task was titled, "Relationship Awareness". This notebook was mainly concerned with analogies and recognition of subsets using a mix of examples across a breadth of subjects.

When Alan saw the first question, he smiled. The question read, "1. Dog , Puppy as Cat , _____". Of course, Alan knew the answer was, "Kitten," however, he also was becoming aware of his own high competence boosting the assertiveness of his answers.

Moreover, he seized this moment to let the secretary's callous words fuel him. He began answering questions in rapid—fire succession. Finally, Ms. Hawthorne said in a voice of resignation, "I'm sorry, Alan, but I can't keep up, can you please slow down?" After Alan gave her a slight smirk, he said, "Okay."

Although subsequent questions grew more difficult, Alan used newfound confidence to calmly and logically sort through challenges the notebook had to offer. As he continually slung aside Ms. Hawthorne's forays, she soon realized that her lunch date would have to be postponed.

Contrary to Ms. Hawthorne's initial impression, Alan's testing process took three full school days to complete. At the end of the third day, both of them were mentally drained and emotionally spent. She conducted 35 tests in a three-day span, with each day beginning at 8 a.m. and ending at 4 p.m., with an hour lunch break.

During that time her respect for Alan grew. As each obstacle she presented, he subsequently hurdled. It was at this time Ms. Hawthorne's emotions got the better of her. She had just concluded the final test when suddenly, and surprisingly, the psychiatrist removed her bifocals and dried her eyes with a tissue.

This turn of events startled Alan. He had just completed the most grueling series of tests he could ever imagine, and now Ms. Hawthorne was crying? Young Alan was very compassionate by nature, so he asked, "What's wrong, Ms. Hawthorne?"

She quickly tried to regain composure, but her voice quivered during her response, "Oh, Alan, I wish I had tested you at the start of the year."

"Why?" Alan asked. "Why!"

While attempting to emanate a more professional manner, she responded, "Because …because, had we known how bright you were we could've…." Her voice trailed off as she looked at the ceiling in disgust. Once again realizing her unprofessional demeanor, she stood up and straightened her beige blazer. She took two steps toward Alan and cleared her throat before saying, "Anyway, Alan, you did incredibly well on the tests and the next step is for me to set up an Individual Education Plan meeting to determine your academic goals."

Alan asked, "When will that happen?"

Ms. Hawthorne put her hand on his shoulder, smiled, and said, "Please excuse me, Alan. I have to confer with Ms. Stern on that." She poked her head out of the office and caught Ms. Stern's attention. After a brief huddle outside her office, Ms. Hawthorne returned to inform Alan that they would have a meeting tomorrow after lunch. She then excused Alan to the departing buses for home.

# CHAPTER 11 - ENLIGHTENMENT DAY

The following day, as Alan's mother waited with her son for the school bus, she informed him that she would be attending the meeting at 1 p.m. in Principal Wilkerson's office. At first, this revelation alarmed him. Generally speaking, whenever your mother meets with the principal, it's not a good omen. Reflecting back to yesterday, however, he recalled that Ms. Hawthorne had set up a meeting for today, so he surmised that mom's statement was related to that.

Sensing his apprehension, Mrs. Jones elaborated, "Don't worry, honey." While comforting him with a hug, she continued, "We're just going to see what we're going to do for you next year because you deserve much better than what they're giving you now." As Alan used the lift to board the adapted school bus, he wondered if by the time he came home that night his life would be forever changed.

That day, Alan seemed distracted during Mrs. Franklin's three-hour morning session. The classroom and classmates didn't change for three periods. All that separated one period from the next was the subject being taught; for example, first period was English, second was social studies or history, while third period was either math or self-study.

On this day, time couldn't run fast enough for Alan. He anxiously anticipated the IEP meeting at 1 p.m. Normally, he was Mrs. Franklin's answer man. But, today, every time she posed her star pupil a question, she would have to repeat herself. She expected a lot more from Alan—far and away the best student in class.

Finally, she shouted, "Mr. Jones, where's your head today? Would you like to join the rest of us back on planet earth?" Her angry tone shocked him more than her words. He had always prided himself on his classroom attentiveness; moreover, her seeming opportunism to jump down his throat angered him and sharpened his focus. From that moment on, every question posed to the class, he answered before she finished talking.

Sensing something was bothering him, she talked with him briefly after class and he told her about the meeting. She gave an understanding nod with a pat on the shoulder, and sent him to lunch.

Understandably, Alan ate lunch faster than ever before. Looking at the big cafeteria clock, it was only 12:25 p.m., yet he felt a need to wait outside the administration office in hopes that maybe his premature arrival would expedite proceedings.

He frantically wheeled towards the aforementioned destination while drawing ire of fellow students whose ankles were victimized by steel foot-rests. However, their cries fell upon deaf ears. A fiercely determined tunnel vision focus of not letting today's potential slip away engulfed him.

Alan arrived outside the administration office at precisely 12:29 p.m., where he sat until 12:45 p.m. At that time, he ventured inside and was greeted by Mr. Wilkerson's secretary. She instructed Alan to wait just outside Mr. Wilkerson's door. Then, he witnessed Ms. Stern and Ms. Hawthorne walk in together while conversing. Next, he saw a couple of ladies enter whom he recognized, but whose names eluded him. Anxiety grew with each passing minute as his mind began running with all of the possible outcomes, both logical and illogical, of this suddenly fateful meeting.

At last, the person who had always comforted and reassured him strode in, confidently smiling. That person was mom, and he knew right then, that everything was going to be okay.

At precisely 1 p.m., Mr. Wilkerson invited the group into his office. Mr. Wilkerson entered first; positioning himself behind his desk, while Ms. Stern and Ms. Hawthorne flanked his right and left respectively. Then, two teachers filled the ends of the semi-circle. Lastly, Mrs. Jones, and Alan took their seats directly across from Mr. Wilkerson.

When everyone was settled, Mr. Wilkerson started the meeting.

Mr. Wilkerson cleared his throat before speaking, "The purpose of our meeting today is to discuss the future goals of this student. It has been brought to our attention that we have underestimated this young man's cognitive potential. Therefore, our goal is to determine what steps we have to take in order to ensure that from this point forward, he receives the academic curriculum best suited to challenge him."

After a brief pause, he turned to Ms. Hawthorne, and said, "Ms. Hawthorne, let's start with your findings on working with Alan."

Ms. Hawthorne opened her brown three-ring, spiral notebook. She raised her reading glasses halfway to her face, but then felt compelled to make a personal commentary, "Before I begin, I'd just like to let you all know what a unique pleasure and surprise it was to work with Alan. I have to admit that, at first, when I heard him slur his words, I made a prejudgment on his intelligence.

"Then, he did something that utterly amazed me. When he realized that I was having a problem understanding his speech, he had me take a piece of scratch paper, and he dictated the alphabet. Next, he pointed to the letters on the paper and found a way to express his thoughts! He actually created a system of communication! That single act clued me in to the possibility my initial impression might've been wrong."

Alan blushed while Ms. Hawthorne continued, "When you spend 21 hours with a person such as Alan, over three intensive days, you really get a sense of who they are. Alan Jones is a very, very, very special individual." She trailed off.

Ms. Hawthorne then went on to detail the test scores. She adjusted her glasses, and began, "On the English part of the test, Alan scored at 11$^{th}$ grade level. On the language and vocabulary part, he scored at 12$^{th}$ grade level. Finally, on the math part, he scored at 10$^{th}$ grade level."

There was a momentary silence in the room, followed by an assortment of gasps, whispers, and rumblings, as the group absorbed the shocking significance of the results. Each of them now realized that Dillon had failed Alan by essentially wasting his seventh grade year. Alan, for his part, could not help but exude a glow of satisfaction, while also noticing stunned looks upon faces of faculty representatives.

Alan felt like saying to them all, "See, I told you so." But, he knew it was the better part of discretion just to smile.

When the rumblings and murmurs died down, Mr. Wilkerson posed an obvious question, "Well, now that we know his cognitive abilities, what's the next step?" With tempered enthusiasm, Mrs. Jones said, "Shouldn't Alan be in advanced placement classes?" However, Ms. Stern was quick to inform her, "Unfortunately, Mrs. Jones, we cannot offer those types of classes at this school."

Mrs. Jones face turned bright red. She thought they were trying to shirk their responsibility in regards to her son, "I don't understand," she shouted, "he passed all your tests. He proved that he deserves an education. Now, you're telling me you can't give it to him! I can't believe this!"

Aware of Mrs. Jones's obvious disgust, Ms. Stern suggested a solution, "What if we enroll Alan in the Sylvester program?" She continued, "He would take first period history with Ms. Goldstein here, then take a bus to Sylvester Jr. High for second and third periods, then take another bus back here for a fourth period audio visual class with Mrs. Whitehead, which he can use as a study period."

Mrs. Jones inquired, "Isn't Sylvester a regular school?"

Ms. Stern replied, "Yes."

Mrs. Jones then asked, "What about feeding and note taking?"

Ms. Stern appeased her fears, "We will supply Alan with his own personal attendant during his time at Sylvester."

Mrs. Jones nodded her head and appeared momentarily satisfied.

At that point, Mr. Wilkerson expressed concerns over Alan's ability to emotionally handle going to school with nondisabled kids. Ms. Stern disagreed with her superior, "He will have to face the real world sooner or later, and the longer we wait, the harder it will be for him when he goes out there."

Mr. Wilkerson scratched his head, took a deep sigh, looked Alan dead in the eye, and said, "Well, Alan, we adults can talk amongst ourselves about your future until we're blue in the face, but, ultimately, the decision is up to you. We can keep you sheltered at this school until you're 21, or you can mainstream at Sylvester: the decision is yours."

The room grew quiet as all eyes turned toward Alan. He felt the enormous pressure of their fixed gaze and he also understood the enormity of his decision. With strained speech, he picked up the gauntlet, and stated with a slow but strong voice, "I want to go to Sylvester."

# CHAPTER 12 - THE GAUNTLET

This is a chronicle of Alan's typical day, from the beginning of the eighth grade to halfway through ninth grade.

An annoying high pitch of a new alarm clock startled Alan awake. Rubbing his eyes, he looked at the neon numbers, and they read, "5:30". He loathed that this new routine required rising at such an ungodly hour; yet, he knew that this was the only path he could take. Before this day is done, he'll ride four buses; take six classes while splitting time between two schools located in two separate towns. Then, upon arriving home, he'll do 3 ½ hours of homework, interrupted by a one-hour intermission for dinner. Next, a one-hour study session is followed by approximately 90 minutes of watching television or exercising. Lastly, Alan will happily fall into bed around 11:30 p. m. dozing off sometime during Johnny Carson's fifth joke.

At 5:33, resigned to his fate, Alan groggily stumbles out of bed and with his eyes half-open, crawls to the bathroom. Still half asleep, Alan attempts to successfully pour the contents of an 80% full stainless steel portable urinal into the toilet without jiggling and causing spillage. While leaning the urinal against the rim of the toilet, he slowly tilts the urinal to pour out the contents.

Ten minutes later, mom feeds him some oatmeal. Although he's never hungry in the morning—and oftentimes slightly nauseous—he won't eat again until lunch at noon. Before then, however, there are three classes to stay awake for, so some nourishment is needed to sustain him.

Approximately a half-hour later, he crawls around the house in order to stimulate a bowel movement. He desperately wants a successful bathroom visit before putting on those dreaded, heavy, long-leg braces and, especially, before the school bus comes. Due to the hectic nature of his schedule, combined with the ineptitude of attendants at school, he knows that his next opportunity to sit on a commode might not come until arriving back home around 4 p.m.

No such luck with sleepy bowels on this day. With only 30 minutes left before the bus comes, Alan and his mother must start the arduous—and time consuming—task of putting on his braces. First, Alan lies flat on his back wearing only underwear and socks. Second, mom lifts the heavy braces onto the bed. Next, he slips his legs through two sets of leg holes and into brown orthopedic shoes that are attached at the end of the braces by ankle screws. After he's in, his mom proceeds to fasten all of the 12 Velcro leg straps – six per leg – and tie the shoes.

With straps and laces securely fastened and tied, his mother puts her custom-made, hand-sewn pants, over the braces. These pants were first purchased extra large to fit over the braces. Then, Mrs. Jones split the outside of each pant leg with scissors. Next, she sewed Velcro strips along the length of each side. This allowed her to quickly and easily put them on Alan. From start to finish, putting on braces takes 20 minutes.

Around 6:45, once Mrs. Jones helped Alan finish dressing, the next task was walking her son out the front door and into his awaiting wheelchair on the walkway. First, she guided him to his feet by holding one of his hands and letting him use his own leg strength to stand. Next, she stood behind him with her hands tightly grasping his shoulders. Then, he began swinging one leg in front of the other, producing a gait similar to that of a convict on a chain gang who is encumbered by a ball and chain around each ankle!

Sitting outside, with 12 minutes to spare, Mrs. Jones sits on the bottom step of their porch and goes over last minute notes for Alan's third period math exam. After mastering the notes, she hugs him and exclaims: "You'll do great!"

The bus arrives a little later than usual. Mrs. Jones pushes Alan toward the side of the vehicle. The driver exits and opens two side doors where a lift is located. He then pushes a button on the inside of one of the doors and the lift slowly descends. Then, he wheels Alan onto the lift's platform and pushes a button raising the platform to the bus's interior level. Alan backs his wheelchair into a slot, which allows the driver to tie footrests to the floor and push handles to the wall.

After securing Alan's chair, the driver closes the lift doors and hops into the driver's seat. As his transport slowly accelerates down the street, Mrs. Jones waves to Alan, and he reciprocates. There are five pick ups left; however, he's dreading the next one. Randall James Boyd III is a cross between an obnoxious ass, a bully, and a momma's boy!

Ten minutes later, Randall -- don't call him, "Randy," – is loaded next to Alan. After the driver ties his chair down, he proceeds to partake of his favorite morning ritual, needling and sucker-punching Alan! Yes, for the next 30 minutes, at least, Alan can look forward to a potpourri of stomach jabs, back slaps, and elbows in the chest, interspersed with witty verbal jabs at his ancestry and testosterone levels. Since Randall was paralyzed from the waist down, Alan found the latter taunt amusingly ironic.

With eight minutes to go before first period the bus approaches the school's loading dock. All five wheelchair users start unfastening their tie-downs. Every second counts when there's less so little time to spare. Furthermore, as an incentive, if Alan manages to extricate himself first, then he not only makes first bell, but he also makes Randall late on this particular day.

A few minutes later, Alan wheeled onto the loading dock, and spun around to give Randall a double birdie. Randall responded with a suggestion of where Alan could stick his fingers! Then, Alan back-peddles through a crowd to a classroom at the end of the second hallway. Upon reaching his destination, he glanced at the wall clock and saw that he made it with just over one minute to spare!

At precisely 8:00, the bell rang, and Ms. Goldstein strode into the classroom and shouted, "Open your textbooks to page eight. " She then proceeded to rant on and on about Nazi atrocities during World War II. To further illustrate her point, about halfway through she put on a documentary that gruesomely depicted the gassing and subsequent incineration of the Jews at Auschwitz concentration camp. Afterwards, she seemed quite annoyed that her students weren't stunned at the graphic imagery. Never mind that it was wholly inappropriate to show scenes of rotting flesh to 13-year-olds. She was bound and determined to exploit her position, and used her classroom as a bully pulpit to advance her own agendas.

In order for her students to make it to Sylvester Middle School in time for second period, they had to make a mad-dash for the buses at 8:40! Those who could walk pushed those who couldn't. This group was given permission to race down the hall full-tilt, to reach two waiting revving buses.

Four minutes later, wheelchairs begin loading. As soon as a wheelchair is loaded, the lift goes back down for another. Meanwhile, either an aide, or another student locks down the last loaded wheelchair. Using this method there's no time wasted instead of letting the driver do all the work.

Amazingly, three minutes later, both buses are loaded and ready to go. The drive to Sylvester takes about eight minutes, with minimal traffic, so needless to say efficiency is essential. Unfortunately, today there was a multiple car accident on the main route, so drivers had to take a detour.

The buses approach Sylvester a scant minute before second period. Consequently, everyone in the group will be tardy. Fully aware of their predicament, before the bus comes to a complete stop, students unfasten seatbelts and help unlock wheelchairs. When the driver opens the doors, those who can walk, scurry to their classes, and those in wheelchairs queue for the lift. Alan successfully jockeys himself to be the first one out, to the chagrin of the other five wheelchair-users.

Mr. Henderson, obviously annoyed, glares at Alan and his attendant Mark, as they enter three minutes late. Normally, Mr. Henderson understands difficulties involved with traveling from one school to another in such a limited time. However, today was the first day for science project presentations, and Alan's tardiness interrupted a presenter. The class focuses on Alan as Mark pulls out a chair and wheels him behind a desk. Alan is chagrined by unwanted attention, and quickly sets his sights on the presenter in an attempt to short-circuit an awkward moment. Mr. Henderson then gestures for the presenter to continue, and mercifully Alan's embarrassment abates.

When class ends, Mr. Henderson motions for Alan and Mark to come up front. Alan is anxiously anticipating a chewing out session. However, Mr. Henderson allays his fears as soon as they arrive at his desk. "Listen, Alan," Mr. Henderson softly began, "I completely grasp how hard it is traveling from one school to the other and back again. All that I ask is that when you are late, and there's a fellow student in the middle of a presentation, that you wait in the doorway until the presentation is finished." Mr. Henderson looked into the young adolescent's eyes and made sure that Alan understood that he wasn't angry at him, he just wanted to minimize the effect that Alan's sometimes inevitable tardiness had on the rest of the class.

Alan knew Mr. Henderson's message was meant to solve rather than scold. "I understand," he helplessly conceded.

Mr. Henderson smiled and cheerfully exclaimed, "See you tomorrow, Alan!" Alan smiled back, nodded, and headed for nutrition break.

During nutrition break, the 27 Dillon students assemble under a covered patio roof on the quad's outskirts. Alan is fed a small oatmeal cookie, along with a juice box. Meanwhile, his best friend in the group, Bobby, decides to seek his counsel.

"Hey! Al!", Bobby began, "How'd your class go, with us bein' late and all?"

"All things considered, as good as can be expected, I suppose," Alan shrugged.

"Why? What happened to you?" Bobby followed up.

"Well, my teacher held me after class and told me to wait in the door-way next time if there's a presentation in progress."

"Did he yell at you?"

"No, and I expected him to yell but he was very calm and understood our situation."

"Man! You lucky bastard! I got my ass chewed real bad by Mr. Black," Bobby trailed off dispiritedly.

Seeing pain in his friend's eyes, Alan made deeper inquiry, "Oh, man, what the hell did he do to you, Bob?"

Bobby's shoulders slumped; he lowered his eyes, and sounded hesitantly nervous in his response. "He called me to the front of the room and yelled at me for what seemed like forever. He said that kids like us should be grateful for having an opportunity like this. And that the least I could do was show up on time."

"Did you explain about the bus?"

"I tried to, but he just told me to shut up and take a seat!" Bobby frowned.

Alan knew that Bobby had been unjustly persecuted and was determined to do something about it. First of all, he wanted to make sure that Bobby was going to be okay. "Look, Bob, you and I both know that there are some people at this school who don't want crips here. And you know what, man? No matter what we do, we'll never win those people over. So, what we've got to do is control the things we can and if someone doesn't like the way we look, or whatever, I say, fuck 'em!" As Bobby broke up in laughter, Alan grabbed him playfully behind the neck and laughed with his buddy.

Mark wheeled Alan towards his third period class a few minutes shy of the 10:30 bell. As they were walking, Alan relayed Bobby's predicament. Mark, aside from being Alan's attendant, is a liaison between disabled students and faculty at Sylvester. Mark told Alan that he'd handle the situation.

Alan and Mark were always on time for Mrs. Johnson's math class. Ironically, however, Mrs.

Johnson was always tardy. With such an unruly crowd, she could hardly be blamed for her lack of promptness.

At 10:33, Mrs. Johnson strolls into the room and slaps down a copy of tonight's homework assignment on Alan's desk, along with notes of her last topic of the period. Because he has to leave ten minutes early in order to catch the bus back to Dillon, it's never an ideal situation to leave any class ten minutes early. However, given the time constraints, it was the only viable option.

This was a relaxing class for Alan. First, he was tops in math. Second, Mrs. Johnson took a liking to him because of his inquisitiveness. Third, he really didn't give a shit how much fellow classmates heckled. (For an in depth look at this particular class see Spitwads)

With ten minutes to go in the class, as quietly as possible, Mark slips Alan's books into the hand- made leather book bag that his mother created. Alan gives Mrs. Johnson a nod as Mark wheels him out the door amid a chorus of boos. The buses back to Dillon depart in ten minutes, so no movement can be wasted. Under the best of circumstances, if they manage to leave Sylvester at 11:50 a.m., by the time they arrive at Dillon, factoring in noon-time traffic, unloading, walking to the cafeteria, and getting in line, we're talking about 12:20 p.m. at the earliest for actually sitting down to eat something!

On this particular day, all of the students are waiting to be boarded at 11:30 but, unfortunately, there are no buses! Word comes to the anxiously awaiting group that their rides are running late due to mechanical problems. One student lightens the mood, "Well, I don't know about you guys, but I say if they ain't gonna feed us, we should ditch the rest of the damn day!" He strongly asserts while pounding his cane into the concrete, ala ex-Soviet leader Nikita Khrushchev. After an uneasy silence, while his mates try to decipher their boisterous comrade's temperament, he cracks a smile and they all have a good laugh.

Fifty minutes later, replacement buses finally arrive, and the group hastily boards them in an effort to minimize the delay. However, they already are aware that they'll be chasing time, no matter how efficiently the rest of the day is executed.

As Alan's bus pulls out, five minutes later, students with sack lunches begin eating. Normally, drivers don't allow this but, given the situation, he lets it go. Furthermore, because of their close- knit nature, there's a teamwork element at play; students with good hands feed those who have difficulty feeding themselves. The only fly in the ointment is that they'll have to eat without beverages, meaning there will be a line at the drinking fountain as soon as they arrive at Dillon.

At 12:45, the buses roll into the parking lot, students begin unfastening seat belts and wheelchair- users unbuckle tie-downs. Those who walk, form a queue at the door, while wheelchairs jockey for position at the lift-gate. A hasty exodus occurs when the door opens as they go for the water fountain. Meanwhile, Alan and the three other wheelchairs wait for the driver to open the gate. Once again, to the chagrin of his fellow silver steed buddies, Alan has successfully gained pole position for the lift.

Once on the ground, a few minutes short of 1:00, knowing that his fourth period P.E. class is on the other side of the school, Alan eschews a nearby drinking fountain in exchange for one residing just outside P.E. bungalow #1. As he furiously peddles backwards, a grin crosses his face for two reasons: first, because he gets out of the wheelchair for the first time in six hours; second, Ms. Andrews was a "smoking hot babe" in every sense of the word; a six-foot blond, blue-eyed, young athletic goddess who had a face that turned grown men into babbling, giggling little boys.

Alan rolls into the door just as the bell sounds to begin fourth period. Ms. Andrews catches a glimpse of his harried expression and shows concern. "What's the matter, Alan, are you alright?" she exclaims. Still trying to catch his breath from the long sprint, he nods in the affirmative. After a minute or so, he explains what happened with the bus, and the domino effect that eventually made him skip eating lunch in order to attend her class on time. The normally easygoing Ms. Andrews suddenly becomes serious.

She crosses her arms, and asks Alan, "Have you eaten at all today?" He responds "no" in a rather matter-of-fact manner. Ms. Andrews then tears off a slip of paper from her notepad and quickly scribbles on it. She then stuffs it into his shirt pocket and authoritatively wheels him out the door. A bewildered Alan can only exclaim "What, why?" She begins, "Mr. Jones. How can you expect to participate in my class when you're running on empty? Now get your fanny up to the cafeteria right now and hand them this note. Alan knew that she was right, but he hated to miss her class. When he hesitated, she forcefully clapped her hands together and uncharacteristically shouted angrily, "GO EAT LUNCH! DON'T MAKE ME REPEAT MYSELF, YOUNG MAN!" Seeing the other side of his favorite teacher's personality, while somewhat disarming, motivated him to not only get to the cafeteria ASAP, but also led him to believe that she at least harbored maternal feelings towards him. He took her show of concern as a lighthouse beacon on an otherwise foggy day.

At 1:10, he arrives at the cafeteria prepared to hand the note to a staff member. To his surprise, however, there's a steaming-hot tray of food and a feeder waiting for him. As he wheels up to the table, in an otherwise empty cafeteria, cafeteria worker Lynette informs him that Ms. Andrews called ahead so he could get a head start.

After Alan finished eating, he still had time to catch the last half of P.E. class and, at the very least, get out of the wheelchair for a while and onto the mat. As soon as he arrived back in the exercise room, he immediately headed toward the big 36-sq-foot Air Flow mattress. This was the favorite piece of equipment among Ms. Andrew's wheelchair students. He plopped right down onto the big, soft, albeit noisy, electronically pumped contraption. Ms. Andrews was completely cognizant of the rigors of Alan's day; consequently, she understood how critical it was for him to use her class as an opportunity to escape the confines of his chair. So, as she put the rest of her students through their paces, she let him rest.

At 1:50, Ms. Andrews dismissed class early so that she could check on Alan. As she sat next to where he lay, she put her hand on his lower-back while inquiring about his status, "Can I give you a little back massage before your next class?" Alan enthusiastically responded with a hearty, "YES!" She gave him a brisk but invigorating rub down, after which, she helped him back into his chair and out the door.

The final class of the day was Ms. Dykstra's leadership class. The original purpose of this hour was to teach leadership skills, but, somehow it disintegrated into a bulletin board maintenance exercise. She seemed ill suited to the task. At the beginning of each class, she'd simply pass out construction paper, scissors and glue. From there, it was up to the students to make up their own assignment. Meanwhile, she would bury herself in a romance novel. When she wanted to read in peace, she'd pass flyers out for the students to post around campus. This activity took about 45 minutes, giving her ample time to discover how her heroine snares a lover.

Everyone paired up with a project buddy. Alan's buddy was a bright-eyed lad named Sam. In contrast to Alan, Sam had a very rosy outlook on life. He walked with a noticeable limp as a result of his own version of cerebral palsy. Alan liked Sam because Sam embodied a certain type of child-like innocence that Alan lost long ago.

Also, to a degree, Sam fed Alan's ego by constantly probing about the latter's adventures at "regular school." Whenever Alan shared details of his travails, Sam's unquenchable thirst for knowledge led Alan to conclude that his friend's true calling just might be investigative reporting.

Time to go home! After a long day, the sweet sound of the final bell is a welcome one to Alan's ears. When the clock is at 2:59, students begin leaning toward the door like track sprinters in starting blocks anticipating a starter's pistol. As soon as he hears the bell, he becomes part of a ritual perhaps rivaled only by Barcelona's running of the bulls! Students run, or wheel, with reckless abandon, in an effort to secure one of the prime seats on their respective buses. Elbows fly, smaller students are body-checked against walls, and an, "Every man for himself," attitude is the only rule.

Unfortunately, Alan was the last wheelchair arriving at his bus. The consequences of being last meant sitting in the very back where good shocks don't reside. To further complicate matters, adjustments were still being made on his new long-leg braces, which he felt were mistakenly manufactured for a girl because the crotch was cut way too high for his liking. Moreover, if the bus hit a bump at a high speed he feared that he might be castrated!

A half hour into the ride home, everything seemed to be going well until unexpectedly, "BAM!" pothole! When Alan saw the bus suddenly nosedive he knew what was coming, yet was powerless to mitigate its impact. When his end of the bus absorbed the shock, Alan bounced six inches off his seat and came crashing back down. Just before he landed, his braces pinched his scrotum, causing him to yell a plaintive," YEEEEEEEEE-OOOOOOOO-WWWWWWWWW!" Upon gathering his senses, he noticed that the affected area was wet. His next realized that the wetness was blood. All he had to do was hang on for one more drop-off, then, he'd be home.

At 4:02, Alan finally arrives home. When his mother gets him in the house, he tells her about his injury. As soon as Mrs. Jones gets his pants off, she gasps, and with a mixture of fear and anger exclaims, "God damn, good for shit-braces! I ought to sue the incompetent numbskull bastards who made this!"

Then, seeing bewilderment in his eyes, she hugs him tightly, while softly saying, "I just hate it when you get hurt, honey!" After she takes his braces off and attends to his wound, she helps him onto the toilet where he can free himself of a stool that's been bugging him for close to three hours.

From this point on, relatively speaking, it's all down hill. Just three hours of homework, followed by two hours of studying, sandwiched around a one-hour dinner. As you can no doubt surmise by now, Alan is unlike most of his peers. He actually looks forward to bedtime, because tomorrow the gauntlet begins anew.

# CHAPTER 13 - TEAM 27

The seventh, eighth, and ninth graders, a total of 27, mainstreaming two classes daily from Dillon to Sylvester, took Ms. Goldstein's first period world history together at Dillon. Ten minutes before class began, there were three minor dramas unfolding, with a common thread linking them. In each case, the combatants had similar disabilities.

Mark and Gary both had a variation of cerebral palsy that affected their legs only. Possessing strong upper bodies allowed them to use metal canes while walking. Although a year younger and 20 pounds lighter than his rival, Gary always challenged Mark for alpha-male status within the group. These two enjoyed swatting at one another with their canes, also known as "cane fencing".

Susan and Maria were both beauties afflicted with brittle-bone disease. They always vied for affections of "hot" guys. Susan had boys basking in her radiance as a striking blue-eyed blond petite girl with a perky disposition. Shiny golden locks, flowing halfway down her back, accented an angelic face.

In contrast, Maria's exotic Latin features, and early onset womanly curves, had boys flocking to her in pied-piper fashion. The two girls were always sharpening their tongues against each other's egos.

The rivalry between Alan and Eric was subtler, but just as fierce. True, both boys used wheelchairs for mobility; however, their relationship possessed multiple layers. The only thing differentiating them was their respective disabilities. Alan had cerebral palsy while Eric struggled with muscular dystrophy. Being far and away Dillon's top students in the group of 27 that went to Sylvester Middle School, mental jousting bouts are bound to occur.

To a casual observer, Alan and Eric seemed to get along great, discussing news events and sports. And while indeed mutual respect existed, on an almost imperceptible level during normal conversation, there were tests.

Eric discussed a science program he saw on television, and tried to catch Alan in a lie by floating a falsehood as fact to see if Alan agreed. Conversely, knowing Eric's weakness was history; Alan did likewise to his counterpart.

As Ms. Goldstein suddenly appeared, authoritatively strutting down the hallway, squabbles ceased and all six combatants glared at their rival upon entering the classroom. While placing her briefcase on a desk, Ms. Goldstein felt an uneasy vibe emanating from her students.

She figured that it was just normal pre-class rivalries and bickering defining this unique group. For six months now they saw more of each other than their respective families. In fact, it could've been argued, that they'd become a family of their own. Little did they know how the day's events would unfold to bring that realization home.

After Ms. Goldstein let them out, they rushed toward two buses carrying them to Sylvester. Without being asked, students who could walk assisted tying fastening straps to wheelchairs. There was such synergy during this time that both buses were almost always loaded and departed in under three minutes. Likewise, upon arrival, walking students didn't head for classes until their wheelchair-using mates had unloaded as well. The beautiful thing is that this behavior evolved naturally over time; no one was asked or mandated to perform given tasks.

Up until last year, Sylvester had been your typical mostly Caucasian, upper middle class school. Winds of change, brought about by district-mandated integration starting in the fall, led to simmering tensions between white and Latino students. Unfortunately, some of Sylvester's parents and students didn't distinguish between six buses of Latino students, and two buses of disabled students. To them, any status quo alteration wasn't greeted with open arms. As a result, occasionally, one or more of the group of 27 would be caught in verbal crossfire.

After second period, everyone headed toward the cafeteria for nutrition break. During the mass migration, a scuffle broke out on the center quad. At first it was limited to a group of four boys: three white and one Latino. When it became apparent that the Latino boy was overwhelmed, his assailants were flocked upon by seven of his brethren. This, of course, brought about a counter assault by many more whites joining the fray. The escalation of participants continued until a few hundred students were drawn into a full-blown riot.

Hell broke loose as Alan departed science class. Peddling backwards, with all senses on high alert, he stealthily skirted any brawls or melees, eventually finding a safe zone where the group always gathered during nutrition break. Once there, he counted 22 other Dillon students, meaning, including himself there were 23 safely ensconced from immediate danger. Yet, simple arithmetic yielded the grave realization that four were still missing.

Quickly, they huddled, took an informal roll call, and determined that Gary, John, Eric, and Maria, were absent from their ranks. Sensing fear and confusion amongst his mates, Mark stepped forward and came up with a plan.

"Hey! Hey! Listen up, people!" he shouted. But, there were still nervous murmurs in the group. "God dammit! Shut the hell up and listen before I jam my freakin' cane up someone's ass!" He screamed vehemently and banged his right cane on the cement three times.

---

There was a group-gasp at Mark's attention-getting statement, followed by dead silence. Once he saw that he indeed had everyone's undivided attention, he took two deep breaths and gave instructions, "Okay. Now, the first thing we have to find out is where our people are. Who knows where to look?"

"We need to know what classes they were let out of." Susan offered.

"Good, how do we do that? Quickly, people! Think! Think!" Mark implored.

"Class schedules," Alan said, straining to be heard.

"Yeah, if we know their last class..." Susan's eyes twinkled.

Bart, Eric's closest friend, knew his pal's whereabouts. "Eric is in the northwest building, room 16," he blurted out. After shy Bart got the ball rolling, in rapid succession each missing person's last known location became known.

"Then, we know where to look! Great thinking, guys!" Mark passionately encouraged his mates. "Now, we have to break up into four teams of four people. One team per missing person. And, remember, always stay together. The other seven will stay here and protect our area."

After assembling into teams of four, each team volunteered to find a specific person. Alan's team, consisting of Mark, Henry, Susan, and himself, assigned themselves to locate and bring back Maria. Her 2nd period class was U.S. History, in the eastern end of the campus. That meant finding their way back through ongoing turmoil between whites and Latinos.

They were rapidly approaching the boundary partitioning civility from chaos with every fearful, but purposeful, stride bringing them closer to both danger and accomplishing their objective.

Suddenly, a metal trashcan came hurtling towards Susan. Alan saw her in peril and instinctively turned his chair to protect her. He knew that even a slight bump, given her brittle bone disease, could land her in the hospital. The can flew into Alan's left rear wheel and bounced away. While causing his chair to temporarily tilt on two wheels, no other damage was done. No words were spoken, but Susan gave him a thankful glance.

Spying an open path, Susan pointed them along until they were just outside Maria's classroom. Upon opening the door, they spotted Maria cornered by two athletic looking white boys. Fueled by a surge of adrenaline, Henry grabbed Alan's handlebars and ran the wheelchair straight at one of the assailants. Alan instantly knew his comrade's intentions. So just before impact, he made sure both footrest blades were reinforced by his foot strength, by slightly standing, and thereby bracing his entire weight on his feet.

Alan's footrests smashed into both ankles of Maria's first attacker and flung him into a wall, where he collapsed writhing on the floor. Rendered at least temporarily unable to stand, he cowardly scurried from further harm by sidling like a crab out the door on hands and knees.

Henry and Alan turned their sights towards Mark, who was pummeling his foe with both canes. He alternated between smashing and severely bruising the poor boy's shins, back, and head. In short order, Mark's opponent had curled up in the fetal position and between sobs, was begging for mercy. Finally, seeing that rage had consumed their leader, Mark's team pulled him off and calmed him down.

All their attention now shifted to Maria who sat huddled in a corner shaking and obviously traumatized. Her blouse was torn across her chest leaving her bra exposed. Quickly, Susan took a sweater from Alan's wheelchair bag and carefully dressed her like a nurturing mother tending to an injured child. She hugged her rival, and Maria broke down in tears, staining Susan's new silk blouse. However, none of that superficial nonsense now mattered to any of them. All that mattered was getting their mate, and themselves, out of harm's way.

"Okay, guys, let's get out of here," Mark ordered.

"I can't stand up! I can't stand up! My ankle hurts!" Maria cried.

"Come on, you have to try!" Mark yelled.

---

**117**

"Sit her on my lap and we'll carry her out," Alan demanded.

"Henry, help me get her on Alan's lap so that we can get the hell out of here!" Mark ordered.

After they gingerly lifted her from the floor to Alan's lap, Alan squeezed her around the torso and tried to reassure her by softly saying, "Its okay. It's okay." This seemed to work as her little body momentarily went limp, with her head coming to rest upon his left shoulder. Now, having her secured and relatively relaxed, he nodded to Mark to proceed.

Mark peered out the window and found that most of the action had moved north of their locale. He guided his troops surreptitiously along until they were once again in their usual nutrition break safe zone. One by one, each team returned safely, having accomplished their respective missions.

As the final team joined them, sirens were getting increasingly louder. In unison, the 27 turned to look as four police cars screeched to a halt at the school's entrance. Teams of armed, uniformed, officers came streaming out with batons in hand. As they raced by, one officer noticed the group huddled tightly in a semi-confined space. He returned and asked if they were okay. They responded as one, "Yes."

The remainder of Sylvester's school day was cancelled for obvious reasons. After a very quiet bus ride back to Dillon, the 27 assembled on the loading ramp. Hugs were exchanged and those who broke down crying were consoled by at least two of their companions.

Mark and Alan each got hugs and kisses from Susan and Maria. They all endured a very harrowing morning and each of them needed support from the other 26 to make it through. Their unity prevailed and they now realized the strength of their team—their family.

# CHAPTER 14 - SPITBALLS

T he Black Knight sat upon his silver steed, grinning from ear to ear while the angry mob pelted him with the weapon of choice amongst those of their ilk. He had forsaken them by committing a treasonous act, siding with their oppressors. Alas, the Knight's betrayal cut deeper because only weeks before he had infiltrated their clan and led them to believe their cause was his. The mob believed their cause was just; they would resist any assimilation attempts. However, the oppressors were an awesome force whose agenda was not only assimilation but also indoctrination of all those who crossed their path. So the battle commenced....

The first week of Alan's first semester at Sylvester Middle School involved an advanced science class followed by a theoretical math class with the latter proving incomprehensible. So, an academic counselor transferred him from one math class to another. That first week both periods at Sylvester had 46 and 40 students respectively; yet, atypical of 13-year-old behavior, those pupils were remarkably quiet and respectful. So, wheeling towards his new third period math adventure, he wondered if the same tension-filled atmosphere, permeating those initial experiences, would prevail.

He finally arrived at his newly assigned classroom and entered. The scene temporarily baffled and amused him! Instantly, that door seemed like a portal to an alternate dimension. There were 30 eighth graders standing at their desks, yelling, laughing, and throwing crumpled paper and other school supplies around the room!

Now, as his mind absorbed this chaotic panorama, a woman posing as a teacher stood up from her desk and wrote her name on the blackboard, "Mrs. Johnson."

Nonetheless, general mayhem continued as students were unswayed by her meager attempt to restore order and commence class. After her introduction, Alan anticipated that she would take control of things by using standard teacher fare—yelling!

But, surprisingly, she began class seemingly oblivious to her surroundings. Over the din, he heard her mumble, "Please open your textbooks to page 32." Alan and a few others complied.

Noise levels eventually subsided to a more civil level. But, blocking out a multitude of side conversations amongst other students while focusing on Mrs. Johnson's low monotones proved difficult. If matters weren't daunting enough, Alan's attendant Mark suffered from a hearing loss. Consequently, because of these conditions, Alan shouldered an additional responsibility of relaying Mrs. Johnson's mumblings to Mark. Attempting to improve things, Alan tried to calm class down by telling Mrs. Johnson, "I can't hear you." This tactic just drew a barrage of spitballs to come flying his way!

Obviously, recent changes in math classes put him a week behind everyone else. So when Mrs. Johnson wrote on the blackboard: "test tomorrow," a numbing chill coursed through his body. Logically, he realized that getting a pedestrian "C" grade would be a great feat on this test. So, that meant cramming a week of missed studying into one night just to have a prayer at a respectable grade!

When Alan arrived home he immediately dived into homework of all classes. He prioritized homework needing to be done that night while setting aside homework that wasn't due for a few days or more. Then, after making quick work of high priority non-math homework, he focused on trying to absorb a textbook that hopefully contained a sampling of Mrs.

Johnson's first five days of instruction. Mom temporarily interrupted the cram session by feeding her son a plate overflowing with homemade lasagna and garlic bread. But, after dinner, he desperately resumed trying decoding that darn textbook until mom ordered him to get in bed at eleven.

Given severe time constraints on study time he was ill prepared for that first exam. So, a few days later, he dreaded Mrs. Johnson's revealing of test scores. That certain queasiness in his gut never predicted good outcomes. To a condemned man, waiting for an executioners ax to fall is often far worse than a momentary sensation of head leaving body.

Now, it must be pointed out that he always expected a lot from himself academically. Therefore, receiving a subpar score on that first exam would be particularly hard to swallow. As Mrs. Johnson read back the scores, there were just a few scores were 75% or higher. This development offered optimism that, comparatively speaking; his result wouldn't be so odious as to come under unyielding scrutiny of the adolescent character assassins.

Alas, embers of hope were soon extinguished as Mrs. Johnson read Alan's score aloud, "63" was the sentence. What immediately followed was a series of jeers and vile epithets that he had heard many times before, but never with a group dynamic. Shouts encompassed the usual range: "CRIP," "RETARD," "SPAZ," and "FREAK." Yes, Alan had heard these words before but never en masse. The assassins' arrows hit their target. But he wasn't going to give those "bastards" satisfaction by showing emotion.

The nature of a junior high culture is one that scrutinizes tiny flaws. Consequently, a disabled boy's fragile pride can be damaged in such a hypercritical environment. In spite of this, from a logical standpoint, Alan knew higher scores were on the horizon; performance would be much better on subsequent exams. Also, because of his recent transfer, there had been only one day to prepare. Moreover, he mused, "If I can get a 63 with just one day, imagine what I can do with a full week!"

As further inspiration, he recalled those taunts and hungered for payback day! Mrs. Johnson's next exam was in six days and 85% of her material had already been mastered. Every night after homework, mom quizzed him for an extra half hour out of his math textbook.

When a question was answered wrong, she marked each incorrect answer with a red checkmark and move on to another question. When their bonus quiz time ran out, she went back to questions with red checkmarks and had him restudy those topics. At week's end, Alan wasn't just ready for an exam; he salivated for one it like a hungry tiger waiting to pounce on fresh meat!

Exam day finally arrived and Alan entered Mrs. Johnson's classroom noticing usual exam day rituals. Kids frantically flipped through textbooks while anxiously dialoguing amongst one another in order to ascertain confirmation of answers. But, there were three students who were just sitting down, with closed books under their desks, appearing calm as can be. The three of them briefly glanced serenely at each other, smiled, and then resumed looking straight ahead.

Mrs. Johnson entered, and without pause, handed out exams. Then, she deadpanned a standard pretest speech: "There will be 20 multiple-choice, 20 fill-in-the-blanks and 10 scratch paper problems. There will be no talking, no peeking. Any cheating will result in an automatic zero and notification of your parents. Alright, ready, begin."

Alan and Mark went to a small room adjacent to Mrs. Johnson's class to take her exam. As soon as Mark sat down, Alan began spewing out answers to multiple-choice questions faster than Mark could fill in circles. When Mark finished filling in the last question, he gave Alan a look of astonishment. For Alan had just finished section one in less than two minutes! Then Alan said, in a slightly impatient tone, "Turn the page!"

A fill-in section presented Alan with his next hurdle. Normally, one would be expected to deliberate more because an answer has to be written in instead of chosen from a pool of five possibilities. Surprisingly, these speed bumps did little to dissuade Alan's dogged pursuit as he maintained a sprinter's pace by completing section two in three minutes!

Now, glancing at the clock, Alan saw that he had a full 50 minutes to complete section three. This section involved word problems, so it could be at least more daunting than previous sections. Word problems, by their nature, take set-up time. And, indeed, it took him 17 minutes to dispose of this section. Nevertheless, he didn't find that section's difficulty level to be significantly higher. After double-checking answers, he handed in the exam, and was excused with 20 minutes to spare!

The following Monday Alan arrived in class with a high degree of anticipation. For he knew that not only had the exam been aced, he also strongly suspected that he received a top score as well! The highest possible score, taking into account three extra credit questions valued at six points each, was 118. Mrs. Johnson's usual classroom mayhem was replaced by an unusual silence as an underachieving throng sat in nervous introspection.

From a distance, faint sounds of familiar footsteps grew louder until Mrs. Johnson walked in. She opened her notebook upon arriving at her desk. Next, without hesitation she announced, "I'll read the scores now so you all can stop wondering." She continued, "Heather Adams, 68, John Andrews, 73," Finally, her recital was nearing Alan's name, "Brian Ingram, 70, Mark James, 56," This was the moment. Alan's name was next. Then, surprisingly, Mrs. Johnson skipped over his name.

Well, as you might imagine, Alan became perplexed and understandably unsettled by this turn of events. As Mrs. Johnson continued with her drone-like execution of meting out reality to those hoping "D" study habits translate into "A" results, his mind rifled through scenarios as to what happened. His thoughts bounced between a lost exam to his score being "too" good. Eventually, confusion and fear grew into defensiveness and anger. Alan felt that she wrongly targeted him for persecution because of a disability. Suddenly, Alan defiantly shot his left hand up attempting to garner her attention. At that moment, a determined champion of justice replaced a normally passive boy. Mrs. Johnson waved her right index finger in acknowledgement and to let him know that nothing was amiss.

---

When Mrs. Johnson read off the last name and score, she broke down class statistics: "The average score was, 62. The low was, 45. The second highest was, 83. Using these numbers, the C-range would be, 55-66. However, there's one score which I omitted, Alan Jones received 118 points."

Instantly, Alan's face lit up, he wanted to let them all know who raised the curve and subsequently ruined their collective day. A voice from the crowd shouted, "OK! What asshole did that?" With his moment of glory at hand, he couldn't pass up an opportunity to rub their noses in how his success magnified their collective ineptitude. Finally, he could wait no longer; he raised his left arm and waved it back and forth while shouting, "Me, you bunch of morons!"

Upon unmasking their conqueror, a hushed, disbelieving pall fell upon them. An unthinkable event just happened and it took a few moments to digest. But, when their collective shock wore off, they decided to congratulate him in a manner in which this group of adolescents punishes those who don't rebel against authority.

The silence was at once replaced by sounds of paper being crumpled. Alan knew that spitballs were being created and that he would be soon pelted. Then, in one motion, most of his classmates stood, turned toward him and barraged him with spitballs, accompanied by a chorus of boos.

His reaction to this turn of events caught even him off guard. Instead of feeling sad and persecuted, he felt pride and triumph! From that point on, every time Alan entered that room boos showered him like a visiting big-time home run hitter. He owned this class now and everyone knew it.

# CHAPTER 15 - DYING CATERPILLARS

As we come of age, there are seminal moments that not only define who we become but also forge an indelible stamp upon all of our future decisions. These moments, like fire upon metal, either make us stronger or label us as also-rans. The true test, however, isn't the severity of the obstacle, but rather how we deal with our predicament. Some have the will, focus, and drive to take on adversity as a challenge, and aren't easily dissuaded from pursuing their passions, regardless of the sacrifice. Unfortunately, others wilt under fire and henceforth use adversity to set limits on themselves and make a convenient excuse for future failures.

In theory, Dillon's staff of 30 personal care attendants provided feeding and toileting needs to over 200 students. But, in reality, about half of these kids were fully self-sufficient in both areas. So, Dillon's true student/attendant ratio stood at a very manageable three to one. Each attendant worked with a group of three students for two weeks, then rotated to a new group. This procedure was instituted for two reasons: to keep students from getting too attached to an attendant and to minimize the risk of abuse.

At the start of spring semester, in Alan's eighth grade year, new attendant rotations were implemented. Students wouldn't be introduced to their new restroom attendant until Mother Nature called. Likewise, their feeding attendant's identity wouldn't be revealed until lunchtime.

Alan's bus arrived back from Sylvester fifteen minutes into lunchtime. So, in order to entertain any hope not being tardy to fourth period, getting comfortable with a new feeder—in an expeditious manner—became paramount. But, for some reason, today, that creaky bus lift felt molasses-like slow while descending.

Feeling like an antsy racehorse being restrained by an iron starting gate, he impatiently muttered, "Come on! Come on!"

Upon finally touching down on solid ground, he bolted towards Dillon's entrance. Furiously weaving his chair through a lunchtime throng, and nearing the cafeteria, he pushed and pried through a stagnant sea of wheelchairs before finally spotting a dude waving at him. Then, slightly panting, he eased on over to a table where Zach was waiting.

Zach came across as a boyish 30-year-old, making him one of Dillon's most popular attendants. Teenage girls were predictably drawn to his meticulously groomed handlebar mustache, slicked back black hair, and overall chiseled Greek looks. Meanwhile, Dillon's adolescent males idolized him as an ultra-cool dude who could get any chick he wanted. He had been working there since dropping out of college in his sophomore year. Suffice it to say, nobody ever registered a complaint about him.

"Hi, Alan!" Zach enthusiastically greeted him with a broad grin, "Do you have your lunch with you or do you have to buy?"

"I have it in my bag. The milk money is in there, too." Alan replied.

After Zach returned with the milk, Alan made him aware of his special time constraints, "Yeah, Zach, uh, on most days, I'll be getting back from Sylvester well past noon, so when I get here it's important... "

Zach cut him off, "Say no more, man, I totally dig. We'll get your pie hole fed, no prob. Are we groovy?" With a hand slap, they assured each other that everything was not only groovy but also totally copasetic.

Alan smiled with satisfaction before devouring a peanut butter and jelly sandwich, banana, and milk. With lunch's last remnants consumed, at a quarter to one, a big time buffer allowed plenty of time to make fourth period. Cruising towards class, Alan smiled knowing that Zach seemed to inherently understand his predicament.

Everything that week went as well as Alan could've dreamed. Zach even paid for milk ahead of time, so there wouldn't be a delay upon Alan's arrival. Of course, Alan reimbursed Zach during lunch. They were so efficient that Alan wasn't even worried about watching the big cafeteria clock hanging far above. At last, he actually could allow himself to enjoy a leisurely lunch.

The following Monday, Alan arrived back at Dillon around 12:12 p.m. So, again, time wasn't an ally and therefore eating lunch efficiently became essential. He took solace in believing that Zach would help compensate for today's time crunch. Upon entering the cafeteria, he espied Zach sitting on a table, one leg dangling, holding someone else's hands. Next, he saw a beautiful young woman sitting alongside Zach, looking softly and lovingly into his eyes. Unfortunately, he noticed one other thing; there wasn't any milk on the table.

Alan rolled up to Zach and waited for his conversation to end. Three minutes passed; Alan cleared his throat. Zach responded by holding up his right index finger. Five additional minutes elapsed; Alan tapped Zach's shoulder. His red-faced feeder whipped his head around while shouting, "Can't you see that I'm talking to somebody? Wait just a goddamn minute!"

Alan impulsively jumped away from the table while feelings of fear, disrespect, and anger played a disharmonious chorus within him. Zach's uncharacteristically angry outburst stunned and embarrassed him. At this point, given Zach's onerous demeanor, ceding to Zach's wishes seemed like a prudent option. He would just have to let his feeder take responsibility for Alan's now inevitable fourth period tardiness.

Finally, at 12:47, Zach's girlfriend left. Notwithstanding that Zach still had to get milk from up front; Alan now had a sparse eight minute window to wolf down lunch. When Zach returned with milk three minutes later,

Alan pointed to the clock. Suddenly aware of the sands of time, panic befell "the cool dude". And, a typically mellow, unflappable, beach boy suddenly transformed into a frenzied, breathless, anal-retentive mess.

"Okay. Okay. We can do this." Zach panted nervously while jam-feeding Alan with a ferocity that would impress secretaries of failing corporations tasked with shredding unflattering documents. Alan tried valiantly to swallow without chewing; there was no point in trying to chew because the sandwich kept attacking him. Finally, he grabbed his feeder's wrist while shouting, "Enough! Just give me the milk!"

Further unnerved by Alan's own display of anger, Zach stuttered in response, "Uh, okay, here you go." After chugging down his drink in record time, Alan raced with disgust from Zach and headed for P.E. class. He wasn't necessarily worried about how Miss Johnson would react if he came in tardy. As a matter of fact, most students doubted if she even knew how to get angry. A striking six-foot, athletic blond, in her first year out of college, Miss Johnson embodied sweetness. When he arrived five minutes late, she smiled while playfully wagging her finger at him.

"Someone's being a very bad boy today," she said, while halfheartedly attempting to suppress a giggle.

"Sorry, ma'am, I got delayed today." He began to blush with tingling embarrassment.

"Just don't let it happen again. Or else!" She barely exclaimed before breaking out in semi-hysterical laughter. Although Miss Johnson made light of the situation, Alan—proud of his attendance record—wasn't accustomed to being tardy. Hoping that today would turn out to be just an aberration on an otherwise spotless attendance mark.

When Alan returned from Sylvester the next day, he fully expected Zach to be ready to go. Upon entering the cafeteria, sure enough, his feeder sitting at a table and apparently waiting. However, Alan's view had been partially obstructed by someone else who squirmed on Zach's lap while apparently giving him a thorough dental cleaning with her tongue. Alan sighed deeply and with a sense of deep dismay, began approaching the lovebirds. He rolled up to Zach, tapping him on the shoulder.

"What?" Zach yelled angrily at the unwelcome interruption.

"I have to eat." Alan said in a lowered tone.

"Oh. Oh yeah, hey, Alan buddy, no harm, no foul, right pal?" Zach said apologetically.

Alan, frightened by Zach's mood swings, cautiously studied Zach's eyes and nodded his head slowly, "Yeah, okay."

While Zach got milk, Alan spent time with Zach's latest conquest. She just posed on the table, and smiled at Alan while letting her legs swing freely. As time passed, she continued gazing at him. At first, her apparent fascination naturally flattered his ego. But, after a couple of minutes of nonstop staring, he began feeling a drill boring between his eyes. Finally, unable to endure her unspoken torture any longer, he asked her a question.

"What's your name?" He inquired.

"Aren't you a cutie pie." she oozed as if speaking to a four-year-old, while rubbing his head.

Recognizing her overt condescending behavior and that her beauty was only matched by her stupidity, Alan shut down any further attempts at communication. Zach came back and proceeded to feed him. However, Zach's girlfriend's constant caresses and tongue licking distracted Alan's feeder. Try as he might to perform his job, Zach eventually succumbed to his girlfriend's will. At that point, he stopped feeding Alan altogether.

Alan left to fend for himself, with half a sandwich to eat, asked another attendant for help. To his surprise, however, instead of feeding him, the second attendant interrupted Zach's make-out session. After the attendant departed, Zach menacingly leaned over Alan's wheelchair and threw a tirade.

"How dare you do that to me? Do you want to get me in trouble? Can't you wait until I'm done with my girlfriend? I told you, I'll feed you when I'm ready. Now, shut up while I kiss her goodbye."

Alan felt too dazed at Zach's rant to form a facial expression much less an adequate response. So he just sat there, pondering future moves as carefully as a military strategist forms a plan of attack. The rest of lunch played itself out on Zach's timetable. Once again, he finished eating well into fourth period. This time, however, as he rolled into class ten minutes late, Miss Johnson's mood wasn't so jovial.

"What's going on, Mr. Jones? Do we have a problem?" she yelled hands on hips, with a laser-like glare that could pierce steel. While Alan finally had his question answered about Miss Johnson's ability to anger, he didn't like being the reason for it. Seeing her disappointment, and a resulting sick feeling in the pit of his stomach, only clarified what needed to be done. After assuring her that this matter would be rectified, he waited until the bus ride home to mull over various options.

On the bus, Alan began going over how to approach this puzzle. Obviously, mom had to be filled in on what his situation. She had always been his white knight against any dragons that a flawed, mismanaged, and out of touch education system had thrown his way. She served nobly as her son's protector, advocate, and cheerleader, but he'd just turned fourteen and a part of him desired to slay this dragon alone.

Right before the bus made its second turn, Alan had a brainstorm. Composing a letter to Principal Wilkerson seemed like a good idea. In the letter, Alan would detail his problem by explaining how Zach's actions and behavior were affecting him. Furthermore, Alan's rapport with Mr. Wilkerson was very good and figured that this is an ideal opportunity to use the principal's open door policy. He began mentally outlining thoughts in a calm, collected, and coherent manner. Being seventh to be dropped off meant that there would be plenty of time to formulate a letter.

When mom greeted her boy, as he rolled off the lift, she laughed softly because she witnessed Alan sporting an expression very rare for him—a smile. She could read her son like a book. Halfway up their walkway, she noticed more excitement in his aura than what he normally displayed after an arduous day. Finally, as they approached their doorway Alan revealed the source of his enthusiasm.

"Mom, I need to dictate a letter to you right now."

"What kind of letter, sweetheart?" ·

"I've got a problem at school and I need to do something."

"Is there anything that mommy can do to fix it?

"No mom, this time I have to take care of it myself."

"Okay, I'll get my typewriter and you just say what you want typed."

After Ms. Jones walked Alan into their house, she disappeared down the hallway. About a minute later, she came back carrying an old, sky blue, manual typewriter that she kept in immaculate condition. She placed it upon the sewing-table; hand cranked a single sheet of paper into the carriage, and nodded in his direction.

Alan began dictating without pause. The speed of his oration caught Ms. Jones – a 90 minute a word typist - by surprise. During dictation, she needed to ask him to pause so that she could catch up. Upon completion of her typing, Ms. Jones first read the finished piece to herself, then read it aloud to Alan.

She knew her son better than he knew himself. He could never hide his true feelings from her, no matter how successful he became at fooling everybody else with a well-practiced poker face. Even though he tried to camouflage his anger, she could tell that he was seething because the strain in his voice and undertone of the letter told her a different story. Next, her innate, mother-protector instinct kicked into high gear. She readied herself to slay yet another dragon at his behest.

"Alan, honey, what do you want mommy to do?"

"Nothing."

"Excuse me, honey?"

"No, it's time for me to start taking care of these problems myself."

"Are you sure? I'll be more than happy to intercede on your behalf."

"I know, mom. It's just that this time I feel and that I need to handle it."

After a pause, he saw a mixed look of melancholy and concern on her face. He hated when she became upset and he knew that his hero needed to know that he wasn't putting her out to pasture.

"Look, mom, I'll always need your support and backup in case things go wrong." Then he shrugged his shoulders, sighed, and lowered his voice before continuing. "It's just that – oh, how can I say this – it's just that . . . this time, I feel a strong need to see what I can accomplish on my own. I don't know how else to put it."

Alan kneeled motionlessly, nervously awaited her response. After a few long, heavy seconds, he got an answer. As Ms. Jones lifted her head, a broad grin washed over a sad expression from only moments before. He found this curiously amusing and wondered what had occurred to precipitate such a dramatic change in her mood.

"Is everything okay, mom?" He inquired, with a nervous giggle.

"Oh, honey, I see you blossoming into a butterfly right before my eyes."

"Huh? What?" He reacted in a dumbfounded manner.

"Oh, never mind, I'm just having a mother's moment. I'm so proud of you. You never stop surprising me. You keep .. ." She dabbed her eyes with a tissue.

"Come on, mom." He cut her off with a roll of his eyes.

The next day, Alan went to school with an envelope tucked into his right inside coat pocket. As the bus slowed before stopping to unload its passengers at Dillon, Alan mulled over how to accomplish his objective without getting expelled. His stomach began making otherworldly noises;

his palms were suddenly cold and clammy. And, worst of all, he even momentarily considered not following through. But, upon departing the bus, courage reemerged by taking a meditative moment to envision the task at hand from start to finish.

Alan purposefully wheeled toward the administration office. Surrounding students, who were making a harried scamper to make it to class on time, were vague images obstructing his path. He finally arrived at Mr. Wilkerson's door where the principal was engaged in a heated exchange with a repeat offender of the no smoking rule.

When Principal Wilkerson finished scolding the violator, his facial expression would scare the white off a ghost. At this point, Alan thought of that old axiom of discretion is the better part of valor. But, before he could second-guess everything, Mr. Wilkerson looked down at the envelope in Alan's hands.

"What's this? Do you have something to give me?" He grumbled lowly.

"Uh, yes sir." Alan nervously exclaimed.

"Well, let's see it. I haven't got all day." Mr. Wilkerson snatched the envelope.

At that moment, Alan, freed from worrying about how to hand Mr. Wilkerson the letter, tried to creep away. However, as Mr. Wilkerson began reading he placed his free hand upon Alan's wheelchair. All Alan could do was wait for a reaction. Mr. Wilkerson carefully read these words:

"Dear Mr. Wilkerson, Over the past week, my relationship with my assigned feeder, Zach, has severely deteriorated. As you know, I arrive from Sylvester Middle School sometime after lunch starts everyday. So, I need to eat lunch quickly. But, for the past two days Zach's girlfriend has been taking most of my feeding time. When I got to the cafeteria yesterday, I found Zach's girlfriend on his lap necking with him.

When I tapped Zach's shoulder he spun around, yelled at me to wait until his girlfriend left, then made out with her until quarter to one. Then, he realized what time it was and tried to cram my sandwich down my throat. If I thought that this would be an isolated event I wouldn't come to see you so quickly. But, this has happened two days in a row and I don't think it will fix itself if left alone. I am asking you to help me. Thank you for your time.

Sincerely, Alan Jones"

Mr. Wilkerson looked up from the letter and loudly moaned. He considered himself an excellent judge of character and knew from previous encounters that Alan wasn't a joker. The principal assured Alan that this matter would be investigated, and that Alan should go to class and forget about the problem until he could talk to Zach.

Unfortunately, telling Alan not to think about a problem is like putting a chocolate cake in front of a diabetic. Sure, he knows certain behaviors can hurt him but eventually impulses overwhelm willpower. So, all during his first three classes Alan's mind obsessed about the various outcomes of his bold maneuver.

When Alan arrived back from Sylvester, he heard an announcement blaring over the public address system, "Alan Jones, report to the principal's office immediately!" Words that strike unadulterated terror in the hearts of all students had finally rung for Alan. Suddenly, everyone around him on the loading ramp grew silent.

His heart thumped in his head as kids whispered about his doom. In spite of the sick, nauseating sensation slowly coursing its way through his body, he pedaled towards Mr. Wilkerson's office. Good or bad, Alan's problems would either lessen or spread in plague-like fashion.

Rolling to a stop at Mr. Wilkerson's doorway, Alan had settled down a bit but still displayed acute pensiveness. The principal motioned for Alan to enter and he complied while noticing Zach sitting to the left of Mr. Wilkerson's desk. Zach's hands were folded in his lap with his head tilted downward. The subdued expression on Zach's face offered Alan a ray of hope that this gambit wouldn't make him public enemy number one at Dillon.

"Alan." Principal Wilkerson began, "I've had a talk with Zach about your letter. He feels really bad about neglecting you during lunch and he has something to say to you. Zach?" Principal Wilkerson stared at Zach.

"Alan, buddy, I'm really bummed about how things went down and I just want to say that . . . " Zach's voice trailed off as he wiped his eyes.

Mr. Wilkerson gently interrupted, "Please, Zach. Continue."

Zach found composure once more, "I just wanted to say I'm sorry for acting that way. And I know that by now you're probably sick of me. But will you do me a favor?"

Alan wasn't very moved or convinced by Zach's seemingly orchestrated mea culpa. However, for fun, he listened to Zach's request, "Okay. What do you want?" Alan asked roughly, tilting his head in suspicion.

Zach struggled in formulating his words, "Will you consider . . .letting me . . .Uh . . . feed you one last time?"

Alan took a good, long look at the emotionally bruised attendant and smiled while responding coolly. "Sure, why not?"

A day after their meeting, word of how Zach had got in trouble had spread around campus. Well, that's not entirely accurate because the reason why wasn't as important to this student body as what bastard got their beloved Zach in trouble. From the first minute he got on the morning bus to the minute he got home, Alan's fellow students reminded him of his treacherous act. Every mentally aware girl at Dillon booed, heckled, jeered, or cursed at him. Three of them even slapped his face.

Yet, Alan kind of expected the day to unfold as it did. Knowing that he risked social ostracism by going after a popular attendant. On the other hand, he never was or, for that matter, cared to be part of the "in" crowd. On balance, the people heckling him weren't able to fully form a coherent thought, so to him their feeble gestures were meaningless—except getting slapped hard by three big girls.

One notable incident did stand out however. Ron, an attendant pal of Zach's, cornered Alan in a secluded area of the patio, grabbed his wheelchair by the armrests, and the following conversation ensued.

Ron leaned over Alan, narrowed his stare, put his finger in Alan's face and silently but unmistakably threatened the eighth-grader who was all of 100 pounds.

"I know how you screwed Zach over, you little bastard. You better watch your little ass. There are a lot of hidden places in this school." Ron warned vehemently.

Emboldened by newly found confidence, Alan looked up at Ron's tattered t-shirt, tied back ponytail, and Jesus facial hair. Noting alcohol aroma emanating from Ron's mouth, Alan said, with a chuckle, "Buddy, you're lucky just to find a job with your drinking problem. Back off before I get inspired to write another letter."

Ron sneered at him, turned and walked away.

# CHAPTER 16 - NARC

Among some of Dillon's attendants, mostly Zach's four similarly mustachioed reefer-smoking buddies, Alan became a marked man. They considered him a rat for getting Zach into hot water by reporting him to Principal Wilkerson for job performance issues. Conversely, they also were keenly aware that as a prized student he fell beyond their direct retribution. Still, every now and then, Alan would be attacked from behind and physically battered by a mentally impaired student with whom he had no quarrel or even acquaintance.

From being gut-punched to getting thrown head first against a tiled floor, to having his face dragged slowly along a stucco wall, Alan suffered a variety of assaults. At first, he thought these were random acts of violence. But, while getting patched up, after yet another attack, one of the potheads flashed him a knowing grin and wink. For a few hours afterwards, Alan dismissed any connection between his attack and Zach's winking pothead friend.

Upon further reflection he surmised that these two events probably weren't coincidental. Pothead posse members were probably assigned to work at Dillon by their respective probation officers. Even so, he never anticipated that they'd cowardly use mentally impaired students to carry out hits to exact their revenge. This realization only made him more determined to put these bastards in their place. Fear? He left fear behind last year. These stupid fools didn't know what he'd been through.

---

Almost a full school year into his first mainstreaming foray from Dillon to Sylvester, Alan's personality had undergone a noticeable transformation. No longer shy or intimidated in day-to-day dealings with students, attendants, or even teachers. Over the course of the year representatives from each of these groups had shown all too human failings.

At a school, such as Dillon, it's easy for abuse to occur. This becomes more likely when approximately 70% of students are unable to communicate effectively, either because of speech difficulty, cognitive impairment, or both. Consequently, bearing witness to various transgressions of inhumanity transformed his spirit from a wide-eyed accepting seventh-grader into a cynical, me-first, survivalist eighth-grader.

Three days after the latest assault, a scene unfolded that would prove to seal his fate as a rat or hero depending on your point of view. During lunch, he happened to be in the hallway when he came across Samantha Rodriguez. Samantha was an attractive girl with severe Cerebral Palsy whose mother always attired her in the finest clothes. Currently, she was in obvious distress outside the girls' restroom, furiously performing the "pee pee" dance in her wheelchair.

Samantha's attendant, Ms. Lawson, a plump 40-something, shabbily attired, dirty blond with a pot-marked complexion, was engaged in a rap session with a young rookie attendant, Ms. MacDonald, a scant three feet away from Samantha. Unfortunately, Samantha's speech was nonexistent so she could only moan. After watching Samantha writhing in agony for a couple of minutes, Ms. MacDonald's expression etched mild concern.

"Don't you think you should toilet Samantha now?" Ms. MacDonald opined.

"Nah," Ms. Lawson scoffed, "She can wait until we're done talking."

"But what if …?"

"She has an accident?" Ms. Lawson finished her apprentice's thought with a dismissive huff, "She knows that I won't tolerate an accident."

Soon after Ms. Lawson uttered those callous remarks, tears streamed down Samantha's cheeks as a puddle of her own urine grew in diameter beneath her wheelchair. He watched in disbelief, as her attendant appeared to be oblivious to Samantha's plight. Anger grew inside him instantly realizing that some attendants perceive disabled students as less than human. Alan wheeled up to Ms. Lawson and pointed at the floor beneath her charge.

Agitated by his interruption, Ms. Lawson scowled at him briefly before noticing that Samantha had indeed lost control of her bladder. Samantha had a knowing fear in her tear-stained eyes as Ms. Lawson violently spun Samantha's wheelchair around and raced her into the girls' room. Ms. Lawson's face was so visibly full of rage that Alan had a flashback to his beating by an attendant at age six. Based on that painful experience, and Dillon's culture of neglect, he feared for Samantha's well being.

After lunch, the disturbing scene he'd witnessed preoccupied his mind. There was no way in hell that he could let this incident go unreported. Now, he had to decide how to disseminate information to a trustworthy third party.

He couldn't report it to the attendants' station for obvious reasons. For a moment he considered reporting it to Principal Wilkerson's office. On the other hand, he suspected that Samantha's inability to collaborate his story would weaken its impact. He had been just a witness this time and not a primary participant.

His mom was friendly with a handful of other moms whose kids also attended Dillon. They'd all known one another since their kids were in fourth grade. Ms. Jones conversed with each woman, by phone or in person, at least once a week.

Alan couldn't help overhearing many of her phone conversations because of acoustics in their house and Ms. Jones's openness with her son. On his way home, that day, he recalled a recent segment from mom's end, of a phone call with Mrs. Rodriguez. In light of what happened to

Samantha during lunch, words from that conversation came to mind helping to instantaneously put the pieces together.

"So, how's Samantha doing in school," Ms. Jones spoke into the phone.

"Oh, that's a shame,"

"How long has she been coming home soaking wet?"

"That's awful. Do you have any idea…?"

After hanging up the phone, that day, Ms. Jones told Alan what he already surmised.

"Yeah, honey, I just got off the phone with Mrs. Rodriguez and she says Samantha is coming home wet lately." Ms. Jones began.

"Oh, really. How so," at the time, Alan barely feigned interest.

"Yeah, she's peeing her pants and not just a little bit either,"

"Oh, well, too bad," Alan didn't want to discuss it further.

Upon reflection, he felt bad for not having had a more compassionate ear. What if he was as helpless as poor Samantha? Once again, remembering how no one was there to stop his beating from that attendant, years ago. Wouldn't he have wished someone had rescued him?

Now, his time had come to speak up and set things right. He harbored no pretense of being a crip savior, superhero, or other such delusions of grandeur. That didn't mean that his conscience would let him suppress impulses of his formerly compassionate being. Therefore, upon arriving home, doing what had to be done wasn't difficult at all.

After stretching out on the living room couch, and settling in, he summoned mom for a counsel, "Mom, we have to talk,"

"Uh, oh, is there a problem, honey?" She sat on the couch beside him with concern in her eyes.

"No, mom, I'm fine but I saw something today that I think you should know about," his voice trailed off.

Sensing his struggle, alarm bells sounded as her mind conjured up dark scenarios. In an attempt to reassure him, she clasped his hands in hers, "It's okay, just tell me what's going on,"

"Well," he sighed, " a few weeks ago you told me that Mrs. Rodriguez said that Samantha was coming home wet,"

"Yeah?"

'I think I know why now,"

"How could you know ..." her face scrunched showing visible consternation.

"Today, after lunch, I saw Samantha squirming in agony outside of the girls' restroom and her attendant just stood right there talking with another attendant,"

"Oh my god, didn't she see that Samantha had a problem?"

"Yes, and the other attendant even pointed it out to her, but she said that Samantha could wait until they were done talking,"

"Wait a minute! Wait just a goddam minute here! Are you telling me that bitch made her wait to pee until it was convenient for her?" she seethed.

"Yes, and when Samantha couldn't hold it anymore and peed herself, the attendant got really mad and cursed her as she took her into the bath-room. It was scary,"

Ms. Jones took a deep breath while shaking her head trying to fig-ure out how to tell Mrs. Rodriguez about Alan's eyewitness account of her daughter's neglect and possible abuse. Her boy never gave her cause to question the veracity of his retelling of events throughout his childhood.

Because of this, her trust in him was implicit and unwavering. Consequently, her obligation was clear. Call Mrs. Rodriguez, relate the ugly truth, and lend support. Meanwhile, with his obligation fulfilled and con-science cleared, Alan closed his bedroom door as he went to study because he didn't envy mom's awkward position.

Although Ms. Lawson wasn't one of the pothead posse, two of them were her friends. Three days after Alan's mom call to Mrs. Rodriguez, Ms. Lawson received official written reprimands from both Principal Wilkerson and Supervisor of attendants, Mrs. Preston. Shortly thereafter, Ms. Lawson quickly deduced that Alan had been the one who busted her.

She knew that Alan and her fellow attendant friend, Ms. MacDonald, were the only witnesses to what happened. Her friend wouldn't report her, so it must've been that little brat who also got Zach in trouble.

As Alan passed her in the hallway between periods, she stared fire spears through him. Being a master of body language, he didn't need to waste any neural synaptic resources to interpret her mood or why she looked homicidal.

Initially, her gaze gave him a rush of fear as intense as a lightning bolt. That fear however dissipated just as fast. After she passed by, he couldn't help suppressing a large grin. A part of him took great joy that she knew that Alan Jones snitched on her.

# CHAPTER 17 - THE OTHER SHOE

Two weeks later, with no signs of further sneak attacks, Alan felt relatively confident that there would be no retributions for his latest act of squealing. Everything settled down, and some of Zach's pothead posse were even becoming cordial toward him. Yet, a nagging little nugget of logic slowly eroded a general mood of contentment. That nugget slowly transformed into a boulder of suspicion as each day passed by without a hint of trouble.

During times of uncertain peril, having a high I.Q. can have distinct disadvantages, especially when it helps stoke a fertile imagination. Alan could create doomsday thoughts far worse than any backlash that might eventually arrive in corporeal form. A multitude of "what if..." scenarios kept looping constantly in his mind fluctuating between feelings of cavalier brashness and anticipatory anxiety. Sometimes bravado took over, making him feel as though he could handle anything the potheads had planned, a kind of "bring 'em on" ego rush. Apart from these moments, an imminent doom scenario obsession prevailed when not otherwise preoccupied.

There wasn't any tangible rationale to Alan's fears however. As a matter of fact, since reporting the last incident, his attendants had been flawless in their respective duties. From feeding, to toileting, to note-taking, all needs were tended to with a high degree of professionalism. Additionally, attendants as a whole seemed more willing to engage in conversation and lighthearted joshing.

After experiencing a few days of this new social dynamic, Alan's confidence to advocate for better outcomes grew. Upon witnessing how speaking up led to a perceived transformation in attitudes amongst the attendant corps, a personal milestone had been reached—mom no longer needed to fight all of her son's battles. Based on past experiences at Dillon however, he wasn't ready to take the hook, line, and *sinker just yet.

Approximately three weeks after reporting Samantha's incident, he needed to use a restroom before lunch break ended, so he went to the attendants' station to have them page his attendant, Brad. Then, he peddled down to the restroom to wait for Brad to arrive. Meanwhile, students were slowly filing into their respective fourth period classes. As a passing parade of walkers, wheelchairs, and limpers dwindled to a handful of stragglers, he saw no sign of Brad. Five, ten, fifteen minutes passed, still no Brad. By now, what had been a minor inconvenience turned into a major issue as his bladder was burning and he was doing all kinds of funny looking contortions to keep from pissing his pants.

Over the years, like many wheelchair-bound peers, Alan became a master at holding urine for extended periods. Anyone who spends a significant amount of time at most disabled schools grows to understand certain realities. Occasionally, he'd have to hold it all day due to attendant incompetence, purposeful neglect, or other extenuating circumstances beyond anyone's control. A "beggars can't be choosers" mentality permeated hiring practices at disabled schools.

Nobody with a halfway decent resume is going to apply to wipe asses and change adult diapers for minimum wage. Consequently, Dillon settled for people whose backgrounds were spotty; an ex-con here, a recovering drug addict there, or someone who just doesn't fit in anywhere else. Dillon often turned into a last chance for many of society's pariahs.

Finally, just when it appeared that embarrassment was at hand, a glimmer of hope appeared on the horizon. A male attendant turned the corner sauntering Alan's way. A tall handsome man with shoulder-length blond shiny hair at the onset of middle age arrived at the scene.

William dressed more flamboyantly than other male attendants, always sporting a poofy multi-colored shirt, gold necklace, and white slacks. Although a full-fledged attendant, he had never been given restroom duty for reasons that were never explained to Dillon's student body. While his gentle mannerisms lent speculation regarding his sexual orientation, nothing substantial surfaced to merit rumors.

William walked up to Alan and immediately saw that the boy was in distress, "Do you need help?" he inquired urgently.

"Yes, I had them call Brad awhile ago but I don't know what's keeping him," Alan said while panting desperately.

"Well, you know, if you want me to help you, I can," William smiled kindly.

"No thanks. I'm sure Brad will be coming any second," Alan's face flushed as his baser instincts about William became readily apparent to both parties in that moment.

"Okay, well, good luck," William scoffed despondently and began strolling away

Alan instantly regretted uttering those words for two reasons. First, he saw a hurt look on William's face. Second, a drop of urine escaped to moisten his cotton briefs. A full-blown accident appeared imminent. Just before his last chance disappeared, he yelled, "Okay, William, please help me!"

William turned running full sprint toward Alan, sparing no time in wheeling him into the restroom and in front of a urinal. By this time the boys' room stood empty because classes had begun. Upon grabbing a bar and standing up, Alan noticed something peculiar. Usually, an attendant simply unzips Alan's fly and casually withdraws his penis without much fanfare. However, William unbuttoned Alan's pants, put his thumbs underneath the cotton briefs and proceeded to pull the confused boy's pants and briefs all the way down to his ankles, leaving him naked from the waist down.

At that moment, Alan's preoccupation with relieving himself took priority. Any awkward or residual embarrassing feelings were set aside. After allowing strained and cramped abdomen muscles to relax, he sighed deeply letting the dam break. He experienced an endorphin high only known to other members of the pee-pee dancers' club. They're grateful for any porcelain, or sometimes other makeshift, receptacles when Mother Nature isn't just calling, but screaming at the top of her lungs.

Near the end of his stream, Alan's mind fully returned to reality while taking note of other tactile sensations. Not only was William wiggling Alan's penis with his right forefinger and thumb but the attendant's full left hand caressed, patted, and squeezed Alan's bottom. While wiggling is somewhat acceptable for shaking remaining drops out, fondling a bottom, let alone a fully exposed one, is a definite no-no for an attendant. Alan felt a hand caress, firmly squeeze his left buttock then traverse across to the right side and do likewise. All those danger signals he'd heard about were on display. Every fiber in his being said scream before this so far minor molestation turned into something unthinkable.

At the last second, however, Alan thought better about making a scene. Since they were alone, with nary a soul for hundreds of feet, he couldn't be heard anyway. Besides, he figured, yelling right now before anything really bad occurred, might just serve to trigger a proportional physical or sexual assault. On the other hand, maybe he simply misjudged William's intentions as one of a sympathetic soul giving comfort. So, he stood in stoic silence trying as best he could to not react to being fondled.

Although he wouldn't ever admit it, after initial shock subsided, he found what turned into a slightly overboard butt massage a not totally unpleasant experience. He'd been sitting all day and did have an achy behind after all. The post urination groping lasted about two minutes.

William then pulled Alan's briefs and pants back up then gently sat him down. At that moment, Alan was relieved for two reasons. First, he didn't have an accident. Second, the cost of enlisting William's assistance hadn't come at too high of a price.

As they parted ways, Alan hesitantly thanked William for helping him out. He wheeled down to fourth period in a daze. On an intellectual level he knew what happened wasn't kosher. Yet, to his bewilderment, there existed a mixture of psychological unease and relief that an adolescent mind isn't equipped to decode.

Although wishing it had been a girl, for the first time in his life somebody acknowledged him as a sexual being and that part of the encounter felt validating. Upon cruising into Mrs. Johnson's P.E. class, he took a full emotional inventory and surprisingly didn't feel mad, afraid, ashamed, or violated at all. Therefore, reporting an incident that would be impossible to prove, didn't seem very traumatic, and would only alienate the attendant corps further seemed pointless. In days that followed, Alan waited for Zach or one of the pothead posse to wink at him in acknowledgement of what had transpired with William.

Eventually, it became apparent that the posse's infatuation with doing him harm waned considerably. Later on Alan discovered Brad's father had an emergency heart bypass that day—forcing Brad to leave work early to be with family. So, Alan chalked all of these events up to a freakish coincidence. Although remaining friendly to William, he made certain that he wouldn't be confronted by an equally uncomfortable situation again. Mrs. Preston agreed to always assign both a primary and a secondary restroom attendant to him.

# CHAPTER 18 - DÉJÀ VU

The Jones family moved to another county just before Christmas vacation of Alan's ninth grade year. Consequently, every carefully crafted mainstreaming mechanism suddenly disappeared; soon discovering relocating to a more rural area had significant drawbacks. Local educators were inexperienced in dealing with a high functioning physically challenged student. Alan and his mother would have to start from scratch, overcoming new obstacles and prejudices in their quest.

On the first Monday after Christmas vacation, Ms. Jones took Alan to Redwood Middle School to meet the principal. As she pushed him into Redwood's administration office, a receptionist—with salt and pepper hair—smiled at him, then politely asked Ms. Jones, "Hello ma'am, I'm Claire. Do y'all have an appointment with Principal Grimm?"

"No, we just moved into the school district and I don't know where else to start."

"Please, take a seat sugar." She gestured toward one of the yellow and orange plastic chairs.

Twenty minutes of library-like silence elapsed before Principal Grimm's door flew open. A man appearing as though he had just gone through a wind tunnel emerged. With his white hair sticking straight up, tie hanging like an old sock, and three top shirt buttons undone, Mr. Grimm looked ready for a scotch nightcap. Then, turning towards Claire, he shook his head with apparent exasperation, while exclaiming, "I'm getting sick and tired of all these parents trying to get those kind of kids in here. Why don't they just stay where they belong?"

Claire's face grew pale as she attempted to rehabilitate her boss' faux pas. Clearing her throat, she introduced Alan and Ms. Jones, "Ahem… Mr. Grimm, this mother and son want to talk to you."

Mr. Grimm glared at the twosome with a practiced consternation. Upon spotting Alan's wheelchair, he began to chuckle softly. Then, he bent down to Claire, while muttering, "They're attacking me on all fronts now."

Turning to face the visitors, he forced a smile while walking up to Ms. Jones, "Hello madam, how may I help you today?"

"We just moved around the corner from your school, so I wanted to talk to you about enrolling my son, Alan."

Mr. Grimm stroked his chin, "Will you please come into my office, madam?"

"What about Alan, can he join us?"

"No, I think, it's best that we speak privately."

Principal Grimm then escorted Ms. Jones into his office and slammed the door. "Just what the hell do you think that you're trying to pull, lady?" He began ranting while pacing like a recently caged wild tiger whose anger was still fresh from being captured. "Who are you? Who sent you here? Are you on welfare? Do you honestly think that you can get away with this?"

Obviously, she was flabbergasted by his tone and subsequent barrage of insulting insinuations.

"Excuse me!" Ms. Jones shouted, her face now red as a tomato, anger welling up inside of her, "What the hell are you talking about? And where in the hell do you get off talking to me like that, mister!" She vehemently retorted. Then, pausing, she lowered her voice, but not her intensity level. Grinding her teeth, and clutching her fists at her side, she spoke in a methodical, measured tone, "As I told you before, we just moved here, and I need to enroll Alan in school."

Taking a deep breath, Principal Grimm circled his office and once again approached her with a fake smile. Displaying Jekyll and Hyde-like behavior, a switch seemingly flipped transforming him from an: out of control, raving, madman, to the valedictorian of charm school. "Ms. Jones, I apologize if I came across a bit harsh. But you just have to understand that, in these parts, all the cripple kids go to Pine Tree Elementary. They have an excellent program over there."

"You mean disabled—not crippled!" She firmly admonished.

"Oh, whatever, I guess I stand corrected," he laughed.

He strolled over and draped an arm around her back then clasped her shoulder. Then, using a slightly condescending tone, he spoke gently in her ear, "Besides, I know you want what's best for your child," he sighed, "you want him to go to a place where he'll fit in and be with his own kind. I'm afraid if Alan goes here, Ms. Jones, the normal kids will tear him apart, tease and torment him, and in general, treat him like an outcast." Then, he released her shoulder so that he could face her, "Which will, in turn, crush his spirit. And I know, as Alan's mother, that's the absolute last thing you want to have happen."

Unfortunately for Mr. Grimm, his incompetence as a principal took second place to an awful poker face. Even a kind hearted, trusting soul— such as Ms. Jones—could recognize an overtly deceitful foray, "You must think that I just fell off the turnip truck, Mr. Grimm." She rebuked. "What kind of lame brain, half-witted, numbskull, do you take me for?" She heatedly inquired. "You just want to do what's convenient for you. I've met your type before, and you're all alike. You, Mr. Grimm, are an old, bigoted dinosaur who needs to be dragged—kicking and screaming—into the 20th century!"

She gave him a cold stare; a look that a mother usually reserves for an unruly child whom she's about to discipline. "Alan had absolutely no problem mainstreaming into his previous school. Why don't you want my boy here?" She slammed her purse on his desk in frustration.

Mr. Grimm folded his arms while taking a deep sigh of utter exasperation. His eyes shifted rapidly – like a bad poker player down to his last few chips. "Aren't you one of those parents, who are trying to force their retards down my throat?" He then stood up and shook his right index finger at her, "Let me tell you something lady," his face scrunching up defiantly, "This is my school. And I'll run it how I see fit. Nobody and I mean nobody is going to tell me what to do in this regard! And if you and your bitch friends don't like it, you can all kiss my ass!" He punched the desk.

He turned away from her; hand combed his hair, opened his top desk drawer and—in one motion—withdrew a pinch of chewing tobacco and put it in his mouth.

Ms. Jones snatched her purse and stormed for the door. As her hand turned the knob, she looked back and warned Mr. Grimm. "I'll be in contact with the superintendent of schools, Mr.Grimm; you can be assured of that."

"You make sure that you do that, Ms. Jones." Mr. Grimm interrupted sarcastically.

"And when I talk to him, I'll mention this little chat we had," she said, acerbically.

"Go right ahead, lady, I've been principal at this school for over 25 years and I've been in the crosshairs of folks a whole lot more ornery and powerful than you. I'll still be here long after you're done jousting at windmills. Good day, madam," he pontificated condescendingly.

Ms. Jones took one last long look at him as she was walking out, turned and resumed her departure. As she strode past Claire, she chuckled, shook her head twice and said, "I feel sorry for you, girl."

Without saying a word to Alan, she grabbed his wheelchair and started pushing him toward the exit. Alan could feel that she had a determined stride in her gait, which told him that the meeting didn't go particularly well.

Alan always had a very close, loving relationship with mom. Their bond possessed almost symbiotic qualities. They were able to communicate thoughts and feelings by reading each other's expressions, sans words. Whenever wanting to discern her true emotions, all he had to do was look at her jaw muscles. If her jaw moved from side to side—that meant trouble. Today, she was grinding her teeth. She only did this when someone or something especially agitated her.

To any onlookers, Ms. Jones displayed serenity and decorum while departing Redwood Middle School. However, Alan knew better. Therefore, even though dying of curiosity about what took place inside Mr. Grimm's office, he somehow sensed that now wasn't a good time to inquire. After all, knowing mom, he figured that she wouldn't be able to contain herself for long anyway.

As soon as Ms. Jones loaded Alan into their car, she grabbed the steering wheel tightly with both hands and yelled, "What a stupid sonofabitch bastard!" She pounded the dashboard six times with her right fist. "Unbelievable incompetence, totally, unfathomable, gutless-wonder that doesn't have a fucking clue!"

While burying her flushed face in her hands, she caught a glimpse of Alan's concerned expression. Taking three deep breaths in an attempt to temporarily compose herself for his sake, she said, "Don't worry, baby, mommy's alright, let's go home now and have a nice talk."

Alan already sensed that Mr. Grimm wouldn't be one of his best buddies. To him, any non-family member who upset mom became an instant nemesis. Because Ms. Jones knew that her son felt highly protective of her, she decided, that for the time being, she'd omit revealing anything that would only serve to anger him. Her best course of action, she thought, would be to filter all emotional conflict out—just relating the gist of what occurred.

As they sat on their living room couch, he nervously anticipated what mom had to say. Employing a stall tactic, she looked away while taking a long sip from her teacup. Alan's imagination could conjure up scenarios darker than those found in Stephen King novels. Therefore, he took mom's hesitation as a sign that her news wasn't just plain old regular run of the mill bad news; it was a looming tragedy of epic proportions.

Playing out all possible permutations in his head, he finally couldn't stand being held in suspense any longer and implored her to release the metaphoric feline from its proverbial container. "Ma, tell me what happened. I can't stand it anymore." He half yelled, half pleaded.

Ms. Jones held Alan's hands with hers, took a deep breath and gave Alan the G-rated, Cliff Notes version, "Honey, Mr. Grimm and I disagree on what's best for you at this time."

Alan's expression showed confusion, "I don't understand, ma. What are you trying to say?"

She fidgeted while desperately searching for the right words. "He doesn't feel that you'd be comfortable going to Redwood, honey." She said softly, hoping against hope that Alan wouldn't launch into a defensive, defiant tirade. Unfortunately, his anger began percolating back in Mr. Grimm's waiting room.

All of Alan's red flags were up; "I climbed a mountain to be mainstreamed, only to have a backward, backwoods hick, relegate me back to a crip school? Fuck him!" His hands were shaking; his face throbbed red. When he got very angry, these were telltale signs.

He clasped his hands together and shouted, "I'm not spending one more goddamn day in a crip school! This is bullshit! Absolute bullshit! We've done this shit before! I took the I.Q. tests two freakin' years ago. I was number one in my math class at the regular middle school. What more can I do . . . ?" He trailed off, while shedding tears borne out of frustration.

Normally, Ms. Jones wouldn't have tolerated such an outburst from her boy. However, understanding that Alan had a perfectly valid reason to be upset, she allowed him to vent. When he finally ran out of steam, she asserted that this new obstacle would turn out to be no more difficult than those they've previously hurdled. She placed her right hand on his left thigh and stared at him, "Look in my eyes, Alan." He complied reluctantly. She continued, "Has mommy ever lied to you?"

Alan slowly shook his head from side to side, and then let his chin rest on his chest while mumbling a barely audible, "No."

She put her fingers underneath his chin until their eyes met again. Using a very soft, nurturing inflection, she tried to reassure him. "Look at me, honey, look at me."

Alan didn't want comforting at that moment. Pride and self-esteem had just been wounded. He pulled away from her because he wanted to stay angry and her touch had always been a perfect antidote for his anger. Moreover, motivational words laced with past triumphs over conquered dragons were not going to cut it this time.

Ms. Jones understood her son's initial frustration but when he pulled away from her she decided not to let self-pity take hold. "What are you going to do now, cry?" she angrily shouted, then continuing her admonishment, she vented a little of her own pain. "Well, if you're gonna cry, go to your room, close the door and don't come out until you can compose yourself. You're not the only one who had a bad day today." She trailed off with a slight whimper.

Seeing mom's pain, Alan's attitude instantly transformed from anger to sympathy. He knelt beside her while hugging her firmly. Next, he completed the role reversal by comforting mom. "Don't worry, momma, we'll fight these bastards just like we fought and beat all the others," he said with a hint of controlled rage.

After a couple of minutes, Ms. Jones outlook brightened considerably and he noticed a mischievous twinkle in her eyes. "Mom... what are you planning?" He chuckled.

Almost giddy in her reply, Ms. Jones gushed, "I know what to do now, baby. We'll be fine." Suddenly, she rose from the couch purposefully striding towards the kitchen. Before leaving Alan she said, "I've got a few phone calls to make, you watch television and go ahead and turn up the sound." He crawled slowly over to the T.V. and turned it on.

Just before he could turn up the volume, he overheard part of mom's first phone call, "Hello, may I get the number of the superintendent of schools?" A smile crossed his face.

One week later, the dynamic duo found themselves in a conference room at Pine Tree Elementary. However, they weren't there to enroll Alan into school—as per Mr. Grimm's advice. On the contrary, Alan was about to be courted by both of the area high schools, as well as Mr. Grimm's school. Alan and Ms. Jones were seated like royalty at one end of a big oval table.

Seated clockwise from them were: school superintendent Mark Jacobs, Principal Gary Moore of Fairlawn High School, Fairlawn High's Disabled Students' Coordinator, Mindy Simmons, Principal Henry Ericson of Lincoln High School, Lincoln High's Disabled Students' Coordinator, Gina Thomas, and last but not least, the infamous Mr. Grimm.

Superintendent Jacobs, a tall, slender, youngish 47-year-old man, opened the meeting by turning his chair so he could look Alan directly in the eyes. "Alan, I went over your transcripts yesterday, I was very, very impressed." He smiled.

Alan could feel a smile of his own coming on.

Superintendent Jacobs continued, "Let's see here, a 3.5 G.P.A. during your middle school career; top student in your eighth grade math class; Dean's List twice. I could go on and on, but we'd be here all day."

A big roar of laughter filled the room. Conspicuously missing from the frivolity was Mr. Grimm. He kept looking down and, in general, sported a demeanor akin to a whipped puppy. Mr. Grimm's new attitude wasn't lost on Alan. He surmised that Redwood's leader received a chewing out of epic proportions.

Mr. Jacobs sensed that he needed to rehabilitate Mr. Grimm's character in Alan's eyes, "Alan, before we go any further, let me be the first one to apologize for Mr. Grimm's inexcusable behavior last Monday. I assure you, Alan, that Mr. Grimm's behavior was completely out of character and he'd be as enthusiastic as any of the representatives here to have you as a student."

Then, he paused, put both hands on the table, and leaned over to the object of his chastisement, "Isn't that right, Mr. Grimm?"

Without looking up, Mr. Grimm simply nodded twice. Alan read between the lines, he wondered why one grown man had to submit an apology for another grown man?

After representatives from both high schools finished their respective presentations, Alan knew that he couldn't say no to Fairlawn's proposal. They were fully equipped to take him right now. On top of that, he liked Mindy Simmons' optimism. Mr. Jacobs asked Alan what his thoughts were.

Alan, normally shy in social situations involving adults, couldn't pass up an opportunity to make Mr. Grimm's discomfort his own personal sport. He took a long look around the room. Finally, his eyes rested upon the beleaguered middle school principal. Talking through his mother, he said, "I don't know. I haven't heard all of the proposals yet," focusing his stare upon Mr. Grimm.

Mr. Jacobs wanted to once again quell any lingering hostility that obviously existed between Alan and Mr. Grimm. Mr. Jacobs spoke softly to both Alan and mom, "If I haven't done so already, then let me emphasize that if Alan chooses to go to Redwood, Mr. Grimm will personally go out of his way to ensure that Alan has everything that he needs, from attendants to note takers to test proctors and everything in between." He gestured toward Mr. Grimm and said, "Right, Mr. Grimm?"

Mr. Grimm uttered a barely audible, "Right, Mr. Jacobs."

Ms. Jones turned toward her son, "Okay, Alan, do you know what you want to do yet, or do you need more time?" She placed a hand on his knee to keep him relaxed.

Again, speaking through mom, he took a deep breath, looked straight at Mr. Grimm, and espoused, "Right now, I'm leaning toward finishing out my middle school career at Redwood."

Alan spotted Mr. Grimm tugging at his tie while uneasily squirming in his seat.

After taking a brief pause to catch his breath, and add drama to the moment, he continued, " But, it would be exciting to go to high school early. I'm going to have to go home, give it some thought and get back to you guys in a day or two. If that's alright with everyone?" He asserted with a newly found brashness.

"Take all of the time that you need, Alan." Mr. Jacobs said.

After the meeting broke up, Ms. Jones and Alan were in the parking lot, about to enter their car. Alan couldn't hold in his enthusiasm any longer, "I'm going to Fairlawn High."

Ms. Jones smiled, "I knew as soon as you saw Fairlawn's proposal you were hooked." Then, she cocked her head to one side and joked, "I know my boy. You just wanted to make poor ol' Grimm suffer." He nodded his head and laughed.

# CHAPTER 19 - LONE WOLF

The cold clean January air heightened Alan's senses. Normally, quiet, serene country mornings are appreciated. But, on a day like today distractions are welcome. When stakes are this high you have to manufacture ways to settle your mind and emotions. How today's events transpired would probably be a harbinger for his high school career.

Sitting by mom while trying to squelch voices of inner demons by studying droplets of morning dew on a bush in front of their home wasn't working. Brashness is easy from afar but on the day of reckoning actions make or break your reputation. What separates the men from the boys is how they handle themselves when the rubber meets the road.

The hand clenching, thumb twiddling, and rapid heartbeat were just the tip of a bigger emotional iceberg. His guts felt like tumbleweeds in a tornado. Today, he would fully mainstream into a high school—with a student body of over 3000—one semester early. Just a scant 16 months ago he began partial mainstreaming with 26 other disabled kids. For the first time, leaning on that peer group wasn't an option.

Finally, a small school bus made came into view and eased to a stop in front of his home. There was just enough time for a final deep breath before plunging headlong into a sea of uncertainties. A portly, middle-aged redheaded woman wobbled out of the bus and joyfully bellowed, "Hi Alan and Ms. Jones!"

Her greeting temporarily derailed Alan's train of thought and snapped him to the present. Upon approaching the just washed vehicle, he peered inside and saw three other students. If a student was the fourth pickup at his previous school they usually were considered early pickups. So, he surmised as much.

"Hi folks, my name is Mrs. Branch, what a glorious morning it is today," she smiled.

"Hello," Ms. Jones warmly replied.

"So, I understand this is your first day of high school, huh," Mrs. Branch grinned at Alan's solemn face.

"Yes ma'am," Alan nervously nodded.

"Well, I bet you'll do fine, right mom?" Mrs. Branch reassured.

"Yes, Alan always is apprehensive going to a new school," Mrs. Jones sighed.

"That's understandable, I suppose, but this is a good town with good folks and good kids. He'll be fine," Mrs. Branch avowed enthusiastically without hesitation.

After Mrs. Branch loaded his chair she quickly got behind the wheel and drove away. Alan kept watching mom until she stopped waving. As they turned the corner his gaze shifted towards fellow riders. There were two other boys in wheelchairs and one boy sitting in a standard bus seat. As it turned out he was Mrs. Branch's last pick up on her bus route. Then, almost on cue, they uniformly introduced themselves.

"Hi, I'm Salvador but people call me Sal," Said one tan-skinned buffed looking wheelchair guy with a smooth Mexican accent.

"Hi, I'm Lar.. Lar... Larry," Said the other wheelchair guy who, like Alan, obviously had cerebral palsy only more severe.

"Hey, Chuck here, how's it hangin," the chubby pasty white guy in the standard seat said. "If you're wondering what the hell I'm doing on a crip bus it's because I'm a hemophiliac and my mom doesn't want me bleeding to death while I'm walking to school," he snickered.

"Oh Chuck, don't talk like that," Mrs. Branch lightly chided.

Alan failed to see what Chuck found amusing about death but forced out an uneasy laugh.

"Hi guys, I'm Alan, how are you all doing," he offered nervously.

After introductions, he sat back and watched how the three other boys interacted. Chuck definitely dominated the conversation while Salvador and Larry simply agreed with anything Chuck opined.

"Hey, guys, look at that new mall on the right," Chuck redirected their eyes, "Yeah, they're painting it pink and green," he shook his head and sneered, "sissy wetback colors,"

Considering Chuck's delicate condition, some of those racist statements would've easily gotten him killed at Dillon, Alan thought. On the other hand, contrary to all logic, all six hemophiliacs he'd known had lived and spoken recklessly. Consequently, all six met an early demise as a result of their cavalier attitude. Chuck appeared to be headed for a premature date with the Grim Reaper as well.

Meanwhile, Salvador and Larry were just mindlessly nodding and laughing at everything Chuck said. Based on their seemingly inane responses, it was hard for Alan not to draw preliminary conclusions about their intellectual limitations. He hated making assumptions about people before really getting to know them. Yet, other telltale signs of mental retardation, which he'd become an old pro at spotting, were glowing like neon signs above both of their heads. This revelation left him feeling hollow and melancholy for reasons he couldn't yet quantify.

A short while later, Mrs. Branch pulled into Fairlawn High's front parking lot. Throngs of students were arriving either by car or by foot. The tidal wave of teenagers and their airport-style bustle left him feeling momentarily overwhelmed. A mixture of competitive ambition and paralyzing fear suddenly battled for supremacy within his soul.

The scholastic orchestra composed of jocks and cheerleaders; nerds and awkward kids looked amazingly self-assured and competent crisscrossing melodically to various classes. They were his true competition, not Larry, Salvador or Chuck. Soon, using a unique backpedal method, he would skillfully weave a wheelchair's base drum rhythms with this ensemble and hope not to strike a discordant note. Surely the double whammy of a wheelchair combined with how it was being propelled would draw unwanted stares and snickers, he thought.

A crowd of perfectly groomed, coifed, and attired boys and exquisitely lush, curvy and appetizing girls strutted about like they owned Fairlawn High. So, obviously, a pimply-faced, spastic, awkward wheelchair pushing kid traveling along in this sea of utopia would stick out like an oil slick. Then, while being lowered to the sidewalk, he remembered the main goal wasn't to impress them or cultivate friendships. No, all he had to focus on was competing with these kids and beating them academically.

Once on the sidewalk, he slowly traversed through wave after wave of kids whose eye level was at least two feet above his head. Understandably, most people who can walk don't typically look down when doing so. The onus, consequently, is on a wheelchair user to keep their head on a swivel to avoid collisions. Using catlike nimbleness, he deftly darted through seams while feverishly looking backwards right, backwards left and repeating the sequence. Finally, with ten minutes to spare, he arrived at room 129. This was first period homeroom for disabled kids.

One by one Larry, Salvador and Chuck joined Alan as they waited for Ms. Mindy Simmons. He watched the passing parade of non-disabled or "regular" kids and their varied interplay. Acute self-awareness of his disability arose while a group of pretty girls gawked at the new freak on campus. In contrast, at Dillon, all of the kids had disabilities so he blended in like a nudist in a nudist colony. Even when he mainstreamed at Sylvester he was still part of a group of other disabled kids. But, now, now he felt naked for all the world to see.

At two minutes of eight, a petite figure came walking up the sidewalk. She was dressed more casually than any teacher he had to that point with a printed tee, denim jeans, and ankle-high imitation leather boots. The pixie had short flaming red hair, freckles, and a confident stride belying her small stature.

She sauntered by them, broadly grinned, unlocked the door and said, "Come on in guys." Ms. Simmons was not only Fairlawn High's Disabled Students' Coordinator but also, apparently and unbeknownst to Alan, their homeroom teacher. Before anyone got settled in their spots she began talking.

"Now, before we get started, I need to make a couple of announcements. We have a new student, his name is Alan, and we expect very good things from him," she patted Alan cheerfully on the back but then, gradually, her facial expressions darkened while walking solemnly toward the front, "However, sometimes change is hard. Unfortunately, we had to make a personnel change for this semester," she sighed, "My longtime assistant and your restroom helper, Linda, isn't going to be working for us anymore," delivering the news as if someone had died. Chuck, Salvador and Larry spontaneously voiced their outrage as their protestations flew fast and furious.

"What the hell?" Chuck yelled indignantly.

"Why, she was great," Salvador cried.

"I loved her, why," Larry pounded a table three times.

"Hey, guys, guys, now settle down, settle down," she talked lower and lower while motioning her palms toward the floor, "I know that none of us likes losing someone we all like but a very practical matter was brought to my attention recently," she said

"What's a practical matter," Salvador's furrowed brow oozed bitterness and confusion.

"Well, a new parent to our program recently said that it is inappropriate for a woman to take teenage boys to the restroom," she stated while standing near Alan thereby, essentially, throwing him under the bus, "Therefore, I've hired a man to replace Linda and he'll be here anytime now,"

"Wait a minute; the only new parent has to be the new kid's mom because he's the only new one here. So it's the new kid's fault," Chuck pointed Alan's way while Salvador and Larry glared in the same direction.

"Okay guys come on now. Get a grip," Ms. Simmons tried feebly to counteract a firestorm of adolescent rage with a logical argument, "This is for the best. Also, after a certain age, you guys should be, I mean really, having a woman in the restroom handling you guys doesn't look right, I mean, really…" she giggled like a little girl.

Salvador and Larry's collective body language spoke volumes. It was impossible to ignore an intense aura of betrayal emanating from both of them. Upon reaching a certain age, physically disabled boys intuitively become deeply aware of their grim social realities. Diminished social standing translates into limited opportunities for intimate moments that their non-disabled peers take for granted.

As a result, their souls are left starving for nourishment. Any kind of touch from a semi-attractive female is oft interpreted as affirmation of one's sense of worth and overall value to humanity. Consequently, anyone who impedes these opportunities is considered a traitor. In other words, as far as Salvador, Larry, and to a degree, Chuck were concerned when Linda got axed, Alan broke a "crip code".

Contrary to the normal unease that someone else might feel in this awkward situation, Alan felt at peace. Like the proverbial Cheshire cat, he simply smiled back and nodded. Like he told himself earlier that day, he was here to compete, not make friends. The only troubling aspect was how quickly Ms. Simmons made him a scapegoat for wonderful Linda's departure. He briefly mused if Ms. Simmons and her former attendant were "life partners". He snickered quietly letting the fanciful idea pass.

Soon after Ms. Simmons gave her admonishment, a man's man walked through the door. He was a tall, light-skinned, imposing figure dressed like a construction worker: checkered shirt, denim jeans, work boots sans tool belt and hardhat. One's first impression was that this dude must've been a body builder in his salad days. Although a senior citizen, a mugger would steer clear of this guy in a dark alley. A rugged and worn expression immediately spoke volumes to an as yet untold biography of someone filled with a plethora of experiences and his own inner demons.

"Oh, hi, you must be Sam, the new attendant, welcome," Ms. Simmons enthused.

"Uh, yes ma'am, glad to be here," Sam gravelly answered.

"Well, Sam, let me introduce you to everyone, first off, you can call me Mindy," she smiled.

"Okay, Mindy," he confidently responded.

"That's Chuck over there goofing off as usual," she playfully scolded.

"Hey dude, how's it hangin'," Chuck purposefully looked away as disrespect oozed from his pores.

"Chuck," Sam extended his right hand but Chuck being Chuck didn't react.

"Anyway, sometimes you'll just have to ignore Chuck," Ms. Simmons sighed.

"I've met his type before, I understand," Sam gave the miscreant a knowing look.

"Next, we have Larry over here," she led Sam to Larry.

"Hi Larry," Sam's voiced went up an octave as he condescendingly patted Larry's head.

"Hi, Sam," Larry struggled with his response.

"Over here, we have Salvador," Ms. Simmons put her hands on Salvador's shoulders.

"Well, hi Salvador, buddy," once again Sam's voice changed as he patted Salvador's head.

"And, finally, we have our newest student, Alan over there," Ms. Simmons nodded Alan's direction as she escorted Sam to him.

Alan didn't want to be given the same puppy dog treatment that Larry and Salvador received. So, before Sam was halfway over, Alan proactively extended his right hand and initiated verbal contact upon firmly grasping the big man's hand, "Hi Sam, I'm Alan," he said while looking Sam dead in the eyes.

Ms. Simmons adroitly surmised from Alan's body language that he wouldn't harbor disrespectful or patronizing attitudes. She quickly intervened before Sam said or did anything that could be misconstrued as either.

"Uh, Sam, Alan here will be taking classes such as, algebra, geometry, honors English, and so on," she blurted hurriedly as her flashing eyes spoke volumes, "You'll be his note taker for two or three periods a day."

"Oh, I see," Sam's demeanor instantly became more business-like while rubbing his chin. He then returned Alan's firm grip with one of his own and the two concluded their handshake, "I look forward to working with you Alan," his robust baritones came through.

"As do I sir," Alan heard sincerity in Sam's voice and returned Sam's respectful attitude with a casual gleaming smile.

"What will I be doing for the rest of the day when I'm not in classes with Alan?" Sam queried Ms. Simmons.

"Well, you'll be helping Larry and Salvador with their work in here or going to woodshop class with them," she responded happily.

"Don't they take other regular cla…"

"Ahem," she abruptly cut him off and shook her head as discreetly as possible.

Unfortunately, Larry and Salvador understood all too well the implied meaning behind Sam's truncated question and Ms. Simmons subsequent delicately nuanced response. Technically Larry and Salvador were students at Fairlawn High. However, for all intents and purposes, they were hardly considered mainstreamed students or part of Fairlawn's community. They remained sequestered in one room, for all but one period a day, rarely interacting with other students.

Although cognitively impaired, both possessed a sort of "crip" intelligence and were perfectly aware of their reality and limitations. On the other hand, here was this new kid who came out of nowhere and suddenly he's being allowed to take "real" classes with the "normal" kids. Keys to the proverbial castle were being given to someone who hadn't been tested yet. As a result, Larry and Salvador's expressions communicated jealousy and resentment.

"Okay, I see," Sam nodded, acknowledging her cue, "Who will be with Alan in the rest of his classes?"

"Either a student volunteer or me," she said.

Yes, an unmistakable aura of bitterness emanated from his fellow wheelchair toting compadres. Then, he realized why he felt hollow and melancholy upon first recognizing that they were cognitively impaired. From afar Larry, Salvador, and him all belonged to the same genus subspecies of Homo sapiens, guy in wheelchair.

Yet, Alan knew that even amongst his own rare breed he was somewhat of an outcast. He could engage in self-deception forever by repeating the mantra that he wasn't here to be popular or make friends. But, at this very moment, being a wolf without a pack felt ominously unsettling and lonely.

# CHAPTER 20 - EXILE

As Alan sat outside his 10th grade English class, on a cold winter's morning, the perplexed sophomore wondered about the circumstances that had sealed his fate. His classmates were being administered their exam within the cozy confines of an environmentally controlled 78° classroom while he had been exiled to take an exam in the elements. His note-taker, Brad, kneeled at his side taking dictation. Since Alan's Cerebral Palsy affected his fine motor skills, he could not hold a pen. As a result, he had to rely on student volunteer note takers for both notes and exams.

Under normal circumstances on an exam day Alan and Brad would use an unused classroom. However, these were not normal circumstances. Alan was the only full inclusion student at the rural high school. While most of the teachers were open and accepting of him, there were a few who had expressed reservations about whether a disabled student could successfully compete or even belonged in a regular school setting. Alan's English teacher, Mrs. Anderson, had become increasingly suspicious about the "A's'" he was getting on the exams.

Moreover, there was nothing to indicate Alan's predilection to do well on exams other than homework, since he had never answered one question in class. This disparity wasn't due to Alan's lack of knowledge or preparation, but simply a fear of having his speech dysfunction laid bare to the world. To illustrate, at the time, if one had offered Alan a date with the prom queen and her court plus a pajama party in exchange for answering one question in class, he would've blushed and smiled but politely declined with a shake of the head.

So, what was Mrs. Anderson to do? She had strong suspicions that Brad had been the one who actually took the tests! On the other hand, she had to wonder if a previously hidden bias had crept into her analysis.

After all she didn't have any hard evidence to support her hypothesis. Although Mrs. Anderson didn't want to directly accuse anyone of wrong-doing, she still had to find out if there were any improprieties. Finally, she devised a plan that would remove any doubt from her mind about the validity of Alan's exam scores.

Earlier that day, Alan and Brad entered class, walked up to Mrs. Anderson's desk, waiting to be handed the exam so that they could proceed to an empty room. However, on this day she had a surprise in store. When she handed the exam to Brad, Alan and Brad began heading outside. Before the duo could reach the door Mrs. Anderson ordered them to halt.

She then informed Alan that today he would be taking the exam in class. After this stunning announcement, she instructed the rest of the class to form their desks in a horseshoe formation leaving the front center of the room open. She then directed Alan and Brad to occupy the newly created open space.

At first Alan's reaction to this sudden turn of events was fear. He thought to himself, "How can I possibly talk in class? There are so many people around; my nerves won't let my jaw relax". Fear transformed into anxiety as he delved deeper into the phobia preventing him from being on the school's debate team. 'They'll make fun of me' he thought, further analyzing the situation.

His thoughts then turned to Mrs. Anderson. Why was she doing this to him? What had he done to perpetuate such unfair persecution? Then just as suddenly, he had an angry thought 'She doesn't trust me' he mused 'thinks I'm cheating, well if she wants proof, I'm not, she'll get it!'

Alan's anger nearly consumed him now. The normally shy and self-conscious young man was bound and determined to put his oppressor in her place! Upon glancing at the exam of: 50 multiple choice, 10 fill in the blanks, 1 essay, he surmised that he knew most of the questions off the top of his head. As she passed out the tests, he listened intently to make sure he understood all instructions for the exam.

Then, as the teacher sat down in front of the class and said "begin", she also motioned for him to commence as well. Alan gave Brad a blank stare, shrugged and sighed dismissively at her. Alan knew what he was about to do entailed a strategy which could embarrass and potentially estrange Mrs. Anderson; however, he felt that any deviation from the plan would in someway compromise his standing at the school.

The first part of the exam was multiple-choice. As Alan answered the first question, he maintained his normal volume, "Number 1: A, Number 2: D", after he answered the second question the rest of the class caught on. The horseshoe formation around Alan became tighter as the class hung on every syllable he uttered.

Seeing his plan beginning to work and sensing Mrs. Anderson would pull the plug on her experiment any time now, Alan fired off the next 15 answers in rapid fire succession: "C, E, E, A, D, D, C, A, A, A, A, C, B, E, B.". Finally, Mrs. Anderson had seen enough and did not want her exam to be further compromised, she stood suddenly and shouted at the top of her lungs "STOP! STOP! FOR GOD'S SAKE STOP!"

With that abrupt and hysterical diatribe, the class collectively froze in their tracks. Pencils hit the floor as students were shocked by the normally poised teacher's violent outburst.

When Mrs. Anderson finally regained her composure, she smiled at Alan and quietly instructed both Alan and Brad to find an empty room to take the rest of the exam. Alan inserted however that exam rooms had to be reserved a day ahead of time. Consequently, finding an empty classroom at this late hour was an absolute impossibility!

Unequivocally in the throes of a dilemma, she wracked her brain for a way for Alan to resume taking the exam. She fully appreciated the gravity of her predicament; any dalliance would further damage her reputation not only in the eyes of the class but also in the eyes of her peers as well. Finally, she turned to Alan with a wry grin and suggested that he take the exam outside against the wall, with a barely audible chuckle Alan said "Sure".

For the remainder of the semester, Alan's homework was often used as a sample of what Mrs. Anderson considered to be correct implementation of the lesson plan. As for Alan's relationship with Mrs. Anderson, let's put it this way, by the end of the semester he actually felt comfortable enough to answer questions that required only one word. Fortunately, for all parties involved, this incident became a catalyst for improved teacher-student relations rather than an instrument to further distrust and disharmonious attitudes towards full inclusion students at Fairlawn High.

# CHAPTER 21 - CROCODILE TEARS

Most distinguishable high school girls are pigeonholed—by their peers—as either pretty or smart. Penelope Grayson, one of the most popular girls at Fairlawn High, easily fell into both categories. Stereotypes such as pretty but dumb blonde or smart but homely brunette are often perpetuated more so in high school then in society as a whole. However, as head cheerleader and valedictorian candidate, she personified an exception to that rule.

The boys lusted after her full blossoms in front and flowing golden locks leading down to her perfectly pert, ripe derriere. Conversely, her 4.0 G.P.A. inspired Fairlawn's coed clan. Yes, Penelope was one of those "can't miss" types who were supposed to turn the world on its ear.

Everyone eagerly anticipated the homecoming dance, on Friday night, after Fairlawn's annual football game against crosstown rival Lincoln. Their gridiron gang rarely enjoyed a winning season; nevertheless, playing Lincoln always stirred school pride and brought old alums from both schools to the contest. As homecoming chair, Penelope orchestrated many homecoming week activities. Each day, during lunch, various events were held on the main quad.

One day, senior girls trounced their junior counterparts in powder puff flag football. Another day, funds for band uniforms were raised through a bake sale. Finally, on Friday, a kissing booth was set up—which gave nerdy boys an opportunity to do something they wouldn't have a snow-ball's chance in hell to do otherwise, kiss an actual girl. Homecoming week became a means for students who otherwise wouldn't interact to have fun and perhaps forge new friendships.

All during that week, Alan soaked in the ambience and marveled at how enthusiastically students participated. Apparently, they could turn off their academic oriented mindsets and just have pure uninhibited fun.

In his mind, fun and school were two words never to be spoken in the same sentence. From a very young age, he learned that there were no blue-collar jobs available for someone with severe cerebral palsy. Therefore, as he was often reminded, grand success in all academic arenas needed to be achieved for a chance at self-support and independence.

Friday, Fairlawn replaced seventh period with a pep rally in the gymnasium. Attendance was mandatory for every student at this "fun", non-academic event. Alan wound up situated next to fellow disabled student Chuck on the sideline near midcourt.

Cheerleaders danced routines in front of them and one even gave him an up close view of her second set of built-in pom-poms. The cheerleader in question was none other than Penelope Grayson. She encouraged him to join in on the fun as she smiled.

"Come on, you can say it! Beat Lincoln! Beat Lincoln! Beat Lincoln!" she said.

At first, he tried to wave her away but she wouldn't leave him alone.

"I'm not going away until you say Beat Lincoln," she smiled.

He shook his head.

"Okay, then, I'll let everyone know you want Lincoln to win," she began motioning for attention.

Alan panicked. In an instant, Penelope revealed her true colors to him and him alone. He had always been adept at unmasking a false persona to see the true person underneath. Behind all her smiles and social pleasantries, lay a young woman aware of her power. She knew how to use her popularity and charms to make or break someone's reputation. Although he wasn't here to make friends, spending the next three years as a double pariah—a gimp and a traitor—wasn't a good idea either.

"Just say it to get the bitch off your back," Chuck talked sideways.

"Okay, okay, I'll say it!" he said aloud with disgust.

"Say what?" she feigned ignorance.

"Beat Lincoln," he mumbled.

"Speak up," she said, cupping a hand to an ear.

"Beat Lincoln!" he shouted to make her happy and go away.

"There, that wasn't so tough now was it," she smiled again, walked up to him and whispered in his ear, "Good cripple boy."

As she cartwheeled back to her group, Alan wondered if others knew the real Penelope. The manipulative, ugly little girl on the inside was well hidden from them. Teenagers are all about outward appearances and popularity. For many teens a small zit on one's nose is considered a tragic event.

So, an emerging, egotistical, diva that probably learned how to wrap daddy around her left pinky by age five, flew stealthily on teen radar.

She wielded her popularity as a tool, which she used to its maximum potential. Like a magician, she only revealed what she wanted them to see. At the time, he wondered if life would always favor pretty people with unbroken bodies. Moreover, how could a disabled person truly find acceptance in such an image-obsessed world?

When festivities ended, Chuck and Alan slowly made their way towards the special-ed bus. Alan's body language told Chuck that Penelope's coercive ploy pissed off his buddy. Generally, Chuck is apathetic if something doesn't directly affect him. Nevertheless, recognizing Alan's emotional plight—as one he experienced many times before—compelled him to comment.

"Hey," he yelled, "Don't tell me you're letting Miss Candy Ass get to you," he slugged Alan's shoulder.

"Yeah, yeah, I know, I know, but I get sick of putting on the 'happy little cripple act' sometimes," Alan moaned exasperatingly, "I just …"

"My man, you've been a gimp way too long to be delusional about your reality," Chuck shook his head in disbelief, "Only the two P's get to have the three P's,"

"Huh?" Alan looked confused.

"Pretty people, two P's, get parties, proms, and pep rallies, three P's," Chuck offered.

"Wow, did you just make that B.S. up or what?" Alan barely suppressed a laugh.

"Kind of," Chuck couldn't contain a guffaw.

Although, Chuck wasn't saying anything that Alan didn't innately know, it's still comforting to hear one's own thoughts spoken by another.

"I appreciate it anyway," Alan finally seemed amused, "Man, if you weren't a hemophiliac I'd sock your arm so hard," half-cocking his fist, "But, I don't want to go to the gas chamber for giving you a love tap," rolling his eyes while catching a glimpse of a new bruise under Chuck's short sleeve shirt, "hey, what's up with your arm there? Did you piss off a guy who doesn't know you're a China doll?"

"Love tap? China doll? Hey, hey, back off, Nancy boy, I'm straight," Chuck channeled Clint Eastwood.

"Come on now, what I meant was…" Alan's face flushed.

"Boy, that's what I'm talking about. You're too easy. Can't you tell when someone's yanking your chain?" Chuck groaned.

"Yeah, okay, sure," Alan forced a smile.

"You've got to learn to chill out buddy," Chuck heartedly chortled, "After all, life's too short."

Alan shrugged and nodded in resignation, "So, like I said, what's up with your arm?"

"Oh, nothin'," Chuck sounded defensive in tone, "Just took a little tumble in class today, it ain't nothin'."

"Considering your condition, do you need to get that looked at by a doctor or something?" Alan said with alarm.

"Nah, like I said, it ain't nothin'. I'll be fine," Chuck offered reassuringly.

Alan mumbled, "Okay." But his concern remained.

Hemophilia is a cowardly disease that doesn't indicate internal bleeding has occurred until the situation is dire. Any seemingly innocuous light tap can trigger hemorrhaging. During his experience at Dillon, Alan knew two other friends who were hemophiliacs. Both died after what would be considered light roughhousing with fellow students. As they rode home, Alan noticed that Chuck was favoring his wound.

On Monday morning, Chuck admitted to Alan that his mom took him straight to the hospital Friday afternoon.

"Yeah, uh, right when I got off the bus Friday, I kinda told my ma 'bout what you said 'bout my bruise," Chuck spoke humbly.

"So, what happened?"

"Um, ma looked at my bruise and rushed me to the emergency room," Chuck said, "Good thing too, doc said it could've gotten serious."

"Oh, wow," Alan shook his head, "Are you going to be alright?"

"Oh sure, they treated me Friday night and kept me in the hospital for observation until Saturday afternoon," Chuck paused thoughtfully and smiled, "I guess I owe you one."

Alan shrugged, "I just pointed out what I saw. No biggie!"

"Yeah, okay, I wouldn't want to owe a punk like you for the rest of my life."

"Well if I'm a punk, what does that make a stubborn ass like you?" Alan laughed.

Upon arriving, at Fairlawn, both boys immediately noticed a disturbing vibe on campus. Students were mulling around in packs of four to eight in highly agitated states. Apparently, a few of them knew what was happening and tasked themselves as disseminators of information. As each group heard its respective speaker's news, many individuals became instantly overwhelmed, collapsed in the arms of another, and sobbed openly.

Chuck and Alan weren't impressed by teenage theatrics currently on display and preceded to walk past the drama to their homeroom class.

"One of the cheerleaders must've missed her period." Chuck opined sarcastically.

"No, I think this is real serious," Alan mocked shock, "It looks like the quarterback got caught cheating on his girlfriend."

"You don't say! Well, hush my mouth! I've never heard anything so scandalous!" Chuck cupped his mouth.

Ten minutes into class, a squealing noise came over the P.A. system followed by Principal Moore's message, "Attention, attention. May I have your undivided attention please," Principal Moore stuttered slightly with his delivery, "I'm afraid that I have some very tragic news to report today," he paused for a good ten seconds, "On Saturday night, Penelope Grayson, one of our most beloved students," he paused once more and sniffled over the open microphone, "Um, Penelope Grayson was in a one-car traffic accident on Saturday night and unfortunately didn't survive her injuries."

Alan and Chuck looked at each other impassively and almost simultaneously uttered, "Huh, if that don't beat all!"

"One car accident? Stupid bitch must've wrapped herself around a light pole." Chuck said.

"She was probably using her rear view mirror as a makeup compact." Alan said.

Ms. Simmons went through the motions and telegraphed her disapproval of their callous remarks, "Hey you guys, somebody you went to school with just passed away. Could you show a little more compassion?"

Alan suddenly felt emboldened to challenge Ms. Simmons seemingly half-hearted admonishment, "Oh, I didn't know that at this school the principal makes an announcement whenever a student dies; how nice of him to acknowledge the importance of every life." He sarcastically oozed.

"Well, this is a close knit community and we care about everybody," she sounded almost convincing.

"Right you mean just jocks and cheerleaders?" Alan cynicism continued.

"Well, no, I mean everybody is important to the …" she was interrupted by another message by Principal Moore.

"Due to the grave circumstances hanging over us today, I'm modifying our schedule. After first period, your second and third period classes will be cancelled. When you leave first period, go to the main quad and you will find a multitude of grief counselors sitting at tables. If you need someone to talk to please, I urge you not to hesitate in talking with a counselor."

After class, Alan went out to the main quad for curiosity sake. Sure enough, he saw rows upon rows of students waiting to talk to counselors. Even though feeling no attachment to this situation, a curious anthropologist residing within was drawn to the phenomenon of communal grief. Slowly, he weaved through a sea of students, counselors, and tables. There were emotions on display as the bereaved were trying to relate what they were going through.

Surreptitiously listening in on various conversations he came away with a surprising conclusion. At first, he believed the superficial aspects of Penelope Grayson's impact upon the student body. A much beloved girl who embodied everything that a normal, insecure teen strives to be: popular, confident, and attractive. Surprisingly, upon eavesdropping, a totally different perspective was gleaned.

A consistent theme centered on of most of the conversations. They suddenly awakened to the unpleasant prospect of their own mortality. In contrast to Alan's experience, most of these kids never personally knew someone who had died—let alone someone their own age. Furthermore, they weren't really discussing Penelope or her tragic end. He surmised that although popular, she was an object of envy rather than a faculty exemplification of a much beloved coed.

She was also, among other things, a measuring stick by which others gauged their own self-worth. A commonly heard plaint went along the lines of: if someone like her, someone so together, someone so perfect, can die by a freak accident, then what chances do I have in life?

On Friday a special assembly took place in the same gymnasium that last pep rally was held. But, this time they would honor Penelope's life. Her teachers and selected students spoke to a jam-packed arena of somber Fairlawn faithful.

Oftentimes, during eulogies and memorial services, a person is given praise beyond their actual deeds on earth. Likewise, all of their human failings are somehow forgotten. This was the case in Penelope's memorial as well. Near the end of the event Principal Moore led a moment of silence during which sobs and attempted muted moans were heard.

Alan sat amongst them and quite frankly didn't know what the big deal was? Wondering why other students were taking so long to move on with their lives. In disabled schools death is a regular occurrence. He had always been told to suck it up and focus on the job at hand—schoolwork.

From age eight, he knew the dreadful realities of many disabled kids who had very tenuous tethers to life, losing many classmates to a myriad of conditions. They could be at school one day and pass away that night. Once, learning about a friend's passing five minutes before taking a midterm and then using that bitter news to sharpen focus in acing the test. So after awhile, as a disabled kid who spent ten years in disabled schools, it's easier to protect yourself emotionally by having friendly acquaintances instead of close friends.

Experience teaches every disabled youngster that when you allow yourself the luxury of having a friend you also leave your heart open to pain and suffering when they die. Ultimately, each disabled youngster must weigh the joy of having a fellow disabled friend against the sometimes-inevitable reality of that their friend's life will be cut short because of their disability. Yes, experience is sometimes a very strict teacher and it taught Alan not to be vulnerable to that kind of agony, or so he told himself.

Eventually the old saying, "life must go on," bore fruit. Penelope would always be somewhere in the collective conscience of Fairlawn's student body. Yet, when school returned from Christmas vacation, the memory of their fallen heroine slowly but stubbornly faded from their immediate thoughts. Classes plodded along monotonously during January and February as somber teenagers joylessly fulfilled their scholastic obligations. Midterms were taken and essays were written.

# CHAPTER 22 - COLD WATER

As March rolled around, everyone at Fairlawn looked forward to Easter break. Traditionally, students use this week off to recharge their batteries for the stretch run to June finals. Alan still had lingering doubts as to how much the collective student body truly missed Penelope. As time went by however, he began to feel optimistic about Fairlawn's culture as it pertained to valuing life. Especially when contrasted against Dillon and other disabled schools.

A week before St. Patrick's Day, on the bus ride home, Alan saw another bruise on Chuck's upper arm.

"Hey, what's up with your arm," Alan interrogated Chuck, "You fall in class again?"

"My stupid teacher flipped his lid and pushed me into a wall." Chuck sighed.

"Pushed you into a wall?" Alan yelled, "Doesn't that stupid bastard know about your hemophilia?"

"Nah, my disease is my problem," Chuck asserted, "It ain't nobody else's concern."

"You're kidding me right? You would rather ..."

"Look," Chuck interrupted, "I don't want and I don't need anyone's goddamn pity! I don't want to be a freak show like the boy in the plastic bubble!" he huffed.

"Let me get this straight," Alan's vocal tones had an unmistakable sarcasm, "You would rather risk dying simply because you want to pass yourself off as 'normal.'"

"Pretty much, what's wrong with that?"

"So, I'm in a wheelchair getting stared at everyday and you're putting your life at risk because you don't want to be a freak show like me!" Alan barked back.

"Oh come on man, you know that's not what I meant!" Chuck moaned.

"Okay, but I still think your teachers should know about your condition."

"Why can't I keep that stuff private? It's nobody's business."

"Yeah man, like I said, a wimp like you couldn't imagine having my cerebral palsy," Alan seethed.

"Why do you say that? What does that have to do with anything," Chuck said with eye-rolling exasperation.

"Because my disability is right out there for everybody to see. I can't pretend to be 'normal' like you can!" Alan's sarcastic side reemerged, "I get around in a wheelchair. I move my arms and legs funny. And, to top it off, I talk like a drunk. If you can't handle people knowing about your hemophilia, which is a hidden condition, you wouldn't have the balls to go out in public if you had cerebral palsy." Alan taunted.

"Okay, shut up. You, you just don't get it." Chuck stammered.

"Oh, I get it. I get it a lot more than you. You chicken shit bastard!"

"Whatever, fine. Just shut up alright," Chuck's voice trailed off as he turned away.

"Fine," Alan relented.

The boys remained silent until Chuck was let off at his home. At that time, Alan thought about reminding him to have his mom look at the new bruise. But he was still angry with Chuck for being so pig-headed. He figured that the moron had survived 17 years as a hemophiliac testing fate with a confrontational personality. Alan had helped him once and wasn't responsible for suicidal people.

The weekend came and went rather uneventfully for Alan. He often used the extra time provided by weekends to catch up on class work or study for an upcoming exam. Typically during homecoming week however, teachers know that their students focus lie elsewhere and don't assign heavy homework loads.

So, Alan and his folks took the opportunity to go to a nearby big cat habitat. He felt an inner kinship with: tigers, lions, leopards, cougars and so forth. Their power and quiet confidence spoke to his soul.

On Monday morning, Alan and mom waited for the bus. For some reason the usually prompt Mrs. Branch was 20 minutes tardy this morning. Finally, her bus pulled ever so slowly to the curb. They glanced quizzically at each other as both found this rather odd because she usually comes to an abrupt stop.

As she departed the bus, he espied her watery, bloodshot eyes and tear-stained cheeks. Suddenly, strong anxiety pangs swirled within him as an unmistakable aura of solemnness emanated from her being. Usually she's quick with a cheerful morning greeting but, today, it was obvious to anyone that she was hesitant and nervous.

Upon walking up the curb, she motioned for Alan's mother to talk with her privately. Ms. Jones made eye and hand gestures for her son to stay put. He obeyed and watched mom go down the driveway to talk to Mrs. Branch. Although out of earshot, he could still study and interpret body language aspects of their conversation.

Mrs. Branch had the same pall about her as an unsuccessful surgeon does relating news to a patient's family. Her hands moved about restlessly from face to neck to hips and back to face again. At some point, Alan lip read, "He didn't wake up," a short time after that he saw mom shake her head in disbelief.

As mom turned and walked back, he didn't need her to verbalize what he instinctively knew. His gut and experience were far better communicators of reality than spoken words. All recognizable elements of death permeated his consciousness.

When one spends more than a decade at disabled schools, with kids who have life-threatening conditions, one develops a sixth sense about death. When Alan left Dillon behind and mainstreamed at Fairlawn, he foolishly believed that death wouldn't follow. But, as mom knelt beside him, he knew his worst fears were about to be confirmed.

"Alan, honey," she began with trepidation, "I'm afraid that I have very bad news, Chu..."

He interrupted anxiously, "I know ma, Chuck's dead, right?"

"Yeah, his mom couldn't wake him this morning," she looked puzzled by Alan's knowledge of his school mate's demise, "Honey, how'd you know?" she bit her lower lip.

"Just a gut feeling mom," he spoke low and stared down at weeds in the lawn, "Chuck wasn't looking so hot on Friday and he's not on the bus. Plus, Mrs. Branch looked all upset, so, I figured..." he trailed off and looked away to hide watery eyes.

Mom tried to hug her son but he pulled back. Under normal circumstances, he always found comfort in her loving embrace. At this very moment of emotional vulnerability however, if she hugged, touched, or consoled him, in any way, he would completely break down.

The mainstreaming experience began three long years ago. But, if this emotionally devastating development couldn't be harnessed and mastered, everything that had been achieved would be washed away in tears. Despising disabled stereotypes, he was determined that nobody would see a weak, frail, cripple. No, too much work and too much sacrifice of his inner child's soul went into proving that he belonged in regular school.

Therefore, he couldn't get on that bus—go to that school—and show any vulnerability. Friends had passed away before and this situation wasn't any different. Using prior experiences as a guide, those awful feelings were quickly corralled into the same pen with all of the others. Without incident, he got on the bus, avoided eye contact with anybody, and arrived at Fairlawn High focused on the day at hand.

First period was homeroom with Ms. Simmons and the two remaining disabled students in the program, besides Alan, Salvador and Larry. He opened a geometry textbook and began studying the finer details of an isosceles right triangle; immersing himself in knowing that an isosceles right triangle has one 90 degree angle and two complimentary 45 degree angles. Focusing on this obscure geometrical concept became a life preserver in a stormy sea of emotions.

During the hour, every now and then, his thoughts would shift towards Ms. Simmons. She appeared seemingly unruffled by Chuck's sudden death. Alan began to feel those old uneasy attitudes about the perceived devaluation of a disabled kid's life. While nobody expected her to break into a southern Baptist type eulogy, it would have been nice to have her make some acknowledgement of his life.

Chuck may not have been a model student. And, sometimes his brutal honesty robbed people of their comfortable, well constructed, delusions of reality. Still, when class ended, with nary a word about their fallen mate, Alan had to talk to Ms. Simmons before going to geometry class.

"Uh, Ms. Simmons?" he got her attention.

"Yes, Alan," she spoke softly.

"Did you know that Chuck died?" he struggled with the words.

"Yes, it's too bad," she deadpanned.

"Too bad? That's a strange thing to say,"

"Why?" she shrugged.

"Because he was a part of your program and usually when a classmate or student dies it's a significant event," he huffed in frustration, "And I figured, based on how the whole school reacted when Penelope Grayson bit the dust, that every time someone died here there was some kind of moment of silence or something."

"What happened at your old school?"

"Oh, I don't know. At my old school, there were tons of disabled kids with terminal or life-threatening diseases and it wasn't unusual to see someone one day and they'd die that night. There were no grand announcements by the principal over the P.A. system. There were no grief counselors lined up in the multi-purpose room," he mocked, "Every kid was expected to suck it up and move on. I understood, it was a handicapped school after all, and that's the reality of that type of school," he seethed.

"And what's new now?" she sighed.

"Well, when queen Penelope croaked the Administrators acted like an actual queen died! I mean the entire school came to a stop because an irresponsible girl didn't belong on the road," he chastised, "We all know the truth. She was equally manipulative with both boys and girls. And, for that, the Administrators practically canonize her."

"Look Mr. Jones, there's no point in pretending Chuck was a saint, and watch your tone young man!" she yelled.

"What does that have to do with anything? I have news for you. The beloved Penelope was no saint! She threatened to make me a pariah during a pep rally,"

"Right," she sneered, "What did she do?"

"I wasn't doing their moronic cheer and she said if I didn't be a good cripple boy, she would stop the pep rally and tell everyone in the gym that I wanted the other team to win."

"So, what do you care?"

"Excuse me, what do I care? Look, normally, you'd be right, I wouldn't care because I know a lot of people don't like me mainstreaming here in the first place," he asserted, "but, if I also become known as: 'the cripple who cheered against the school' it would make life harder." He snapped.

"I still don't understand why that would affect you," she said, "I mean you've been through worse at your last school. Okay, just for argument's sake. What if your fears came to fruition and the whole school despised you for the remainder of your high school years? What changes from your current situation?"

"Well, for one, I'm constantly watching my back waiting to be attacked," he said.

"Oh come on, get real! This isn't your previous school," she laughed, "Besides, this is a good school in a good town and you're fortunate to have this opportunity." She scolded.

"Oh, right, I forgot, silly me," shaking his head with a mocking grin and snort.

"Okay," she sensed sarcasm, "I know I'm going the regret asking this, but why are you silly?" she raised an eyebrow while crossing her arms tightly across her chest.

"I guess you expect me to be a grateful crip boy for being allowed to go here…"

"That's not what I meant, I…" she said apologetically.

"Let me tell you something Ms. Simmons," he saw vulnerability and pounced like a tiger, "and if you need to report me to the principal for my 'tone' then do it," he paused, "I earned the right to be here with my grades. And, as such, this school is legally required to provide me with an education. You aren't doing me a favor. You're doing your job," he glared.

"Hey, talk to me with respect young man!" she growled back.

"Tell you what, I'll give you respect when you give me respect and you acknowledge that Chuck was a human being worthy of some words being said of his death."

Ms. Simmons never saw Alan this adamant about anything. She now knew that all of this could have been avoided if she said a few words to eulogize Chuck when class began. Yet, at present, Alan appeared so angry there was no point in continuing her defense. All she could think to do was send him to the next class.

"You're already tardy for second period, you better get going," she said quietly and walked away.

Without saying another word Alan just shook his head and slowly wheeled out the door. He gave her one last hate-filled stare before slamming the door in her face. Peddling towards geometry class the anger that was reserved for Ms. Simmons turned inward. He felt like a stupid fool for breaking his own rules and getting emotionally invested with another disabled kid.

How could delusional thoughts be allowed to pervade a normally cold, calculating logical mind? How did childish optimism establish a beachhead on the frontal lobe? Did he really think for one second that a life of a disabled kid was at last viewed as equal to a "normal" kid by a school system that fought so mightily to keep disabled kids from mainstreaming in the first place? The stark contrast between Penelope and Chuck's situation—and how each evolved—confirmed what Alan already knew. Sometimes you need to be doused by a bucket of cold water to snap you back into reality.

# CHAPTER 23 -
# COMPETITIVE DRIVE

Frank Saunders a tall, lanky, man in his early 50s, had a genuine passion for American history. Today, as he did every Thursday, Mr. Saunders separated his class into six teams, with each row representing a team. Then, he would ask 50 current event questions and students would raise their hands to answer. Each member of the winning team received ten "test points" which were then applied toward Friday's exam.

For example, if a winning team member earned 78% on a given exam, he or she would in effect be given 88% once extra credit had been factored in.

As he sat in Mr. Saunders's history class, one question kept gnawing at Alan, "Are the other five people on my team really this stupid?" As usual, not only was Alan's team behind, they were in their perpetual state of dead last, a full 15 points in arrears of row five, led by Will Harris, with just 25 questions left.

As Mr. Saunders's best student, Alan really didn't need any bonus points. But, Alan Jones didn't get where he was by passively watching his competition earn higher grades! However, up until now, his speech problem dissuaded him from actively participating in the weekly contest.

With each passing week, the gap between Alan's fear of being ridiculed for speaking aloud, and his utter frustration for points lost narrowed. He always answered Mr. Saunders's questions in his head. Somehow, he had to summon up enough courage to verbalize the answers. Still, speaking was one challenge, making himself understandable was quite another.

Moreover, finding a mechanism allowing him to answer questions while using a rationed vocabulary could be tricky. Finally, an idea came to mind on how to solve his language barrier dilemma.

Most of the questions were multiple choice, which allowed for an, a, b, or c, response. Before Mr. Saunders's next question, Alan clenched his hands together in nervous anticipation because – against better logic - he could no longer hold his tongue.

Immediately following Mr. Saunders's recitation of the next question, the teacher saw a sight, which startled him so badly that he temporarily lost composure. Alan Jones had his left hand jutting straight up and looking like he actually wanted to answer a question! A perplexed Mr. Saunders inquired hesitantly, "Yes, Al. . . Alan, did you want to answer?"

Alan nodded, and anxiously uttered, "Yes"

"Well, then, Alan, what's the answer?"

"B!" Alan excitedly exclaimed, while scanning the room for hecklers.

"That's correct, Alan! Absolutely correct!" Mr. Saunders chuckled, while Alan waited for the next question.

Alan didn't stop at one. Oh, no. After answering five of the following six, he saw an opportunity to do something extraordinary. With his team still trailing by eight points and just ten questions to go, he went for broke. After each question, he decided to stick his hand in the air first, no matter what. He mused that, at worst, his team would lose again; conversely, if he ran the table, not only would his team get ten points but, he would become a legend.

Alan answered the next two questions correctly. But, then, a member of the leading team protested. With eight questions left, and Alan's team down by six, the teacher was interrupted, "Excuse me, Mr. Saunders, Mr. Saunders, sir," a voice rang out.

Mr. Saunders slowly slid his focus from paper to questioner.

"Yes, William. What is it?"

"Mr. Saunders, I don't feel it's fair that one person answer all of a team's questions. Also, he's taking over our entire contest!"

"Well, William, what do you want me to do about it?"

"Make some kind of rule that one person can't answer more than one in a row!"

"We're more than halfway into the game. I can't change the rules now just because you're wary of a little competition, Mr. Harris."

"That's not fair!" William shouted angrily.

"Mr. Harris, sit down and shut up or you'll find yourself sitting across from vice Principal Thompson! Do I make myself perfectly clear, Mr. Harris?" Mr. Saunders yelled, with hands on hips.

"Yes, sir!" William responded sarcastically while shooting a dagger-eyed glare toward Alan.

By this time, Alan's mindset wasn't going to let any intimidation that Will Harris could conjure up stem his momentum. His competitive drive already was cruising in high gear. Furthermore, any personal reservations regarding his speech had long since dissipated.

Also, his team members – who'd never even spoken to him before - made themselves useful by becoming his cheering section. They figured that they could ride his coattails for an easy ten points – and this sorry group needed all the help that they could get! Every time he answered correctly, they'd slap him on his shoulders or rub his head.

Alan's strategy of raising his hand first seemed to be working. So far, he'd known all of the answers well before Mr. Saunders had finished his inquiry.

With three questions left, and his team's lead trimmed to a scant one point, William decided to employ desperate tactics. As Alan raised his hand to answer yet another question, William tried to rattle him by using mockery.

Before Alan could respond, he heard an imitation of his voice coming from across the room, "Duh, duh, whhaaaaaat cooouuuldd da answer beeeeee?"

With all eyes now on him, William took his mocking behavior to new heights of contempt by rolling his head in a circle and drooling down his chin. The class shared a group giggle, borne more out of nervous response than William's comedic foray.

Unfortunately, William's tactic worked. Alan totally forgot what the question was, and instead of asking Mr. Saunders to repeat himself, he reflexively took a guess. "B," he shouted hastily.

Mr. Saunders shook his head because Alan had answered wrong due to William's deplorable tactics; consequently, he had no choice but to accept Alan's response. "I'm sorry, Alan, that's not correct," Mr. Saunders grimly related.

Then, to add insult to injury, William raised his right hand and said, "I believe the correct answer is c, Mr. Saunders."

The red-faced teacher glared at William, and stated coldly, "Correct, Mr. Harris."

The normally good-natured, mild-mannered educator had been pushed beyond his boiling point, which is saying something, considering that he'd never shown even a hint of annoyance in the previous ten weeks. Mr. Saunders rose from his chair, and with a deliberate gait, marched over to row five, seat two.

Now, standing over William, he pointed toward the door and shouted, "Get out of my class, now!"

William became too rattled at his teacher's outburst to obey in a timely fashion. Mistaking William's unresponsiveness as further insubordinate behavior, Mr. Saunders grabbed his pupil's left elbow and unceremoniously dragged him out. "Sit your butt against this wall. I'll deal with you after class, mister!" his voice boomed through the wall. When he re-entered, a traumatized classroom sat in stunned silence. Mr. Saunders, however, calmly picked up where he left off.

The sideshow had one positive side effect. It gave Alan plenty of time to regain his focus. Moreover, he figured out how to handle any additional hecklers who might try to interrupt his train of thought.

"Now, where were we?" Mr. Saunders asked rhetorically.

Alan knew that he had to be absolutely perfect from here on in. Down by two points with two questions left, there was no room for error. So, he blocked out everything else that was happening and focused solely upon Mr. Saunders's next question.

Then, right before he answered, a coughing epidemic hit the students in the other five rows. Oddly, each of these coughs were followed by an utterance of the words, "choke," or "loser."

To the hecklers' chagrin, however, Alan was prepared for their taunts. He simply smiled at Mr. Saunders to assure him that everything was fine. The teacher found a way to silence his charges, "The next person who speaks out of turn gets a ten-point deduction from tomorrow's exam."

As quickly as you could say, "pop-quiz," a hush once again fell upon the room. His path now clear, Alan answered both remaining questions to tie the score.

With no questions remaining, Mr. Saunders threw his hands up, "I guess we have a tie. I'll award five points to each team."

However, Alan wasn't satisfied with this solution. He raised his left hand, and after Mr. Saunders acknowledged him, he said two words, "tie breaker".

His teacher gently tried to persuade him to split the points; however, Alan would have none of it, "All or nothing," he clearly stated.

Seeing that his star pupil wasn't going to back down, Mr. Saunders decided to accommodate Alan's wish. "Okay, here are the rules. I'll ask one question. Whoever raises their hand first, must give me the correct answer; otherwise, their team loses."

Then, he threw Alan a nasty curve, "This will be a fill-in-the-blank question."

Alan's heart raced a little faster, a sweat broke out on his brow, and he suddenly had trouble getting enough air. He was comfortable answering questions with one letter. Now, out of the blue, he'd be forced to clearly enunciate polysyllabic words!

Mr. Saunders could see Alan's trepidation over the selected format. So, without further ado, he asked the tie-breaking question. "Trenton is the Ca. . . . . ?"

Using the same strategy he employed for multiple-choice, his hand was in the air before Mr. Saunders could finish.

As soon as he saw Alan's hand, Mr. Saunders truncated his speech. "Yes, Alan," he said, while pointing at his suddenly brazen young ace.

Alan, taking his time, folded his hands, took a deep breath, and said, "New. . . Jersey."

Mr. Saunders took a sip of his coffee, sighed, and deadpanned, "Well, Mr. Jones, you just won your team ten points."

Then, breaking into a smile, he enthusiastically shouted, "Congratulations, Alan!"

Each member of his team high-fived him as they thanked him for helping them out. He heard them say,

"Alan, you're the man!"

"That was fantastic!"

"You're the greatest!"

When Alan wheeled from the room, he passed William, who was sitting against the wall. William wasn't in a cordial mood, to say the least, "You cost me a B on the test, you sonofabitch bastard! My mom is going to ground me if I bring home a C." Glaring at Alan, he threatened his new adversary, "I'll get you for this, count on it! You sonofabitch!"

Alan couldn't help but laugh at William. Alan had a penchant for reading people; William seemed like a typical loudmouth. These types never have the ass to back up their words.

Alan looked down at him, and said, "I killed you in there. I own you. You're my bitch!" Alan then wheeled to English class.

After that day, Mr. Saunders instituted the, "Alan rule". According to this rule, "Alan is prohibited from answering more than two questions in a row." In spite of this constraint, Alan's team still won every contest.

# CHAPTER 24 - COWBOYS

By his junior year at Fairlawn High Alan's social standing had long since been established. Being the only mainstreamed disabled student in a school of 3000 was bad enough, but his speech problem and standoffish, introverted personality served as a deadly combination to further exacerbate his isolation. Outwardly, he understood his role of not only performing at an academically high level but also becoming a standard bearer for disabled students who would follow him. However, secretly, he yearned for a friend, a girlfriend, and some sense of belonging. Along with the nerds, geeks, and other assorted freaks, he officially became a clique of one.

In order to accomplish any goal, sacrifices have to be made. He devoted his entire focus on nurturing and cultivating the fruits of academic pursuits. Consequently, allowing prime social maturation years to wither and die on the vine.

Fairlawn was a spacious, outdoor campus with no hallways. All of the classrooms had picture windows framing magnificently manicured lawns. During nutrition and lunch breaks, each clique would assemble on an area of the quad claimed years ago by their forebears.

Jocks would hang out near the weight room and preen; cheerleaders would goof around, strutting and teasing jocks, and so on. There were about ten separate cliques, from "Chess club" to "Stoners". The largest of these was a group approximately 40 strong called, "The Cowboys", who took up residence on the entire northeast area of the quad.

On these breaks, Alan would roll past the Cowboys down a long, steep hill to a recreation room. He liked to frequent a lonely bumper pool table in a deserted corner. Being a good geometry student allowed him to foster an appreciation for the nuances of the game. A bumper pool table has eight sides, four bumpers in the center of the table, and two pockets at opposing ends flanked by two bumpers. Each player has three balls, which he must successfully pocket on his opponent's end.

Since straight shots are impossible until the ball is right in front of the pocket, the trick is using geometry to bank the balls off the sides. He liked playing bumper pool by directing the ball with his clenched fist since he couldn't use a cue stick.

As usual, when the second period bell clanged at 10 a.m. Alan eagerly rushed out toward the rec room. On this day, as he dashed past the Cowboys, something unusual occurred. The biggest Cowboy got up and followed him down the hill. As Alan was entering his favorite hangout, the Cowboy trailed five paces behind.

Four minutes after Alan began his practice session, a big shadow covered the table–he knew it was the Cowboy. Before he could look up at his mysterious pursuer however, two five-dollar bills floated down upon the green felt. Then he heard a booming voice. "I'll give you ten bucks if you can sink that ball from the other end," the stranger proposed.

Alan lifted his eyes in an attempt to ascertain the stalker's intentions. What first registered was the size and wardrobe of this guy. He definitely looked like a cowboy, from his size-16, worn leather boots, faded jeans with holes, an old hand-me-down leather belt, adorned with a wide, showy buckle, an unremarkable tattered vest covering a checkered shirt, and to complete the look, a top of the line hat which cost more than the rest of his ensemble.

Alan tried to look the red-bearded stranger in the eye, but his hat was tilted forward, covering the upper half of his face. At this point, Alan lost patience with the mystery.

"Let me look you in the eyes, sucker, I don't have time for bullshit," he strongly asserted. The stranger tilted his hat up until his entire face was revealed.

"Howdy, I'm Tom," he said softly.

Unfortunately for Tom, Alan was in no mood to be played with. While Tom's intentions may have been good, Alan's own experience had led him to believe that everything has a catch and everybody has an angle. He backed away from the table in order to assess his predicament. While the two Abe Lincolns lying on the table looked intriguing, he wanted more information from Tom.

"Okay Tex," he began with a hint of cynicism, "Let me get this straight. If I sink this shot, that money is mine, right?"

"First of all," Tom sighed, his eyebrows arching, "my name ain't Tex, like I said before, I'm Tom. And yeah, if you sink that ball, the money is yours."

"And if I don't make the shot? What then? What's in it for you besides having a little fun at my expense?" Alan snapped back.

Tom's voice softened as he said, "Look. All I was wondering is if you might want to spend some time with me and my boys."

"And just who are your boys, and why in the world would I want to hang out with you guys?" Alan continued his antagonistic bent.

"My boys are the Cowboys, and I'm their leader. We're a bunch of nice dudes who shoot bull and make fun of all the pretty people who walk by acting like fools, from pompous pom-pom cheerleaders to asshole jocks."

"Oh, the Cowboys. Aren't you the guys who have an average 2.1 G.P.A. or something? What kind of childish prank are you guys playing on me?

Oh, I get it. Sucker crip-boy into believing he's real. I bet the rest of your posse is lurking in the shadows waiting for the punch line."

"I thought that you could contribute to our group, but you seem like a pompous ass in your own right, so maybe not," Tom said, with resignation in his voice.

Instinctively, Alan considered dragging his 3.5 G.P.A. into the discussion but quickly realized that such an action would only confirm Tom's hypothesis. On the other hand, he wasn't going to turn down what he considered to be easy money.

So, without further fanfare, he calmly wheeled up to the table, lined up his shot, coolly sank the ball, and scooped up his winnings. Then, he gave Tom his over-practiced, long, hard, piercing stare, only used whenever he wanted to scare somebody off. However, Tom didn't scare easily and he wasn't done with Alan.

Then Tom dug deep into his pockets and pulled out two more dollars plus a couple of dimes and four pennies and placed the currency on the outer table ridge. Alan was puzzled by this sudden offering and pondered starting his wheelchair and going to sit outside of his next class. It seemed to him that Tom wasn't going to leave him alone until he derived some satisfaction from their encounter.

"So, what do I have to do to get you off my ass, man? Alan snarled.

"One more bet. If you make that shot again, I'll never bug you again," Tom replied.

"But," Alan interjected.

"But, if you miss, then tomorrow you have to spend your entire lunch period up on the hill with us, deal?" Tom queried.

Alan pondered the offer for a long minute and finally agreed, but not before being assured that Tom would hold up his end of the bargain. There were two balls left on the table. One ball was behind two bumpers. The other was practically a tap in just left of the hole. Tom let Alan choose which one to shoot, so naturally he opted for ball two. As he lined up his sure thing shot which would net him a whopping two bucks and twenty-four cents plus not being harassed again, he wondered if he was being shortsighted. He took a moment to ponder the big picture; what would happen—if he missed?

After all, he pondered, would it be so awful to try something new? Maybe, just maybe, this could be the type of group inclusion he'd been craving all along. If he makes the shot, nothing changes. He'll remain safe in his isolation, yes, but are there better opportunities in the long run if he aims just right of the pocket? He had too much stubborn pride to accept Tom's offer outright. If he missed the shot on purpose, he'd have to make it look not too obvious as to arouse Tom's suspicion. So, he took a chance.

The next day, the bell clanged signaling lunch break. True to his word, Alan headed toward "Cowboy Hill" in order to fulfill his obligation. Approaching the center of the quad, he wondered how he would be received. Would they greet him with open arms, or would he have to brace for an hour's worth of razzing and ridicule? In any case, he mentally prepared to accept his fate no matter how embarrassing.

Finally, he arrived at Cowboy Hill and rode his wheelchair onto the lawn. At first, the boys were preoccupied with a heated but friendly debate over their favorite football teams. Then, as Alan settled in a spot next to Tom, the group's attention fell upon the newcomer.

Tom turned his head toward Alan and flashed a huge grin. "Well, I see that you're a man of your word," he chuckled. Then he slowly stood up, raised his arms, and whistled for quiet, "Hey, guys, I've got an introduction to make. Hey, listen up now." He put his left hand on Alan's left shoulder and Alan wondered what was meant by it. Either he was going to be an object of a group beating or he was going to be accepted into the brotherhood. At this point, he figured that there was no in-between.

Then, Tom answered his question in resounding fashion, "Guys, this is my friend, Alan. I just met him yesterday but I already know that he's a great guy. He can be a bit ornery, but he's not a complete ass."

The group laughed uproariously. Then, Tom, half-kneeling, softened his voice slightly and concluded his intro, "But, overall, I know that he'd make a great addition to our group. Now, I want each of you to introduce yourselves to him one at a time."

As each Cowboy shook Alan's hand, the skepticism that previously resided within him slowly transformed into a very strange sensation. Although a foreign feeling, he derived a tremendous sense of warmth and well being from it. For the remaining two years of high school, he had buddies. After all those years as a social pariah, he could finally say that at least once in his life he was truly accepted.

# CHAPTER 25 - SANS SHERPA

After transferring from community college and taking a semester of general education classes at State U, Alan applied for entry into their nationally acclaimed School of Business. Upon receiving an acceptance letter, he was assigned a Business School advisor named, Ms. McPherson. When he finished the letter, he shouted, "I made it! I made it!" Simultaneously, emotions of excitement and tearful happiness coursed through him. At once, memories, both good and bad, flooded his mind. Finally, years of: never-ending study sessions, two-hour bus rides to and from school, having to prove his worth time and again to an endless stream of doubters and doomsayers, had paid dividends. At last, he wouldn't have to deal with incompetent dunderheads, or so he thought.

A week before spring semester commenced, Alan had a strategy session scheduled with Ms. McPherson. He arrived outside her office door at five minutes before ten. He peered through a pane of glass and espied a woman drinking out of a coffee mug while casually reading a People magazine. Willing to accept that he came early, and that she didn't have to acknowledge visitors yet, he patiently waited. Moreover, the last thing that he wanted to do was to piss her off. At the moment, he believed that in her role as an academic advisor, she had the power to make his life hell.

Ten o'clock came and went. Alan didn't get overly concerned until the clock read 10:15. He tried to make eye contact with her but she still had her head buried in the same magazine. Not knowing what else to do, he lightly knocked three times. She put the magazine down, sprang from her chair and trotted towards the door.

Upon opening the door, she met Alan with both of her eyebrows arched high, mouth wide open, and scratching her head. His eyes fell upon a tall and very attractive young woman in her late 20s or early 30s. Her lustrous brown locks, which ran freely down to her shoulders, served to perfectly frame her face. He soaked in her deep-set bright blue eyes, high cheekbones, and small sloping nose, finished off by a warm ear-to-ear smile showcasing glistening white teeth. Gazing at her blank expression, Alan gleaned that she had absolutely no clue as to his identity or purpose for being there.

"Hi, I'm Alan, your ten o'clock appointment," he said, in a questioning manner.

"Uh, I don't think so. Maybe, I don't have my appointment book handy. Let me look for it."

She motioned him into her office. As soon as he entered he had to stop his wheelchair in its tracks because the floor had been swallowed up by a tsunami of books, files, and manila envelopes. Unfortunately, her desk seemed to have been hit by a tornado, and he saw little hope of her finding her appointment book. As she furiously rummaged through her possessions, he had a fleeting moment of doubt. What if he had come on the wrong day? However, he quickly dismissed the trespassing thought as masked anxiety rearing its ugly head once more.

"Ha, ha! I've found the little bugger!" she yelped.

"And, am I in there?" he pleaded hopefully.

"Yeah, here, are you Alan Jones?"

"Uh, huh." He nodded.

"Great, I have you penciled in for 10 a.m. Well, what do you know?" She mused.

"Penciled in?" he wondered.

"Good morning, Alan!" her voice transformed into a young, pleasant, feminine voice with enthusiastic verve.

"Come, come in, please," she cheerfully gushed while clearing a path for his wheelchair from the door to the front of her desk.

When they both settled into their respective positions, she began her scripted opening speech. She had recited this same tired diatribe countless times. Therefore, her boredom with the monologue came through in her delivery tone.

"All students in the school of business are assigned a career counselor. The counselor's function is to serve as a guide to the student throughout said student's academic career. Furthermore, my job is to ensure that you have every opportunity to cultivate and develop relationships with recruiters and companies through various meets and greets, as well as internships and other functions. However, if at any time you feel that you would be better served by another counselor, you are free to exercise your prerogative. Do you understand my role and your rights?"

Alan nodded warily, still trying to absorb what he'd just heard.

With formalities now out of the way, Ms. McPherson's demeanor returned to its previously jovial state. She playfully spun around in her chair as she gleefully shouted, "Now, let's see if we can game plan towards graduation!"

"Game plan?" Alan thought that her metaphor was a bit screwy but he was willing to play along. He had never been in a big time university setting before and figured that catch phrases were part of a counselor's lingo. Everyone has their own Mt. Everest to scale, and on any expedition, not heeding your guide's advice is foolish. So, he leaned in, followed her lead, and attentively participated in game planning his future.

"The first thing we have to do is figure out your option," she said plainly.

"Option? My major is business," he stated, with bewilderment.

"Yes, however, within the general business major you must concentrate on a specific field of study."

"Such as?"

"Oh, let's see, accounting, business law, decision support systems, economics, finance, management information systems, and a few others."

"Wow, that's quite a selection. How do I choose?"

"Well, according to your Junior College transcripts you took a lot of computer courses."

"Yes." He pulled forward in his seat. "My major was information systems." He beamed.

"Yes, yes, I see that. Very good."

"Thank you."

"So, can I assume that you'd want to continue on that path of study?"

"Most definitely."

"I guess the only question then is whether Decision Support Systems or Management Information Systems is the best option."

He shrugged his shoulders.

"What does that mean, Alan?"

"It means I don't know." He looked at her with befuddlement in his eyes, "You're the counselor. What do you think?" He sighed

"Which one sounds closer to your field?"

"Management Information Systems, I suppose."

"What do you base that on?"

"Well, I don't have the course descriptions in front of me like you do."

"And?"

"And, that means that I only have the option titles to go by."

A chagrined expression suddenly combed her face as she realized her indefensible position. "I'm sorry," she chuckled, "Here I am looking at the catalog, and expecting you to be a mind reader." She shook her head.

For the next 20 minutes, they scrutinized course descriptions together. Every sentence was parsed in order to find a deciding factor that would swing them one way or the other. To their ever-growing dismay, no matter how hard they tried to differentiate between the two, a stalemate seemed inevitable. Just when one course swung the balance for one option, a counterpart would seem as viable. In the end, with all other modes of decision making exhausted, she proposed that they employ a time-tested method.

Ms. McPherson reached into her desk drawer and withdrew her purse. She retrieved a tiny quarter-size object from her purse. Alan thought No, it couldn't be! She stood up and kept a straight face as she addressed him.

"Okay, I've got a shiny new quarter."

"What?"

"Heads - Management Information Systems, tails - Decision Support Systems." She opened her right hand showing him the shiny quarter of fate.

His laughter betrayed his disgust. Here he was at one of the top business schools in the country and his future comes down to a coin flip? How could this happen? They're supposed to know what the hell they're doing! Why not a game of rock, paper, scissors? Why not pluck pedals off a dandelion? He lightly chuckled, rolled his eyes and with a sigh of resignation mumbled, "Okay…"

The quarter bounced thrice before slowly rolling on its end underneath her desk. They both heard something hit against a baseboard of a wall. She looked behind her chair and muttered, "Stupid, stupid, stupid," she raised one eyebrow, scratched her head vigorously and uttered, "Hmm…"

Anxiously awaiting a verdict, Alan's attempts at ascertaining her body language were to no avail. He looked at her and wondered why she seemed so hesitant. How could the outcome of a simple coin toss cause her such consternation? Furthermore, given that either outcome seemed equally desirable, why didn't she just tell him heads or tails sans melodrama? His curiosity quickly turned to irritation as he tired of her indecisive behavior that plagued their meeting.

"Well?" He smacked his hands together.

"Uh, I think it's tails?"

"What do you mean, you think it's tails?" He sarcastically oozed.

"Um, there's more than one quarter here." She nervously mumbled.

"Then, how do you know?" He huffed, no longer trying to mask his annoyance

"I'm sorry; I guess I'm having a bad day, huh?"

Slouching against the wall, there it was, a wide-open shot. She let down her guard and revealed her fragile ego. An open invitation for him to give her a hard verbal jab that would destroy her—maybe even make her cry. However, no matter how tempting it was to crush her, he once again realized that acting on that impulse wouldn't achieve anything. For better or worse, he still needed her approval on any course selection. Consequently, he surmised that it wasn't in his best interest to tear her down.

He turned his motor on and moved behind her desk. He instantly saw her dilemma. There were no fewer than ten quarters scattered behind her desk. Obviously she had resorted to this crude method many times before. Alan suddenly realized that he'd just learned a valuable lesson; incompetent dunderheads are an inescapable part of life. Once she saw that he'd seen the quarters, her face flushed beet red and she tried to speak, but no words came.

His anger turned to pity for her. Trying to lighten the mood, he laughed loudly in an attempt to transform the situation from a steaming pile of crap into something funny.

"Don't worry about it." He chuckled lightheartedly.

"Really? You're not upset?"

"Nah." He lied, with a plastered-on smile.

"What are you going to do?" Slinking like a repentant child to her chair.

"I've made up my mind and I'll take Decision Support Systems."

"Oh, okay, that sounds good." She perked up.

He left her office and headed to the bookstore to buy a school catalog. He knew that he'd have to study it cover-to-cover until he could recite it in his sleep. He'd have to climb this Everest without a Sherpa.

# CHAPTER 26 - JAWS OF DEFEAT

T hose who fail to quickly adapt to their ever-changing environment are doomed to perish. While one might assume that this axiom certainly holds true in the jungle, it has a broader scope as well.

Alan's encounter with academic counselor Ms. McPherson shocked him awake with a bucket of ice water about realities of university life. By his second year at State however, he grew to embrace that scholastic achievements at academia's elite levels were lonely, survivalist quests. During a typical semester, business class sizes dwindled from standing room only to just enough students left to fill one-quarter of the chairs.

Some students, like Alan, were committed to their sheepskin pursuits. But, there were others who behaved like pace cars and dropped out after lap one. He also adapted and became immune to fickle, temperamental professors going on power trips. Still, occasionally, a sequence of events unfolds in such an unexpected way that it pushes even a seasoned student to sanity's outer limits.

For better or worse, Alan's Friday night ritual consisted of religiously studying State U's catalog before retiring. Past experience taught him to trust his own research rather than asking the inept Ms. McPherson anything. Therefore, he not only knew what classes were mandated for graduation but, also, their tiered prerequisites. As a result, future semester schedules became branded on his brain.

Many students don't possess foresight beyond their next frat party. However, Alan couldn't afford such myopic serendipity; on campus, he was his only support system. With a sparse eight weeks left in his junior year, Alan came across a paragraph in the catalog entitled: "Upper Division Writing Exam". He glanced at the section and thought it warranted closer scrutiny.

His pulse quickened upon discovering that passing this exam is required to receive a degree. Then, after further, and intensive, reading, he ascertained that every junior or senior was eligible to take this exam once per semester. Disbelief rapidly transformed into anger upon realizing that one opportunity had already gone by the boards. The only thing his afore-mentioned bungling adviser seemed qualified for was giving seminars on "How to keep a job when you're a moron."

He immediately understood what Ms. McPherson's latest bout of utter incompetence meant. One of four opportunities to take the test went sailing away. And, to compound matters, time was running down for the second—and final—chance this academic year. He didn't want to enter his senior year with an extra burden. The longer that he thought about this predicament the more enraged he became.

He sarcastically chuckled and wondered how she kept her job, "She must know where a lot of bodies are buried." In one motion, he snatched and threw State U's catalog against a far wall. His face pulsed red while screaming, "That stupid, good for nothing, bitch!"

After the following day's geology class, he switched his power chair into high gear. Eschewing sidewalks, he made a beeline – over the plush lawn - to Ms. McPherson's office. As he drew closer, he reminded himself to stay as calm as possible. On the other hand, a part of him really wanted to take a fraternity paddle to her hindquarters.

Her screw-ups were now beyond a point of diminishing returns. He entertained a delusion that she worked undercover for a competing business school. And, her mission seemed focused upon derailing his academic goals. Nonetheless, she needed to understand, in no uncertain terms, how her actions were jeopardizing his graduation chances. However, upon arriving at her door, he decided to channel his rage more constructively.

The door swung open and Ms. McPherson greeted him with a broad grin, "Hello, Alan, come in! I didn't expect to see you today. Do we have an appointment?"

"No, Ms. McPherson. I have a serious problem."

As she closed the door behind them, her expression went from happy-to-horrified, in a blink. Her whole mannerism changed as she slowly took her seat, looking like a child about to get a severe scolding. Then, he reached into his wheelchair bag and retrieved the catalog. Quickly, he turned to the earmarked page and placed it on her desk.

"Uh oh, what did I miss now?" She mumbled nervously as her eyes frantically searched where Alan found disaster. Finally, he pointed out the troublesome section to her. As she studied intently, her body noticeably tensed up more and more with each passing sentence. Then, she slowly pulled away from her desk, turned away from him, pounded her right fist into her forehead while yelling, "Stupid, stupid, stupid!"

Although glad to see that she recognized the situation's gravity, her attempt of self-abasement underwhelmed him.

After her predictable mea culpa, he espied her contemptuously. There wasn't any way that she could misinterpret his facial expression and body language right now. She could feel his thorough disgust with her and she couldn't blame him. This just epitomized her total failure as his counselor.

She put her head in her hands, and with a more convincing level of contriteness moaned, "Oh, Alan, I'm very sorry."

Flogging her any further was, at this point, just an exercise in mental masturbation. Not only had the proverbial horse, long sprung from his unsecured quarters, he was running at full gait toward the nearest glue factory. No, now wasn't a time to assign blame for what went awry. Now was the time to find solutions, and he knew that he needed her help.

"Okay. Can I still take the exam this semester, or is it too late?"

"As a matter of fact, there's one more chance," she enthused.

"When?" His eyes widened

"March 25th."

He threw up his hands, gazed at the ceiling, and sighed, "You're kidding me, that's in two days!"

"Oh, that's right, today's the 23rd. Wow! That's real soon, isn't it?" she oozed.

She just lobbed a big, fat, stupid softball over the home plate of ignorance, but he decided not to swing his sarcasm bat.

"Yeah, and I've got to set up a proctor and reserve a test room."

"You don't have any time to prepare. What will you do?"

As her statements devolved into inanity, his need to see her break down and cry grew. Yet...

"Look, if I can manage to find a proctor and a room in two days, I'll just wing it and hope for the best," he said, with a degree of resignation in his voice.

Before heading home, Alan stopped by the Disabled Students Office. After lengthy negotiations, he managed to secure both a proctor, and a room, for the 25th, at five o'clock in the afternoon.

Alan had high confidence in his composition abilities. This knowledge – combined with the fact that it would be pointless to cram for a test such as this – left him feeling as though he had nothing to lose. After all, he thought, under the circumstances, nobody could expect him to pass a test for which he had no time to prepare. No, Ms. McPherson would take the heat for this one.

Two days later, he arrived at the testing facility 10 minutes early. He always liked to get a feel for his environment before game time. The secretary allowed him into room No. 7; then, she closed the door upon exiting.

So, there he sat, alone in a tiny 10 x 10 room. No windows, just a closed wooden door and a ceiling vent that didn't seem to be blowing much air. His subconscious anxiety of being unprepared suddenly came forth, symbolically, by being trapped in a room that could easily be mistaken as an interrogation facility.

Finally, after what seemed like hours, the door eased open. In walked a short, thin, Asian lad with thick, horned-rimmed glasses that were taped together at the bridge.

In broken English, he introduced himself, "Hi, I Wang. I help write you good today. Okay?"

Alan found it nearly impossible not to laugh out loud. Between his own speech problem and Wang's obvious newness to English, he couldn't help but admire fate's sense of humor. He figured that if he was destined to go down in flames, he might as well enjoy the descent.

After they settled in, Wang was curious about Alan.

"So, you like school?"

Alan nodded.

"What your major?"

"Computer Information Systems."

"Oh, wow, computer that good. My major. . . "

Alan interrupted, "Let me take a wild guess."

Alan despised stereotypes, but...

Wang chuckled, "I bet you never guess."

Alan looked up, threw his hands up and blurted, "Uh, engineering?"

Wang's mouth hung agape, "How you do that?"

"Just lucky I suppose."

As Alan read the instruction sheet, Wang sat quietly gazing at his pencil. After a couple of minutes, he told Wang to open the test book.

Then, as he began dictating, he noticed that Wang wasn't writing in a fluid motion. Instead, his proctor seemed to be stuck on the first word. He sighed deeply and mumbled, "This is going to be a long day."

He chuckled when he saw Wang's addendum to his original sentence, "This is going to be a long day."

"Do you understand me?" Alan asked.

"Not good," Wang admitted apologetically.

"Okay, I'll talk slower," Alan slowly stated.

"I hear harder, promise."

With renewed focus and determination to clearly enunciate every syllable, Alan once again strove to make Wang understand. However, in the middle of dictating the third sentence, he noticed that the words being put to paper weren't matching the words that he spoke. He suddenly stopped talking and told Wang to tear out the page. Wang looking puzzled, said, "What wrong? I no write good?"

Alan knew that he was in a jam. According to the clock on the wall they'd already managed to fritter away 15 precious minutes. He had to find a way to minimize their dual language barrier. While Alan's challenge was speaking clearly, Wang found understanding any English whatsoever a daunting task, regardless of who's talking, let alone someone with speech problems.

Fortunately, Alan had a wealth of experience dealing with test time adversity. Therefore, he thought of a solution that had worked for him in the past. He instructed Wang to rip out a blank sheet from the test book. Then, he had Wang write the alphabet with two spaces between each letter. After accomplishing the given task, Wang looked at him with disbelief. However, Wang was willing to play along.

Alan pointed out each letter to form: words, sentences, and para-graphs. Wang slowly began to see the method to Alan's madness. Knowing that the clock was his omnipotent foe, he feverishly pointed out one letter after another in a seemingly hopeless Don Quixote-like effort to joust at the minute hand.

Yet, no matter how fast he went, that ruthless minute hand kept squeezing his seconds. Wang could barely keep up as sweat now poured from both of them. Alan finally came to the conclusion that he could only defeat his enemy – time - by ignoring it. With a mere eight minutes left, and two paragraphs plus a summary statement to go, he put all his energies into concentrating on what he had to write and pointing at the appropriate letters.

Halfway through his summary, a one-minute warning buzzer sounded. He not only had to finish writing, but he then had to emulate renowned speed-reading maven, Evelyn Wood, and scan Wang's chicken scratches for spelling and punctuation.

While he completed the former, completing the latter proved to be an insurmountable endeavor. He managed to edit three pages of the six-page essay before someone stormed the room and yelled, "TIME!"

After leaving the building, Alan's body and mind were too exhausted to worry about the test. He knew that his writing style would pass muster. The only thing that they could nail him on was punctuation, and Wang's poor penmanship might be a factor as well.

With these things in mind, he went home and went to bed after suffer-ing the slings and arrows of outrageous fortune.

The following Thursday afternoon, Ms. Jones brought mail to Alan's bedroom.

"What's this, mom?" He asked.

"Looks like it's from State U."

Alan's eyes lit up as he excitedly snatched the envelope from her grasp. He savagely tore the envelope, removed its contents, and unfolded his fate.

"Dear Mr. Jones, on this exam, two English professors grade your essay and assign it a number from one to six. Six points being the highest and one point the lowest. If the combined scores are equal to or greater than eight, then you pass the test. If, however, your combined total is less than eight, you must retake the test. Mr. Jones, your score on the Upper Division Writing Exam is 9. Congratulations! On a side note, you may want to be more careful with your punctuation and penmanship. These two deficiencies prevented you from obtaining a higher score. "

Alan rolled on the floor laughing, knowing that he'd snatched victory from the jaws of defeat.

# CHAPTER 27 - END OF NIGHT

C ost accounting is a term eliciting yawns and confused stares from almost anyone not sporting a three-piece suit and a pocket protector to work every morning. Even amongst corporate types this function of the business model isn't greeted with much enthusiasm. Essentially, cost accounting is a necessary detail every business mustn't ignore if it has any hopes for success. Because it's their milieu, CPA's are about the only ones who are fascinated with the nuances of this dry topic. However, some business schools include it in their core curriculum to the dismay of non-accounting majors.

Alan knew that sooner or later he'd have to bite the bullet and confront the dragon. While managing to get by in preliminary accounting courses, he was wary that this beast might lay waste to any aspirations of a coveted university degree. To complicate matters, State U. had been recently recognized as having the nation's top accounting school. Many classmates had their academic careers burnt to a crisp trying to slay "Ol' Costy". With just three scant semesters left until graduation however, he could stall no longer.

From day one, in Ms. Upton's Cost Accounting 320 class, he felt lost. He couldn't keep pace with the speed of her lectures. The only thing giving him solace was the fact that he wasn't alone. Most of his classmates spent a good portion of each hour exchanging confused gazes.

Mrs. Upton didn't so much teach her subject matter as throw it at you. If you couldn't grab the bull by the horns, she figured that was your problem! Finally, after five weeks, he completely tuned her out and let his mind ponder more pleasant thoughts because he gained no benefit from listening to her droning monotonous tones.

Every night he'd open his accounting text on the bed, read and try to grasp concepts that seemed as alien to him as voodoo. As far as he was concerned, there wasn't any rhyme or reason that he could cling to. The moment he thought he began to grasp a theory another one would seemingly contradict it.

His mind fogged over and his attention span waned, as the black clouds of failure grew increasingly malignant in his frontal lobe. He constantly found himself rereading entire passages and chapters because his eyes would cross and his mind would drift. Each study session ended with a violent flinging of the text.

Thus, three quarters of the way through spring semester all his fears were coming to fruition. Miserable performances on both midterms left him in dire straits. His entire academic future rested on him achieving a C or better on Ms. Upton's final exam; and, in a normal class that wouldn't seem to be a monumental task. When the class average is a D plus however, attaining a full grade higher can be a Herculean feat. To make matters worse Alan didn't come close to passing either midterm.

Seven hours into an all night cram session on the eve of his final, reality smacked his face. There wasn't any way in hell that he was going to pass. He could be stranded on a desert isle for ten years just reading that fucking textbook and it wouldn't make a damn bit of difference, he thought.

Taking a step back though, he discovered that he was trying to manufacture an appropriate emotion for the given situation. He wasn't really overly sad or angry or felt any kind of what might be considered a normal emotion about the impending demise of a once stellar academic career. As a matter of fact, ever since his neurologist had upped his anti-seizure meds to six Phenobarbital pills a day, last year, everything seemed more foggy than usual.

As his mom drove him home, after the final, her senses were permeated by his innermost fatalistic mood. He didn't have to say a word or make an overt facial expression for her to recognize her son's true emotional state, even if he wasn't capable of acknowledging core emotions anymore. She knew this particular class had been an uphill struggle all semester and that Alan wasn't accustomed to failure in the academic arena. As a loving mom, her primary instinct was to offer comforting, consoling words to sooth a wounded ego. On the other hand, she never let him wallow in self-pity and wasn't about to make an exception. So, she began speaking in practical terms.

"I came across an article in the newspaper the other day and I think you should look at it when we get home," she began.

"What's it about?" He said half heartedly, guilty of subconsciously stewing over his failure.

"The article says that they've made a connection between Phenobarbital and compromised cognitive alertness."

"You don't say," his attention suddenly fully focused on her words.

"Yeah, honey, perhaps we should have a little chat with your neurologist, Dr. Saxena."

"Wouldn't that be nice if the pills were hindering me," he mused, "But, that won't fix…"

As she pulled into the driveway, she slammed on the brakes, looked him sternly in his eyes and lectured, "Hey, stop that shit right now mister! That class is over, done with and beyond your control right now. Whether you pass or fail there's no point in obsessing over it. We can only control what we do from this point forward, understand?"

"Yes mom," was his short, stunned response.

After changing into pajamas he asked her for the article. Carefully absorbing the findings, a new reality became apparent. The drug he had depended on all his life was indeed complicit in depleting his potential. Symptoms of his current malaise were finally validated by scientific evidence. Increased grogginess, low attention span, indecisiveness were but a few culprits he recognized. Upon finishing, he sat in exasperated silence for a few minutes while pondering what to do next.

"Mom," he called out, "We have to talk."

"What is it honey?" she said while trotting in from the kitchen.

"I've just read the article and everything in it fits how I feel,"

"Well, then, we should set up an appointment with Dr. Saxena,"

"Agreed," he sighed.

Three days later, they sat patiently in the office of Dr. Ophira Saxena who'd been treating Alan's seizure condition for ten years. She had earned their trust by maintaining his seizure free status during that time. Once a year, he'd visit her to get his Phenobarbital blood levels tested and answer her inquiries regarding his overall health.

She was always personable and cheerfully answered any concerns that either Alan or his mother had. After a fifteen-minute wait, an Indian doctor in her early 40's wafted into the room beaming a huge welcoming grin.

"Hi you two, how are you guys doing today?" she politely opened.

"Oh, were fine, thanks, Doctor Saxena," Ms. Jones gave a default response.

"So, we're not scheduled for our annual appointment for another few months. Is there something wrong that needs my attention?" she sat with a wrinkled brow.

"Well, doctor, we feel that it may be time for Alan to get off Phenobarbital,"

Doctor Saxena's facial expression showed that she was visibly flabbergasted by Ms. Jones statement. After taking a moment to gather her thoughts, she struggled, yet managed, to articulate a tactful response, "Please excuse me but with all due respect to you Ms. Jones, why in the world would you want to stop a course of treatment that has until now successfully prevented Alan from having seizures."

"Well, doctor, we came across an article in the paper the other day and it links Phenobarbital to decreased cognitive potential. Ever since Alan's meds have been upped from four to five and now six pills a day, he's been more sleepy, lackluster, and unemotional. Also, he can't seem to concentrate on his studies without great effort. I just wonder if he needs seizure meds anymore since he hasn't had one in over 20 years."

Doctor Saxena's gaze shifted toward Alan. She needed his input after all because he was her patient, not Ms. Jones. She had to make sure that he understood the pros and cons to any course of treatment. A responsible neurologist won't blithely cede to a patient's whimsy without playing the role of a well-informed devil's advocate. She pulled her chair directly in front of his and put her hands on his knees.

"Alan," she began, "I want you to understand that this is a very serious discussion we're having. Getting off Phenobarbital isn't simply a matter of not taking the pills all of a sudden."

"What do you mean?" he asked.

"Well, you've taken this drug for almost your entire life and your body has become, for lack of a better word, addicted to it."

Alan put up his hand to collect his thoughts before speaking, "What do you mean addicted? Am I like a drug addict or something?"

"An innocent, unwilling one, but yes, technically you're a drug addict," she sighed, "Phenobarbital is more addictive than Heroin and you'll have to follow my instructions to the letter if you want to succeed in fully detoxing off it," she studied him for a moment before delivering a final admonishment in a slow, measured tone, "Alan, I need to make certain you fully grasp how serious this decision is. If you decide to go through with this, even if you follow my instructions perfectly, there will be tough times.

There will be times when your body will crave Phenobarbital. Unfortunately, there are no shortcuts, no quick remedies. Also, you may have a seizure. However, if you can make it through the next few months, you'll be fully detoxed. As I said previously, the final decision is yours," she awaited a response.

Looking down at the floor, he tried to find a serene place in his mind to think. He knew what had to be done before he even entered her office. The status quo had become untenable and wasn't working anymore. However, he knew that once his thoughts were given voice everything would change.

This decision would drastically change his reality and severely challenge his honor, commitment, and fortitude. In essence, an all or nothing proposition fraught with perilous obstacles along the way. Finally, he looked back up and answered her in a strong voice.

"Yes, I need to get off these pills. Let's start today!"

Doctor Saxena took his answer in stride and proceeded to outline the details of his detox. "Now, Alan, for the next three weeks you'll take five pills a day. After that, if everything's okay, you'll take four pills a day. Then, after three weeks of four pills, I'll see you again to check you out."

"And, then what? Three pills for three weeks and so on?" he interrupted.

"Yes, yes, I believe you have the gist," she smiled, "Every three weeks we'll take the next step down as long as you don't have a seizure or any other setback. As I alluded to before, there will be rough moments and how you handle those is up to you. Just remember that even though you're not alone, you're the only one who can have the strength to make it through to the other side. No one can judge you and you don't have to prove anything," she spoke slowly and directly, "What I'm saying Alan is if this gets too hard let your mom and me know. Are we clear on that?"

"Yes, doc," he said without hesitation.

# CHAPTER 28 - REFOCUS

Five weeks into his detox program from Phenobarbital, Alan was feeling more alert than ever. Transitioning from five-to-four pills a day hadn't caused the negative reactions he feared. Horror stories abounded in certain circles about the shakes, DTs, cold sweats, and a host of other nasty withdrawal symptoms inflicting their carnage on addicts who finally desired to shed their pharmaceutical pacifiers and deal with reality. Because of this, he lacked sympathy for drug addicts who were whining and crying about detox. All he knew was that his perspective became brighter by the day.

Upon entering his senior year at State U, he had to start preparing for his working career. All seniors are expected to plan a year ahead for this eventuality. Most take a summer internship at a company that draws their interest. Alan, however, had his course mapped out by the State's Regional Center; supposedly, they had perspective employers lined up after graduation. But that's another story.

So, he followed their directives to the letter. As a result, mom and him drove to the university to meet with a workplace ergonomics specialist. As it had been explained to them, this person would evaluate how Alan worked on a computer and make recommendations on how to maximize his efficiency and comfort. He wasn't completely sold on the science's validity but as long as it was coming out of Regional Center's pocket he didn't care.

After parking the van, they wound through back corridors before arriving at a small, shoddy bungalow. Euphemistically, or jokingly, this converted RV was referred to as "The Disabled Students Services Center". At that time, State U. wasn't what you would call a disabled friendly school.

Being a state-supported institution obligated them to provide at least a modicum of governmentally mandated services for disabled students. Beyond meeting bare bones acceptable standards, however, each university had the freedom to divvy up the budgetary pie. Suffice it to say, the Disabled Students Department was left scrounging for monetary crumbs every year.

Upon arriving, they were greeted by a lanky, grey–haired woman who dressed like one of State's coeds. "Hi guys! I'm Patty. Glad to meet you!" She gave each visitor an enthusiastic handshake before escorting them both to a computer workstation. Her choice of age inappropriate attire, informal greeting style and introducing herself as "Patty", a kid's name, in lieu of "Patricia", led Alan to believe that his initial feelings about this being a time-wasting encounter were correct. Patty came across as a transplanted flower child from another era. But, like he told himself before, Regional Center was footing the bill. So, he just decided to play along.

"What exactly do you do, Patty?" Ms. Jones asked solemnly.

"Well, Ms. Jones, I'm here to gauge if we can make any improvements on how Alan works. I'm just going to ask him to work at this terminal awhile and then I'll have a better feel for what adjustments, if any, have to be made."

Alan interjected, "I'm sorry, Patty, but to be honest with you, I don't see how you can help me," he shrugged, "I mean, look, I type with one finger, always have and I always will. So, frankly I…"

"Hang on now, give me a chance and don't dismiss me out of hand. Maybe you're right and I can't help you," she shrugged, "But as long as you're here, it won't kill you to give me a shot. What do you say? Are you willing to have an open mind about this?" she chuckled playfully.

Alan had played this tired old game before. He had been burned too many times either by callous individuals who had no intention on following through or by kind souls who lacked the competence to produce tangibly significant outcomes. People with good intentions and hollow promises are a dime a dozen. Conversely, those who actually deliver results are but a precious few. He locked eyes with her for a few hushed seconds before softening his appearance, making a deep sigh and acquiescing to her wishes. "Okay, I'll give it a shot."

"Love your enthusiastic vote of confidence," she laughed again, "Now, I want you to read off this sheet of paper and type it into the word processor. First, adjust yourself at the keyboard like you always do and then start typing."

As Alan positioned himself at the keyboard, Patty took up residence almost directly opposite him in order to examine his style. He read the first sentence twice to make sure he copied it correctly. Then he held his left wrist with the right hand and typed. Meanwhile, something odd caught her eye when watching him read the first sentence. She quickly dismissed it as an aberration. When she caught him doing the same thing while reading the second sentence, alarm bells rang loudly in her head.

"Stop. I want to try something else for a second," her manner darkened.

Patty instructed Alan to come out from the workstation and sit directly across from her. She had him read the paper silently while watching his eyes. What she discovered startled her. After being convinced of her suspicions, she sighed and looked at him in a mixed look of amazement and appreciation. Now, all she had to do was explain why there was a goofy expression on her face.

"I…I can't believe it," she stammered.

"What's the matter?" Ms. Jones antenna knew something was wrong.

"Well, I don't know how to tell you this but quite frankly I don't know how Alan ever learned how to read let alone make it through a competitive university," she said.

"What are you talking about?" Ms. Jones said defensively.

"Come here, Ms. Jones, and watch his eyes closely as he reads," she said.

Ms. Jones stared intently at her son's eyes as he read the page. After a few seconds, however, she failed to understand what seemed so readily apparent to a person that they just met, "I'm sorry, Patty, but I don't see what you see. What are you talking about?" she sighed exasperatingly.

Patty leaned over and whispered in Ms. Jones ear, "Watch his left eye as he scans from left to right," Alan's mom nodded twice, "Now, watch his right eye and see if it's making the same movement," the specialist waited for a light to go on in the mother's mind.

Then, suddenly, like discovering a previously unrecognized subplot in a favorite old movie, it hit her. While his left eye was smoothly moving back and forth, his right eye seemed a bit off center. Although, she couldn't quantify the problem, she knew that something was amiss. She shook her head in disbelief and regret, "After all these years, how could I have missed…"

"Missed what?" Alan said.

Patty, ignoring Alan, nodded with satisfaction upon seeing that Ms. Jones saw the problem. What concerned her now, however, centered around making certain that the slightly guilt-stricken mother understood that her culpability in this matter didn't exist, "You have to understand, I'm a trained professional and there wasn't any conceivable way that you could've detected this. A typical optometrist wouldn't have spotted it either. This disorder was just discovered about 10 or 12 years ago and few optometrists have a working knowledge of it."

"Really?" Ms. Jones eyebrows arched.

"Oh, yes. You'd be surprised at the number of optometrists who are ignorant of the topic."

"Is there anything that can be done about it?"

"About what?" There was a strain in his voice.

Again, Patty ignored him, "Fortunately, a handful of ophthalmologists, who specialize in treating this condition have cropped up. As a matter of fact, there's one about 15 miles from campus. Before you guys leave, I'll try to run down his phone number for you."

"Okay, we'll give him a try," Ms. Jones said.

Everybody has a sore spot, a subject that they'd rather not have brought into question. In Alan's case, he always felt that he had to overcome negative first impressions that were made by his wheelchair and speech problem. Moreover, part of his drive had been borne out of a desire to prove his true value to society. Therefore, he took Patty's assessment as an insult.

Finally, with his patience about tapped out, Alan shouted so that he could be heard, "Hey! Excuse me! Will somebody tell me what the hell you two are talking about?" Then, he tilted his head mockingly at Patty's amateur physician's diagnosis, "Look, lady, I don't know if you like to play doctor or pretend or what, but I don't have time for sick head games," he wheeled closer to her, "I'll speak slowly so you understand, I… don't have a reading problem, got it!"

The experienced specialist studied him carefully. She knew what an automatic defense mechanism was and how to bring it down. All she had to do was convince him that her interests were purely focused upon acknowledging and building on his success. To that end, she asked him questions that she thought would accomplish her objective.

"Listen," she began softly while leaning forward, "What you have done up until now is amazing and I'm not calling that into question whatsoever. I have a great amount of respect for you and what you represent. However, I'm now asking you to respect me enough to prove that I can help you. Will you at least extend me that courtesy?" she smiled.

Her words, and the way in which they were conveyed, eased his posture yet again. Still, he didn't feel that she could help him but there was a detectible sincerity in her eyes which he couldn't ignore, "Okay, you're right," he nodded while still simmering inside.

"Let me pose a few questions to you then, if I may. And try not to over-analyze why I'm asking them. And don't tell me what you think is appropriate. You're not on trial here," she chuckled, "Just, give me your first, gut reactions, okay?"

"Okay," he sighed.

"First off, do your eyes ever begin to hurt while reading?"

"Yes, but doesn't everyone's?" he scoffed.

She wrote in her notebook, "Alright, do you ever have to reread a line or even an entire paragraph because you lost track of where you were?"

Alan's back instantly straightened and attention heightened, he'd never told anybody about these things because he deluded himself into believing that it was normal, "Well, uh, yes, I have but I figured, you know …"

"That it was normal?" she finished his thought.

"Yes, I suppose," looking chagrinned and suddenly more receptive.

"Yes, okay, that goes with my theory," she stroked her chin three times, "Let me follow up on that," she asked her next question in a very deliberate tone, "Do you ever make sure to remember the last word of the previous line in order to make sure that you don't reread that line again."

Alan threw his head back, looked at the ceiling and broke out in near hysterical laughter. Her flawless interpretation of his heretofore-unrevealed vision abnormalities gained her instant credibility in his eyes. No pun intended.

She didn't need a verbal answer. His reaction told her all she needed to know, "I guess I can take that as a yes then. Right?" she chuckled.

Back in control again, Alan nodded twice while softly laughing out a, "Yes"

Ms. Jones cut in, "You could decipher all that just by looking at him for a couple of minutes?" her mouth agape in astonishment.

"Yes, I've been working at this for some time now and to me it's hard to miss," Patty shrugged.

"I always wondered why it took so long for Alan to read a chapter or a newspaper article. Well, that would certainly have to slow him down," Ms. Jones sighed.

"Like I said before, what amazes me is the fact that, given these obstacles, he learned to read at all. I mean, in almost all of my case studies of people who have this problem, they never attain literacy. All I can say is that Alan must have one hell of an internal drive," Patty shook her head.

"I have to admit that I didn't come here with an open mind but you won me over," Alan conceded gracefully.

After their meeting, Patty handed Ms. Jones a piece of paper with a phone number on it. One week later, Alan and his mom were meeting with Dr. Robertson, an ophthalmologist who specialized in vision disorders. During their visit, Alan's specific malady was identified and Dr. Robertson prescribed a course of therapeutic eye exercises that could be done at home.

Three times a day, without fail, Alan and mom diligently carved out 20-minute sessions for his eye exercises. Though frustrating and monotonous at first, after two or three weeks, Alan's scanning ability improved dramatically. By the start of fall semester his reading speed increased greatly because instead of reading a single word at a time he was seeing and comprehending one or two sentences instantaneously. Now, all he had to do was to complete detox to feel fully locked and loaded for the first time in his academic career. Unfortunately, those hibernating detox demons, arising from their slumber, had other plans.

# CHAPTER 29 - A NEW DAY

Alan awoke with a fast thumping heartbeat but didn't know why. Despite there being a mild breeze from outside which kept displacing the cloth vertical blinds, he felt smothered. In his mind there wasn't enough air in the room. His body and linens felt like somebody laid a huge, hot, sopping wet beach towel on top of him. His gut told him that there was someone wielding a knife overhead waiting to stab him in the heart. He spun out of bed and kneeled while leaning on his dresser in an attempt to gain control. Yet, waves-upon-waves of imminent disaster kept washing over him, seeping insidiously deeper into his consciousness.

The nightstand's digital clock served two purposes at this moment, reading 3:07 a.m., and casting ambient light in an otherwise pitch-black room. Frantically, he ran his hand along the wall for a light switch. Moving hastily, he stubbed a knee on a doorjamb and was catapulted into the open bathroom door, which he careened off of before his momentum finally landed him prostrate across the toilet.

The physical pain temporarily allowed him to focus on tuning out his panicky feelings and turning on the bathroom light. With that suddenly, seemingly Herculean task accomplished, he pressed his back against the wall.

Looking around, he saw a lighted bathroom and, surprisingly, everything seemed in its usual place. Towels were hung neatly; shower curtains weren't slashed to pieces—no sign of violation whatsoever. Yet, his heart raced as oxygen seemed in short supply. "What's wrong with me? Why am I sweating? Why won't my heart calm down? Is there a killer in our house now?" These four questions kept compulsively looping through his mind while he trembled uncontrollably.

This intense sensation of doom felt completely foreign. Any logical person can always unmask an evil, underlying rhyme, or reason, puppeteer behind any fear. Unfortunately, Alan's usual rational mind didn't coming to his rescue this time. Knowing that most people who die in their sleep do so at 3 a.m., he became convinced that death loomed near.

Leaning hard against a wall seemed to be his only comfort right now. After making sure that there wasn't anyone else in the bathroom, he quickly slammed its door and locked himself in. Suddenly, the walls seemed to ripple like a lake does when a pebble is skipping upon it. The house wasn't shaking, however, which meant an earthquake wasn't occurring. Not knowing a logically sound explanation for these odd sensations caused spikes of nausea, which felt like they were running laps from head to toes.

Splashing cold water on his face seemed to bring the heartbeat down somewhat. Now, feeling relatively safer and calmer, it was time to try to get a grip on what the hell was wrong.

Crickets were mightily chirping away on a balmy July night. He had heard that cricket sounds are usually good indicators of the status quo. Usually, if they maintain a good rhythmic chorus, everything is deemed all right. Conversely, trouble is assumed to be afoot if their midnight serenade ceases without warning.

Because of helpful insect friends outside, and not hearing any stirring within the domicile itself, he began dismissing any paranoid fantasies of becoming a homicide victim. He still felt extremely unsettled though and just couldn't quash that omnipresent feeling of doom. With the walls still rippling, he pounded his forehead, attempting to shake logic awake. All he wanted to do now was keep it simple, and not pass out, or have a seizure.

Then, a revelation hit him clear as day and caused a chain reaction in his mind: seizure, Phenobarbital, detox, and shaky feelings from detoxing. As he linked them all together, he realized at once what was happening. He was having what drug addicts call the DTs, or what doctors call withdrawal.

Secure in this knowledge, he scurried from the bathroom, turned on the bedroom lights, and checked his wall calendar. Sure enough he'd just gone down from four to three pills a day five days ago. He'd been detoxing for six weeks total, but hadn't had a problem until now.

Going from six pills daily to five didn't faze him in the least. While there was some anxiety going from five to four daily, he still handled it fairly well. But right now the monster he'd heard about, and knew was coming, had his sanity against the ropes.

With his enemy now identified, he knew what had to be done. All he had to do was fight the images, sensations, fears, and nausea, until this episode ended. That would be easier said than done, however. To complicate matters, intricate patterns on bedroom walls only served to intensify wall-rippling effects. Unfortunately, because his bedroom walls were far more lavishly adorned with various artwork, bookshelves, and posters, they provided a far more intricate canvas for optical delusions. But he didn't dare turn the lights off. No, that would be much worse.

He turned on the television in a desperate attempt to provide much needed distraction, and hopefully a calming influence to his troubled mind. Frantically flipping through channels like a hummingbird on steroids, he happened upon a home shopping channel. An attractive middle-aged woman was speaking in soothing monotones. For some reason, listening to her pitch suede leather jackets seemed to snap him back into reality or a facsimile thereof. While visions and sensations didn't abate, he began to feel more grounded.

As he kneeled by the bed, eyes glued to models wearing jackets, he felt a warm, furry body rub up against his right thigh. Instantly, calmness came over him because that sensation was very familiar. Shadow, an 11-year-old cat he had raised and nurtured since she was a kitten, decided to visit. As soon as he gazed downward he saw that she had concern in her demeanor. She kept rubbing on him and meowing like she knew that trouble was afoot. Finally, she flopped down on her back—her way of communicating that she wanted daddy to rub her belly.

When he adopted her, people who never should be allowed to own a pet or raise children had already traumatized her. The extent of abuse and neglect during her first six months of life made Shadow wary of humans, to put it mildly. When she first arrived at Alan's home, she quickly scurried from the cage and hid under the couch. Only after everyone went to bed did she dare explore her new digs in earnest.

Three days into her stay, Alan came out at two in the morning to get a drink and caught her doing the same. Not long after that, she learned to trust him and she granted him the privilege of rubbing her belly that he took as her acceptance of him as a friend. It took a few years of loving touch to purge the last vestiges of her trauma.

Now, roles were reversed. Previously, rubbing her belly was good calming therapy for her. He was the one who now derived greater benefit from their ritual. Normally, Shadow wouldn't tolerate more than five minutes of petting or rubbing.

This time, however, she sensed Alan's dire straits and just let him pet her for as long as he needed to. Eventually, they both sat atop the bed and witnessed sunrise. Then, secure in the knowledge that he wasn't dying and would indeed live to see a new day and many days thereafter, he laid down and quickly fell asleep.

A few hours later, he woke to a beam of intense sunshine piercing through his blinds. Upon looking around the room, everything looked the same as it always had but somehow seemed different. He felt more awake, alert, and alive than at any other point in his life. Yet, this new heightened sense of being made him restless and insecure.

Fine details in carpet textures, wood grains on doors, even subtle hues in a tree outside, never noticed previously, made him wonder what kind of foggy existence the first twenty-seven years had been. Seemingly, anxiety from last night had morphed somewhat into this new state of intense awakening.

Many more nights of tumult ensued and played on variations perpetuated in that first night. The first week of, "Night Frights", were excruciating as he struggled with his new terrors and manifestations. Try as he might to ignore or fight his fear, he just couldn't manage to exorcise those evil, pervasive gremlins from his mind. Shadow was his lone comfort and connection to reality during these times of dread. Some nights, he'd stroke her for at least an hour before calming down.

As much as he appreciated her loyalty, however, he knew by week two it was time to grab this bull by the horns. The turning moment came two weeks into his new routine. He woke up having the same symptoms that were getting all too familiar. This time, however, he got angry, and found his bedroom mirror. "You wanna fuck with me! You wanna fuck with me! Come on you cock-suckin, sneaky, coward bastard. Let's go, I'm ready now!" he yelled, as he pounded the sink.

Then, he ran to the opposite side of his bedroom and turned his stereo on loud and cursed some more, "Oh, you don't like competition, do you, you cowardly little asshole? No, you wait 'til all's quiet, huh?" Though still anxious, he definitely felt more in control.

Two months later, he was completely off phenobarbital. As a result, his increased mental acuity, and corrected vision, helped him achieve a full point higher GPA in his senior year. That night's category five, hurricane of terror, stirred with anxiety and doom, never fully manifested itself again. Instead, remnants of it kept sporadically visiting Alan like an irksome in-law for at least a decade.

Whether in the form of a hallucination, or a transitory doomsday feeling, or good old-fashioned paranoia, those little detox gremlins liked to attack just when Alan thought he was in the clear. Silly boy. In the long run, however, eschewing phenobarbital's safe, but foggy, and disengaged existence, in exchange for a future of complete awareness with occasional anxiety, turned out to be a no-brainer.

# CHAPTER 30 - SLINGSHOTS

The summer before entering his fifth, and hopefully, final year at State, Alan fancied himself as an Indiana Jones of Academia, perilously pulling through such thrilling escapades as, "Survive at all 'Cost Accounting'", "paralysis by sadistic 'Statistical Analysis'", "demonic 'Advanced Macro Economics'", and of course, who could forget, ""evil Professor Igor and the Bell Curve curse"". Yes, after conquering such formidable foes, the finish line for his quarter-century-long academic career was in sight. Yet, as he staggered past the 25-mile-marker of this marathon, he rediscovered a long, forgotten obstacle. The last mile would be run up a steep treacherous hill on," Speech 101 Avenue".

For any other business student a course like "Speech" is considered a comparative breeze, and a welcome reprieve from business school's rigorous courses. All one has to do is get in front of a class, say a few words semi-coherently, and not freeze or fall down. Yes, all one has to do is talk, one of the most natural functions for a human being. Granted, some people are introverted, or shy, but invariably these individuals find a way to focus on the task at hand.

Five years ago, upon perusing State U's course catalog, he discovered with dismay that, at some point, a speech class would be in the offing. Being saddled with a severe speech impairment is challenging enough, but now he was at the mercy of some pervert, with a sick sense of humor, who constructed the General Education curriculum. As a result, he was forced to take a class called "Speech 101".

Now, with a full load of business classes on tap for his senior year, he could stall no longer, and silently chuckled at fate's twisted plot to kill his pursuits. Akin to David's predicament against the invincible Goliath, some way, somehow, using whatever tricks he had left, speech class had to be conquered. However, like David, he wasn't without a proverbial stone, or three, to be more precise.

Transfer credits are very valuable commodities for any university undergraduate student. Every undergrad is allowed to carry over, or transfer, up to sixty applicable credits from a junior college. Fortunately, Alan had only used up fifty-seven transfer credits, meaning that exactly three of these precious jewels were left. This became a significant turn of events. Even though this did nothing to change the fact that speech had to be taken, it did reduce what he perceived to be a steep climb to a more manageable ascent, because this meant he could take a speech class at his old stomping grounds, Fairfield Community College.

Alan enjoyed three mostly wonderful years at Fairfield C.C. A comfort level existed there amongst his hometown people in a more relaxed atmosphere, when contrasted against State U's cutthroat, ultra competitive environment. Many friendships and bonds were forged during that time.

Now, having to deal with numerous failures by State U's support staff for the disabled, he longed for the days when Fairfield's staff made everything transparent. From dealing with teachers, to setting up test proctors, to giving private counseling for venting frustrations, all he had to worry about was succeeding in the classroom. Comparing them now, he marveled at how Fairfield's under-funded disabled students support staff was one hundred times more competent than their big state-run university counterparts.

One week before summer session commenced he was on campus to enroll for an early morning speech class. Even though it had been over four years, a rush of cozy familiarity washed over him when touching down on the Fairfield parking lot blacktop. The college had a wide-open countrified look and feel.

There were handsomely manicured, luscious green lawns and high trees that flowed and cascaded like gentle lakes and waterfalls throughout Fairfield's hilly landscape. As a matter of fact, campus buildings were designed in such an unobtrusive way that they naturally complimented their surroundings. All these sights, smells, and sounds, eased him into a state of tranquility as he reminisced on how much fun college used to be.

Suddenly, like a splash of cold reality, one week later there were no more excuses, or delays, or stays of execution from State U's dean. The first day of summer school had arrived, and it was Alan Jones's time to vanquish Goliath. Otherwise, chances for a university degree would be mercilessly crushed into dust and cast to the winds of sorrow. Again, like David, only two simple choices existed for him: triumph over seemingly insurmountable odds, or more likely, perish at the hands of an omnipotent foe.

There were available spaces near the back of the classroom, where he took up residence. As other students filed in, a palpable thickness permeated the dewy morning air. There formed visual cacophony consisting of various finger taps, foot taps, thumb twiddles, and an array of other tics that people subconsciously employ to redirect nervous energy. Like any other artistic or musical medium, this unique orchestra had an unmistakable theme. To varying degrees, they were all scared of taking a class based on public speaking. Reading his new classmates body language gave Alan solace that he wouldn't be competing against professional keynote speakers.

At five past the hour, a level of uneasiness amongst the group became apparent. Collectively, they were unsuccessfully suppressing nervous giggles and chatter. The teacher was late, and some in the class were hoping that he wouldn't show up at all. The general rule is, if a teacher doesn't arrive in fifteen minutes, a class may leave. After five more minutes had elapsed, everyone began counting aloud with each motion of the minute hand.

All hope for early parole was shattered, however, with two scant minutes remaining. In walked a youngish looking, smiling chap in faded jeans, a Hawaiian shirt, and with a noticeable spring in his gait. One could reasonably surmise by his jovial emanations that he just got lucky with the Missus before coming to work.

Before the man uttered a single word, Alan had already got a gist of this guy's personality. Whether intentional, or not, the new teacher had given veteran students a blueprint on his instruction style and personal demeanor. Typically, hard-ass teachers are always on time and some won't even permit a tardy student entry. This young dude looked so laid back that Alan wondered if he had enrolled in a surfing class by mistake.

"Welcome to Speech 101. My name is Mr. Dalton. I realize that most of you aren't here by choice, but because you need to take a General Education requirement either for Fairfield or a university. Now, I'm not a sadist; I understand that to a lot of people, public speaking and public spanking contain about the same level of embarrassment. With the one, your heart pounds, your breath gets labored, your cheeks get very red, you might break down and cry, and you promise anything to anybody just to get it over with," he paused, " then there's public spanking…" he said nonchalantly, with a disarming devilish grin. The class broke out in hysterical laughter dissolving any lingering tension.

Mr. Dalton went on to detail what was required to pass his class. Each student had to deliver three speeches during the six-week course. Topics would be handed out one week before a speech had to be delivered. During their first speech, a student had to argue the "pro" side of a given topic. Conversely, in the second speech, the "con" side, of that same topic had to be given just as compellingly. For their third and final speech, students could freelance and take that opportunity to discuss a subject that stoked their passions.

During that initial hour, Mr. Dalton discussed basic points of effective oration; issues like bullet points, sign posting, posture, head movement, focal point, and summarization were covered. As class was dispersing at hour's end, he still felt a general uneasiness amongst his new pupils, wondering how many of them had ever spoken to more than a handful of people at a time. Thus, he felt an urgent need to delay granting their dismissal in order to give a pep talk to those who were on the fence.

"Wait! Wait! Come on back, people. I've got one more thing to say," he sighed as they froze in their tracks, "Look, I'm still sensing that a lot of you are still very unsure about this class," speaking in gentle tones, "Each of you is afraid of getting up here and making an ass of yourself. Well, I've got news for you! So is everyone else in here! Take it from me because I've taught this course for five years now."

He continued, "Unlike other courses you have, Speech 101 isn't a class where you hope for other students to slip up. On the contrary, in this class, each of you will draw confidence from seeing your fellow classmates overcome their fears. I've seen it time and again. In a very short while, you guys will become supportive of one another. Now, have a great day guys, and I promise, if you give yourselves a chance, that by the end of this course you'll be a more confident person."

Alan and his attendant waited for everybody else to file out. He wanted to talk with Mr. Dalton privately.

"Um, Mr. Dalton, can we talk?" his attendant translated.

"Sure, what's on your mind?" Mr. Dalton greeted them with a welcoming smile.

"Well, as you can tell, I have a speech impairment."

"Yes, and you're probably wondering how in the world you're going to pass this course. How am I doing so far?" he nodded knowingly.

"Right on the money," Alan sighed, "I've been putting this off for four years but my university insists that I take speech. So..."

"Let me try to put your mind at ease here, okay?"

Alan shrugged.

"I know that there are certain things beyond your control because of your circumstances. With that being said, however, I also know that in order to come as far as you have, you had to overcome many, many obstacles, right?"

Alan saw where this was going but nodded anyway.

"I can't imagine what some of these obstacles were, but I can assure you that in time you'll realize that my class is a molehill rather than a mountain. Just prepare your speeches on paper, practice at home, take your time and put one word in front of the other. Before you know it, you'll be done."

"Okay, well, that sounds good in theory, but…" he shrugged despondently.

"But what? Listen, when I found out that you were going to be in my class, I got excited," his eyes flashed.

"Why?" Alan looked away cynically.

"Every semester I get students who allow their fears to take control. They get in front of this class with their head looking down and speaking just above a whisper. When they're finished, they quickly scurry back to their seat. But your presence changes everything."

"How?"

"Your presence doesn't allow those students a convenient out. When you get up here and talk, everyone's going to be silently pulling for you. The baseline of your success will be a springboard of confidence for others," he asserted enthusiastically.

Alan fully appreciated the effort Mr. Dalton put forth in his pep talk. Still, words of encouragement ring hollow when spoken by someone who's not been there, done that. No one wants to talk about the other side of being a pioneer, a trailblazer. There are no mentors, or maps, or road signs, when you're the first explorer. All any onlookers can really do is pat you on the back and offer best wishes. Yes, family, friends, and kindly strangers can lend emotional support. Ultimately, whether or not an individual will triumph in their personal pursuits is decided by character and will at a series of pivotal moments.

Once at home again, Alan dug out mom's old tape recorder from a closet. After setting it up on the kitchen table, two paragraphs of a newspaper article were used as practice. After completing each cycle of dictation, he hit the rewind button to get instant feedback.

Here's where a lifelong paradox reared its ugly head. He always understood himself as he was talking. Yet, whenever hearing himself on tape, he never associated the voice as his own. To his exquisite frustration, at every tape rewind and subsequent playback, all he heard was some addle-brained wino speaking in slurred, slow motion. After about the 29th dictation, mom, who'd been casually listening while cooking, offered a suggestion.

"Honey, instead of talking as fast as you can, just focus on saying one word, then the next, then the next, and so on," she continued dicing tomatoes for her homemade spaghetti sauce.

The manner, in which her words seemed similar to an idea Mr. Dalton had earlier, finally resonated as a plausible method. Once again, he rewound, hit record, and tried a new technique. Speaking as deliberately as a preschooler learning how to read, Alan made sure that he enunciated each syllable and pronounced every word.

Upon playback, both of them noticed considerable improvement. The next week was focused on honing this method and using mom as a practice audience. However, during one practice session, he discovered that she was more than willing to give voice to her critiques.

"Stop looking down and look forward, Alan!" she chided.

"But I have to read the …" he began explaining.

"You're giving a speech to me. Forget the paper, you're only supposed to use the paper as a reference anyway, right?"

He nodded.

"Okay, then, talk to me like you're trying to convince me of something or sell me on a viewpoint, and by the way, your body language sucks! You look like you're getting ready for your own execution." She huffed.

"Well, mom, I'm nervous, I don't know if I can pull this off," he shrugged.

"Then, why the hell did you enroll in that class, Alan?" her arms crossed.

"I don't know, ma,"

"Bullshit!" she yelled.

"What the hell,"

"That's right, bullshit! What makes this class so fucking harder than any of the rest? Just because you have to talk to a group of people as scared out of their minds as you are? Come on! Get real!

This isn't goddam calculus, or economics, or none of that shit! And those classes were scary! You beat all those scary shit classes and now you're getting anxious over a pissy-ass speech class at a community college? Come on! Do what you always do, get angry, get focused, and ace this thing!"

"How the hell am I supposed to do that, mom?" his demeanor morphed from resignation to anger, " Please tell me, because unless a fucking miracle happens by next week, I'm going to get up there, and not be understood, and get laughed at! That's my fucking reality and nothing you say can change that fact!" he yelled as he pounded the table.

"Alright, just go ahead and quit, you big baby. And why stop there? We'll get you out of State U. while we're at it. There's no use going there anymore either since you can't pass a stupid speech class. You're just a quitter," she mocked.

He got down from his chair, scampered on his knees to his room and slammed the door so violently he had to shut it a second time. Since only moms know how their kids are wired, they seem to possess unique insights on how to effectively push emotional buttons to affect change in their adult offspring. Because they were so close, each of them knew the other's manipulation playbook. However, right now, he was too steamed to rationalize what she'd just done, and why. All he could process was anger, frustration, and wounded pride.

Predictably, at first, he seethed while pacing the room, not comprehending why she'd laced into him so contemptuously. After all this time and all his accomplishments, why did she meet his fears with sarcasm during an expressed moment of doubt?

As many minutes passed, emotion gave way to logic upon realizing mom had done what she had always done during a crisis, personal or otherwise, motivate by not letting her kids wallow in self-pity. Mulling her words now with a cool head, he chuckled and acknowledged that mom's message was right on the money. After an hour of self-imposed solitary confinement, he emerged, and said, "Mom, let's kick this sucker's ass!"

With renewed determination, focus, and anger, he practiced speaking five hours a day. Every speech was broken into paragraphs, sentences, words, and yes, even syllables. Also, nonverbal aspects such as posture, eye contact, and confidence in argument were addressed as well. Each practice session yielded its share of inspiring triumphs and frustrating setbacks. Finally, on the night before he had to speak before the class, his mom put away all the practice materials, and simply stated, "You're ready, honey."

The next day, he rolled into class with fire in his eyes. Since Alan couldn't process anger and fear simultaneously, anger became a far more useful emotion, at least for today. Knowing that you're about to do something risky heightens awareness of everything and everyone around you. Therefore, as Mr. Dalton walked in and shut the door, every fiber in Alan's body wanted to put his wheelchair into high, and bolt without looking back. A moment later, with composure regained, panic was once again supplanted by searing intensity.

As a young woman timidly delivered a speech on air pollution, his attention span wavered. Suffice it to say, smog and ozone depletion aren't first and foremost on your frontal lobe when you're consumed by your own angst. Words of his imminent oration cycled furiously like a hamster on a wheel. Occasionally, he'd take note of her incessant shifting of feet and lack of eye contact. In essence, she did everything you're not supposed to do when giving a speech. Then, during a moment of introspection, he heard, "Alan Jones, please come forward,"

Without hesitation, he flipped the wheelchair on and quickly assumed a position behind Mr. Dalton's desk. The attendant placed Alan's yellow index card in front of him and walked away. Suddenly, it was as if a giant vacuum sucked out all sound and air.

The only sound audible at that moment was his heart trying to beat out of his chest. Then, all of those eyes, all of those judgmental eyes, watching and waiting for this crip to flop, and have a seizure. Most people can't look away from a car accident, especially if a freight train is about to smash a Honda Civic and Alan was the Civic.

Rushing things would only make matters that much worse. Accordingly, he paused, took four long breaths and made them all wait. Absolutely nothing was going to be uttered until he felt ready. Mr. Dalton cleared his throat in a not-so-veiled attempt to prod Alan to begin.

Without being overtly disrespectful, Alan stared down young Mr. Dalton, and put up one finger. A professional student exercises every advantage as laid out by the syllabus. There were no set limits on time, so this speech would be delivered at his time and pace, and nobody could say anything about it.

Then, he thought of colorful Uncle Lou and how the glad-handing lout loved to be the center of attention by telling stories at family reunions. Some relatives saw him as a big oaf who lacked many social graces. Lou knew what some thought of him but he couldn't care less. Out of nowhere, Alan thought it might be fun to sort of channel his colorful relative. So, he scanned the class and began passionately pontificating about poverty in America.

His focus temporarily overcame any remaining anxiety by enthralling his audience with amazing clarity. Using the one-word-at-a-time method, his speech came across strong and confident. Everything Mr. Dalton taught was employed to near perfection. From sign posts-to eye contact-to posture, everything fell into place. Well-timed hand gestures were even employed to further spice up certain points for dramatic effect. Then, suddenly, he stuttered on a word and almost locked up.

They say that every war, or game, or drama, has a tipping point where the day is either won or lost. Upon scanning the faces of those who saw him flinch and were anticipating his likely demise, he took a moment to give himself a mental ass kicking, "Come on, damn it, just plow through and keep talking no matter what!" Alan took yet another breath, got angry again, and proceeded to deliver a suitable summarization of his speech. The audience was thanked for their time as its speaker methodically returned to his seat.

The class rose as one and gave Alan a thunderous standing ovation. He felt goose bumps as he finally parked his wheelchair. Like a successful marathon runner, he was simultaneously ecstatic and emotionally spent. Yes, Indiana Jones of Academia had overcome staggering odds yet again.

# CHAPTER 31 - MOCKING MIMES

After he graduated from the State University, Alan was physically as well as mentally exhausted from the past two weeks. Cramming for and taking finals had exacted its usual toll of a 10-pound weight loss from an already slender 130 pound frame. This signaled the end of an academic career that spanned a quarter century.

Alan, and his friend Earl, planned a weekend trip to San Francisco in part to celebrate this milestone. The two friends had known each other for almost a decade, going back to when Alan was a freshman at the local community college, and Earl drove a van for the disabled students program. Earl, a shy, straight-laced, introspective man, was somewhat atypical for a musician. He had always wanted to see the renowned San Francisco symphony orchestra. Meanwhile, Alan had always been intrigued by this city's vibrancy and culture.

They embarked on their journey at 8 a.m. during a typically beautiful, but brisk June day, when the foliage was losing its glistening from morning dew. The drive up the coast highway featured many a spectacular sight, especially on a fog-free day. Whenever these two got together, topics of conversation were never lacking. These factors made the 430-mile-trip seem shorter than usual.

Upon arrival, they checked into a motel and rested for an hour before finding a bite to eat for dinner. Walking down the street in search of a restaurant, they stumbled across a coffee house also serving sandwiches. To their pleasant surprise, however, the place doubled as a performance venue for aspiring entertainers. So, while eating, they saw everything: from poetry readings to singing, stand-up comedy, Shakespearian scene interpretation, and more!

Afterwards, the duo strolled through the now silent and abandoned business district until discovering a nightclub. However, the club was up a flight of stairs and had no ramp! Seeing their predicament, a tall, attractive young lady in her mid-20s intervened. She was a looker, with shoulder-length, lustrous sable hair, piercing blue, soulful eyes, and high cheekbones that accentuated her cute matching dimples.

"Hi, I'm Lisa. Do you guys need help getting in?" she asked.

"Yeah, but I don't see how we can get this power chair up those stairs!" Earl lamented.

"Wait right here," she retorted mischievously with a wink.

Before two minutes passed, four burly young men, walking behind six, tall, attractive women, approached the troubled twosome. Without saying a word, three women stood on either side of Alan, then simultaneously put their arms under him and easily carried him up the stairs. Meanwhile, the four guys hauled up his wheelchair.

So, there he was, being manhandled by six, tall, gorgeous, full-breasted women who were willingly and happily taking him into their domain. Needless to say, Alan was in heaven! The highlight of what turned out to be a great evening came when Lisa whispered in Alan's ear,

"You owe me, mister! Now, you're dancing with me, like it or not!" At once, her declaration startled and excited him; he wasn't accustomed to being propositioned.

Then, she raised her hand and snapped her fingers. Next, two women assisted him to his feet and began swaying him side-to-side while Lisa danced provocatively, only inches from him. They danced three songs, after which his legs became wobbly and he had to sit down.

Before walking away, Lisa put her hand on his shoulder, bent down, and kissed him on the cheek.

"Thanks, sweetie," she cooed. When Earl and Alan went back to their hotel, and retired for the evening, Alan fell asleep with an ego boost, a smile on his face, and images dancing in his head, of those three women.

Earl had already risen and dressed by the time he woke Alan at 7:33 the next morning. Alan, not a morning person, half-opened one eye at the clock, and grumbled,

"What the hell are you doing? It's too early to get up, leave me alone!"

Earl knew that if he left his pal to his own devices, Alan, a habitual late sleeper, wouldn't get up until lunchtime. At once, Earl ripped off the blanket and uncharacteristically asserted himself,

"Come on, lazybones!" Earl shouted playfully. "We've got a full day of sightseeing and I don't want to waste daylight waiting for you to drag your butt out of bed!"

Alan growled, "Alright, alright!"

Then, he slowly crawled onto the floor and into the bathroom to prepare for the day.

Their first stop was at Pier 49, a popular haunt for tourists and locals alike. Along this boardwalk is a plethora of shops, attractions, sideshows and eateries. However, upon arrival, they realized they had made a mistake by underestimating the chilling winds off the bay. No matter what time of year, these winds knife right through unprepared visitors.

Wearing only printed t-shirts, they were forced to buy a pair of overpriced $30 windbreakers. Notwithstanding, they enjoyed their time here by eating too much, impulsively buying trinkets, and watching shows.

Upon departure from the pier, they decided to remain on foot. Strolling through the tourist district, they came upon an area of performance artists.

Each performer had their own sidewalk space, and a tin coffee can for donations. Alan enjoyed, and Earl envied, the talents of a saxophonist for twenty minutes. Alan dropped $5, and Earl $3, in the can.

They both were entertained to varying degrees by all but one performer, a mime. There stood a lonely white-faced mime, with an empty can, and no audience, performing his invisible box act, looking like the end result of a republican budget cut. Earl felt sorry for the poor guy.

"Let's go over and cheer him up," he said.

Alan growled, "Mimes are stupid, that's why he's alone." However, when Earl insisted, and Alan caved, they went to check out the performance. A young mother and her six-year-old daughter arrived with them.

The idea of a sane person standing on a public sidewalk, intentionally drawing attention to themselves, by flailing around, was a concept that escaped, and annoyed Alan. Because one of the side effects of his condition involved involuntary arm movement, he worked hard at keeping still in public. The battle to appear as "normal" as possible became just one way to gain respect from others. Consequently, He felt that mimes were indirectly mocking him.

Alan thought, "While I try my damnedest for human interaction that doesn't involve my freakin' wheelchair as the primary topic of conversation, here's this joker making himself look like a moron on purpose."

The mime, evidently inspired by his newly found following, decided to tailor his act. He catered to the little girl by doing skits and impressions that appeal to kids. Unfortunately, to his chagrin, she didn't appear to be interested in animal mocking or slap stick. Her interest seemed more to lay on the man who sat in a pretty chair with big wheels.

While pointing at Alan, she asked her mother, "Mommy, what's wrong with that man?"

The mother turned a rather dark shade of red, obviously embarrassed by her child's innocent question. Immaturely, she transformed a potential learning experience into an opportunity to scold her youngster. While giving her daughter a quick slap on the backside, she shouted,

"Don't look at those kind of people like that. It's not nice!"

Suddenly noticing that she had become the focus of disapproving scowls, she scurried away with her now bawling charge.

Alan had always felt sympathetic toward anyone in obvious distress. His compassion toward the girl's plight multiplied because he knew that he was at least partly responsible for her pain. Because of this, He feared the girl might form a negative impression of disabled people. At the same time, he was livid at the mother.

He thought, "She was the one needing a swift spank, and if she was within arms reach I would've spanked her!"

This wasn't the first instance of a mother scolding and shielding her child from, the man in the wheelchair. Even though he had grown accustomed to the Middle Ages ogre treatment by now, he never got used to feeling like an outcast whenever it occurred.

Alan consoled himself by reflecting back upon the previous night, when every man in the nightclub envied him. Then, shaking his head at the two starkly contrasting situations, he found a kinship with the misunderstood performer. Like the mime who couldn't hold the girl's attention long enough to convince her that he was in an invisible box, Alan would always struggle in making his true self visible to others, whilst their focus is drawn to his box. He took solace in knowing that his efforts did bear occasional fruit.

# CHAPTER 32 - MOUNTAIN TOP

"Are you almost ready honey?" Ms. Jones shouted from the kitchen, "We have to be there by six,"

"Yeah mom, I'll be right out, " Alan responded while kneeling in front of his bathroom mirror.

Before another ten seconds had elapsed however, mom popped in to lend a hand.

"I just got done dressing you," she sighed, "Now, stop worrying and fussing, and let's go!" Encouraging Alan out to their van with a firm pat to his backside.

He peered into the mirror again to make sure his tie and vest were straight. Suits were Alan's least favorite attire because they felt unnatural. So they only saw light of day when a societal ritual, such as a relative's wedding, mandated they be worn. Other than these rare formal shindigs it had been kept in a mothproof garment bag.

Knowing her son was more comfortable in a t-shirt and sweats, Ms. Jones sought to ease his wardrobe angst while expressing her true feelings.

"Wow, you'll have to beat the ladies off with a stick tonight!" she hugged him, "I can't tell you how handsome you are," she blushed and smiled pridefully.

"Thanks mom, you look great too," he expressed while noticing her mid-calf green dress, matching pearl necklace and bracelet, accenting her naturally beautiful olive-skinned face and soulful eyes.

Although uncomfortable dressing up, Alan had every right to embrace not only tonight's awards dinner but tomorrow's graduation as well. Every dragon, pitfall, setback, and other obstacles were conquered. Yet, he didn't find solace on a stage. Truth be told, he half-wished he could just stay home and get his degree in the mail. But, you know how much proud moms love pomp and circumstance—especially when their kid is being honored.

He majored in business administration with an option, or specialty, in management information systems, M.I.S. for short. Tonight M.I.S. graduates w ere being honored in a separate awards ceremony. Tomorrow was the traditional graduation for all business majors. In any case, listening to scores of middle-aged university administrators pontificating about success in "the real world!" isn't something one eagerly anticipates.

Moreover, in Alan's experience a plurality of school administrators were at their current posts for a single reason. They didn't demonstrate competence to be otherwise employed in "the real world." But, at this point, enduring a couple of rituals seemed like a minuscule price to pay in exchange for recognition of nearly a quarter century's worth of struggles.

"Alan!" Ms. Jones shouted, "Stop admiring yourself and get your butt in here! We're going to be late."

"Okay, mom, I'm coming right now!" Alan said loudly.

He got in his power wheelchair then descended a cement ramp that was part of a handicapped accessible living area. This section of the house was added on five years ago as a mother's loving gesture. He traveled through their backyard, and gate, stopping in the garage. Ms. Jones already lowered the van's lift-gate, so Alan didn't slow down driving into the vehicle.

Travelling along a familiar sixteen-mile stretch of highway, mother and son shared a moment. Alan just happened to turn and smile at mom as she did likewise. For these five university years their van had taken them to so many classes that it could almost make this trip sans driver. During these five years, there were struggles, highs, and lows. And, many a sleepless night spent questioning whether or not competing at this level was realistic.

One person he could always rely on, especially in this last stage of the journey, was mom. She believed that Alan's perseverance could aid in accomplishing a great many things. Yet, she also knew that disability or not, earning a degree from a top business school was no mean feat. So, whenever he needed encouragement, she built him up. On the other hand, she also knew occasional lectures curtailed episodes of laziness and procrastination.

Upon pulling into Hilton hotel's parking lot, a valet motioned for Ms. Jones to drive up to an open disabled parking space. When their van's ramp extended, Alan's concentration split between descending safely versus taking in a vibrant atmosphere. A magnificently conceived implementation of architecture towered high in the night sky. With Hollywood premiere style spotlights illuminating their path, each honoree strolled a marble-tile walkway ending at handsomely adorned shimmering doors.

The ambience of this moment in time heightened his anticipation for the night's festivities. Scanning people wandering about, he spotted many familiar faces but something was noticeably different. People who were classmates for half a decade looked completely transformed and more approachable.

Guys who usually came to class donning baggy jeans and perpetual five o'clock shadows, looked dapper in their suits with nary a whisker. Girls, who up to now, had only been seen in sweats or shorts—depending on weather—wore: designer dresses, jewelry, and glowed as if they had spent a good portion of the day in a beauty spa.

Alan's gaze widened to loved ones of each honoree. There were moms, dads, some siblings, and even spouses. Every graduate had their own support system of people who valued and encouraged them.

Some families openly displayed affection with hugs; others were more socially reserved. But, overall, witnessing this scene softened his heart. These weren't the same cutthroats who did whatever it took to stroke a professor's ego. They appeared to him now, as individuals desiring to make a better life for themselves.

Alan and mom maneuvered past other soon to be grads, coming to a halt at a four by eight foot neon sign, flashing: "WELCOME & CONGRATULATIONS TO STATE U. CLASS OF 1991!"

Waiting for doors to open, a couple of male classmates, Bryce and Omar, approached him employing hesitant gaits. When they stopped two feet in front of him, all of his defense mechanisms instinctively came online, preparing for any insult, wiseass quip, or flippant remark.

"Hey there Alan, so what do you think of this shindig they're having for us?" Omar smiled.

Alan studied Omar's face trying to derive his true intentions, "It's nice, I suppose, if you're a person who needs external validation—right?" he curtly responded using his mom as a translator.

"Right, right," Omar nervously giggled as Bryce forced a smile.

"I mean this is for our folks and family. They eat this stuff up. My mom here can't stop smiling tonight," Ms. Jones affirmatively nodded, "As for me, I can't wait to get home so that I can take off this noose and monkey suit," strongly asserting while adjusting his tie.

Omar shifted his weight from side to side uneasily before changing topics, "So, what did you think of the hypothetical problems on Mr. Nomo's final?"

Alan rolled his eyes and laughed, "That egotistical clown needs a flowchart to decide whether or not he needs to use a restroom."

"No Alan, don't hold back, and tell us what you really think of the guy!" Bryce deadpanned before they all broke out in laughter.

Their merriment ceased with doors swinging open; guests were invited inside to a spacious dining room that appeared as though it could seat 1,000 people. Again, Alan and mom adeptly seeped through the throng and sat a table a few feet from a rear exit. He commonly took tables by exits for wheelchair accessibility and safety purposes.

Menus, for soirees of this nature, don't deviate a whole lot. You can either have a chicken, fish, or vegetarian entrée. So, Alan picked the chicken meal and hoped for the best. Nobody expected a gourmet feast by any stretch of the imagination. This part of the evening's festivities served to give event staff more time to prepare the main auditorium.

As expected, when meals were served, most people picked at their plates, eating just enough to be polite. Alan valiantly tried eating dry poultry by taking a bite of a biscuit in between. Often employing similar techniques to eat dry or hard to chew food. After awhile however, mom acted like a boxing referee in a one-sided fight; her son wasn't going to give up but it was painfully obvious that he could choke at any minute.

"It's alright honey, it's alright," she said reassuringly, "This chicken is giving me a bad time too. You don't have to eat it."

"I can do it mom," he snarled defiantly.

"Come on Alan," she whispered in his ear, "It's lousy food and we can pick up your favorite hot dogs on the way home."

"But, I think I'm making a dent in it, "

"Look, I know that you treat everything like a contest," they made eye contact, "But, tonight is for you. You don't have anything left to prove. Just enjoy tonight—okay?"

He sat back, exhaled, and smiled in resignation, "Okay mom."

A total of eight people sat at Alan's table. Classmate Margaret O'Shea and her mom sat immediately across from the Jones'. At 5'10" Margaret stood out amongst other coeds. Her long, lush, flowing, red hair accentuated fine fair skin and emerald eyes—turning heads from men and women alike. Margaret's mom, a very attractive lady in her own right, decided to break the ice with Ms. Jones.

"So, I take it that you're Alan's mom," she grinned, "Am I correct?"

"Yes, I'm Ms. Jones, " she smiled politely, "How do you know about my son?"

"Oh, I'm sorry," she blushed, "I failed to introduce myself. I'm Penelope O'Shea—Margaret's mom. Maggie talks about Alan's accomplishments." Alan playfully winked at Margaret causing her to smile bashfully and look down.

"Wow, that's nice to hear," Ms. Jones sighed contentedly, "Alan's never been a social animal, so I assumed that he just blended into the crowd."

"You're quite the jokester Ms. Jones," she chuckled, "Your son is the only business student in a wheelchair and he can't even take his own notes," she said, "How can he not stand out."

The two mothers went on to talk about generic topics that new acquaintances find comfort in discussing. Meanwhile, Alan attempted to deconstruct a snippet of conversation that just took place. Until now, like his mother, he had believed that his time at State U. had largely gone as any other anonymous student. However, if attention had been garnered from someone like Margaret, could this long-held perception be wrong? Not that he cared mind you.

After dinner, graduates were led to a backstage area for last minute instructions. Their families were escorted to an adjoining convention hall. Looking around, Alan only saw three classmates engaging in conversation. Everybody else kept thoughts unexpressed while maintaining downturned glances.

Alan felt a collective group anxiety permeating his sympathetic synapsis. Noticing that every student seemed to be suffering varying degrees of pre-ceremony jitters didn't require a degree in psychology. This revelation perplexed him; instinctually, he believed that anybody who wasn't visibly disabled could mask internal fear of these situations with relative composure.

Graduates were scheduled to be on stage at eight o'clock sharp. Yet, at fifteen past eight, they were still in a holding pattern. Every two minutes a hotel staffer would say, "Any minute now." Alan sensed growing apprehension amongst his classmates. From fingernail biting to hyperventilating and everything in between, many manifestations of nervous behavior were on display.

Additionally, dealing with his fear of being put dead center—for all to see—was daunting enough. Yes, it was sixth-grade graduation all over again. Every involuntary movement made would draw unwanted attention, curiosity, and scrutiny from audience members. Only this time, there wasn't a girlfriend—such as Emily—to soothe jangled nerves. On the other hand, a mature 27-year-old man supposedly has more composure than a 12 year old boy. So, temporarily, psyching himself into believing that this is easy, a measure of bravado came flooding in.

Out of the corner of his eye, he spotted Margaret, six feet away, whispering to two staffers. She pointed directly at him while expressing her points. As their chat ended, the trio smiled while nodding in agreement. Because they were looking his way, he briefly became curious about whether or not the conversation's outcome affected him. Finally, at nearly half past eight, silence was obliterated.

"Alright people," A man's authoritative voice boomed, "Let's get this awards ceremony on the road," a stout, balding man in a three-piece took control by smacking his palms together. "I want you guys and gals to form two parallel lines. Then, you'll all walk out on stage and maintain those lines until you arrive at center stage."

"Next, you'll peel off two at a time to your seats—understand?" He then walked directly to Alan and bent down, "Alan, I want you to be the last one in line so you'll occupy the center spot—okay?" Alan, too stupefied to react, simply nodded in compliance.

Alan instinctively thought, "Center spot? Are you kidding me?" His heart pounding caused head throbbing and temporary blurry vision. Unlike sixth-grade graduation however, he focused on breathing and averted a panic attack. Upon calming down, his senses became aware of a young lady rubbing his back and saying, "Relax Alan." Turning his head slowly, he saw the heart-melting smile of Margaret O'Shea.

"Alan," Margaret began, "I'll be sitting next to you on stage," her placid voice soothed him, "I'll rub your back when you get anxious—okay?"

"That's very kind of you Margaret, but you don't even know me," he shrugged, "Why would you do this?" he asked humbly.

"I know you'll probably hate hearing this," she hesitated before looking into his eyes, "You're an inspiration to not only myself but to a lot of us here," she continued, "I've been in many of your classes over the years, and I know how tough they were," she closed her eyes while nodding her head, "Odds are that none of us will see each other again after tomorrow. And I, well, I just wanted to make sure that you enjoy tonight, because you've more than earned it," she smiled.

The raw truth of her feelings touched his core being—throwing him for a loop. A wave of new emotions coursed through his body and ended their journey in Alan's tear ducts. In order to maintain dignity, he instinctively turned away from her while surreptitiously wiping tears away. She astutely recognized what was happening, backing away until his composure could be regained.

The curtain opened and he cautiously wheeled onto stage. Reaching center stage, he mistakenly glanced at the audience and immediately wished he had opted to get his award by mail. The crowd's size seemed comparable to a sold out sports arena.

After pausing to breathe, he continued to a designated spot looking downward. Knowing that mom was in the third row, he quickly located her and they locked eyes. She mouthed the words, "You're doing great honey, smile." He giggled softly.

Everyone filled their assigned seats and Margaret sat by Alan. After the Dean made a brief welcoming address, he introduced the first speaker. An obese grey-haired gent in his early 50's labored up to the podium and sighed. After pausing two minutes to catch his breath, a typical speech on the evils and pitfalls of the "Real World" was delivered using a pontificating fire and brimstone style. But, he offered little practical advice on how he carved out success in the same "Real World". Listening to this cynical blowhard felt more like a punishment than a reward.

Grads eventually tuned out the noise while a parade of speechmakers took their turns spinning similar admonishments. Miraculously, one orator even managed to achieve a modicum of comprehensibility. Honorees found quietly conversing amongst themselves to be more palatable than listening to these hasbeens. Speeches given by people who define their self-worth on past perceived glories ring hollow. Like old dogs barking, they mindlessly spew a barrage of polysyllabic words just to hear the sound of their own voice.

Finally, after one hour of useless oration, the emcee took proceedings in more festive direction.

"And now, without further ado, It's time to recognize the achievements of a great class," he paused as the crowd lightly applauded, "Ladies and gentlemen, I proudly present State U's M.I.S. class of 1991!" The audience rose as one and gave the grads a rousing ovation.

Understandably, there was a gamut of reactions amongst grads. Some blushed, smiling shyly, while others nonchalantly took it in stride. Alan knew that applause was intended for everyone on stage; still, pesky little feelings ambushed him. This massive outpouring of recognition from people whom he'd never seen before and likely wouldn't cross paths with again was touching. And, yes, he had to take a couple hard gulps.

As roll call began, Alan quickly detected an unusual pattern. One would anticipate names would be called in either alphabetical or sequential seating order from left to right or vice versa. And, when the presenter called out, "Laura Banks," who was sitting at the extreme left side, every-thing seemed to be going according to plan. However, "Robert Adams," who sat up extreme right side, was the next name heard.

Subsequently, people seated second from both extreme ends were summoned. One by one, upon seeing the third, fourth, and fifth repre-sentatives on each side stand up, acknowledge applause, and receive their award—he realized his fate. Being the fourteenth person in a queue of twenty-seven means that you are dead center. With thirteen individuals on his right and left, combined with the roll call system employed, his name would be called last.

Eyes became more drawn towards center stage, and on him, as grads received their awards. Usually, during moments such as these, negative thoughts would creep in—preventing Alan from experiencing joy. Margaret saw him holding rigid and surreptitiously rubbed his back, which proved to be a great elixir. Soon, any existing nervous energy morphed into an emotion that he tried not to acknowledge too often—pride.

Without warning, memories flooded Alan's mind as it became evident that just two names remained before his name. A 25-year academic jour-ney flashed like a highlight reel in his mind, smiling while recalling every: triumph and setback, acknowledgement and doomsayer, in seconds. Then, as if touched by higher wisdom, he had an epiphany. Sitting perfectly still on stage wasn't something to be concerned about at all.

When the daydream ended, he saw Margaret walking back to her seat after accepting her award. So, Alan knew the moment was at hand. After applause for Margaret abated, the presenter said, "Alan Jones," with a booming voice that reverberated throughout the room. As Alan turned his chair on to go to the podium, Margaret turned it off and said, "Stay here."

Temporary befuddlement quickly vanished as the presenter walked from behind the mahogany platform slowly approaching Alan.

Alan's nerves simmered down deep in anticipation of a moment culmi-nating his life's purpose—up to that point. Then, almost on cue, something unusual occurred as he was handed the award. The entire M.I.S. graduating class mobbed him.

They shouted, "Alan, Alan, Alan," while patting his back. Margaret, and a succession of girls, hugged and kissed him. Guys squeezed his shoulders while voicing admiration. Suddenly, this outpouring of emotion and recognition became overwhelming.

Tears poured from Alan's eyes and the façade was shattered. His choice wasn't to ascend this mountain alone. And, getting external validation was never something he expected or thought that he needed. But, right now, all he felt was pure joy. This was his shining moment and mom's words rang true—he didn't have anything left to prove.